UP IN
TELLURIDE

J. MICHAEL MILLER

For Greg

Always my co-pilot

CONTENTS

RECKONING

SANTA FE, NEW MEXICO
FEDERAL OFFICE BUILDING

D*ammit, get a grip. Do not give this chicken shit one gram of satisfaction.*

Harold Ciro is standing at the far end of a mahogany conference table that shines with a dark glow. I look at his hazy reflection in the table because I can't stand to look directly at him.

I hear Billy's voice. "Darren? Darren?"

"Harold, can you give us just a minute alone?" I hear Billy ask.

I clear my eyes and focus on his face that I know as well as my own. Thank God he's here. For longer than I can remember, he's been my advisor, my confidant, and my friend. And now, my lawyer. There's a reason people say "if you did it, get Mercado". But in my wildest dreams—nightmares—it never occurred to me that he would be sitting next to me...representing me...fending off a prick like Ciro.

Harold's nasal whine rings out. "Okay, Billy, five minutes. But when I come back, Darren signs. That's it. No more stalling."

He leaves and closes the door, but I can't quit glaring at the space he occupied. I have never hated anyone so much. And, lately, I have learned to hate some people, believe me.

I feel Billy's arm around me. "Darren, you've got to focus. I know this is a bitter pill to swallow, but--you know this--swallow you must."

Tears come into my eyes. Tears of rage, I suppose. I say "I suppose" because the only time I have ever cried was when I got beat at something. The first time I felt this way seems like yesterday—I struck out my first time batting in Little League. Definitely the same feeling, just magnified by a million.

"Darren? Talk to me. What's going on?"

"I don't know if I can physically sign that...," unable to find words for the unspeakable.

"I just don't know if I can."

"Darren, you don't call me consigliore, but you might as well. That's what I am. And much more—you are like a brother to me. You...are...out...of...options. You have to sign this *Consent Decree.*"

Dammit, this is not what I want to hear. Here we sit knuckling under to a toady, while he gloats at my predicament. Him and his state school law degree. What a load of shit.

"Sign the damned decree!" I leap out of my chair and slam the table. "That's the best Billy Mercado, the meanest junk-yard-dog lawyer in America can come up with? And don't tell me I am out of options. Nothing pisses me off more than telling me I have to do something."

Billy shocks me. He grabs my face with his beefy hands and pulls it within inches of his, eyeball to eyeball. "Listen to me, Darren, like you have never listened to anybody before. If you don't sign the decree, a very public trial, no matter the outcome, is going to ruin your life. Come on, man, put away your child's mind and use your lawyer's mind. You have to know what I am saying is true. Not giving up is one thing, but flat ignoring reality—that is dangerous."

"So, Billy, are you going to come with me to tell my dad I don't want to be in politics anymore? Hell, he's already got 'Darren Jacobs for President' pins printed somewhere."

As always, Billy stays patient with me. "Would you rather tell him that you are going to be prosecuted for serious felonies and have been running a drug distribution network?"

The door opened and Ciro stepped back into the room.

Asshole! Just like him—it hasn't been five minutes.

"Times up," he says, sounding like an old maid schoolteacher. "Senator Jacobs, are you all right? You don't look well?"

You condescending prick. You don't care one iota whether I'm okay. Special prosecutor, my ass. Beto could put you down—forever—with one punch.

Sweat drips from my forehead, pooling on the table. Cold drops run down my back, as I reach for the pen. *Jesus Christ, I can't get my breath. My tie is strangling me.* I yank it open— but I still can't breathe. The walls in this little room are closing in. *Oh, God, my chest is exploding. I am dying! I am dying!* Black spots dance in front of my eyes. I try to stand, all goes black. I feel myself falling and hear Billy yelling.

CHAPTER 1

FRIDAY, MAY 19

I had every intention of getting a good night's sleep when I went to bed around one in my Canyon Road home in Santa Fe. But I was so excited to get up to Telluride, I tossed and turned a few minutes, said "to hell with it" and took off, stopping only to fill a thermos of coffee at Denny's.

At three fourteen--I distinctly remember seeing the white needle hands on the black clock face--I was screaming along a back road, every twist and turn of which has been embedded in my memory from countless trips between Santa Fe and Telluride. I topped a hill the other side of Pagosa Springs doing something north of eighty, reveling in the exhilarating feeling of being momentarily airborne, my stomach free-floating in its cavity which was, itself, straining against the seat belts; and then, the front tires settling sweetly into the downside of the bank. Porsche, there is no substitute!

Expecting to see a soft rollout turn to the left, I was set up for a power slide. Instead, I remember blinking momentarily and when I opened my eyes, my headlights were shining—so it first seemed to me—on a copse of young aspen trees that had amazingly grown up in the roadway. *That doesn't make a lick of sense! How could even young trees grow up since I was last here two weeks ago?* Raising my view slightly, I was confronted with an even stranger mystery: the "trees" were attached to giant, solid bodies with gnarled branches extending upward and the entire mass was moving. I think that I lifted from the accelerator, but I know I didn't hit the brake and, yet, miraculously, time slowed to a breathless crawl. The only sound I heard was a soft flowing, like air coming out of a duct. I looked to my left and saw a pair of knobby, hairy legs with hooves backing away from me in super slow motion. I could see individual hairs and black shiny spots where hair didn't grow. Mesmerized, I continued my inspection upward and found myself staring into a pair of dark brown eyes, round with surprise, set in a ridiculously angular head upon which was perched a pair of antlers that--it occurred to me at that moment--seemed to be an impressionistic sculpture.

I methodically inspected every visible inch of the giant animal when something caused me to shift my vision skyward and to the right. Out of the darkness, two white, dancing angles moved across the top of the windshield trailing massive trapezoidal clumps. *Well, I'll be damned. Legs and hooves!* The one closest slid quietly out of view. The second, however, I saw inching toward the top of the windshield by tiny fractions, and then, it struck the glass with a loud "crack" that instantly broke the silent spell and returned time to its frantic pace.

Instinctively, I jerked my eyes forward and, to my profound amazement and joy, the headlights were blazing down an empty highway. I slammed the brake pedal with all my might, and my little darling, true to her 911 dna, lifted her shapely rear-end off the ground and spun herself around one and a half complete revolutions, coming to stop dead in the middle of the road, facing backwards, the headlights shining on the largest elk herd I have ever seen. The massive animals--more than a hundred, I am sure--plodded across the road, seemingly paying no attention (perhaps pretending that it didn't exist?) to the shining projectile that had momentarily joined the herd and then moved on.

I know my telling of this event is hard to believe, but what I have recounted is exactly as it happened. It is hard for even me to understand how I survived that encounter without a scratch, but I have lived my whole life with Da Jewel and, so, I am conditioned to believe that only the best can happen to me.

What's "Da Jewel" you ask? A Brooklyn-ized pronunciation of D.J.U.L.—Darren Jacobs' Unbelievable Luck. What started almost as a joke when I was a teenager has been elevated in my mind to the protection of an impenetrable cloak.

I restarted the engine, disgusted with myself for having failed to kick in the clutch during the skidding, spinning stop. *Dammit, Darren, you know better.* The rest of the drive to Telluride I remember as almost other worldly, my chariot and I bound together in a rhythmic and graceful high-speed dance. At some point, it occurred to me that I probably should have felt abject fear and then the relief that comes from surviving. But I didn't. I had never felt fear in my life. I had seen it in people under stress from different situations. I had read about it in books. But, personally, I didn't know what fear felt like.

Even how I got my beloved vehicle is another great example of Da Jewel. Last year, I was up in Denver at the Rocky Mountain Mining Conference, ostensibly to hear the latest regulatory stance from mining officials but, in reality, to participate in one of the storied annual drinking binges by miners who had known each other for decades. Mid-morning the last day, the coffee was having no impact on my hangover, so I decided to step outside the Brown Palace and get a breath of fresh air. A cabbie was closing the trunk of his yellow cab after having dropped off arriving guests.

"You up for a fare?" sprung out of my mouth, because up until that second, I hadn't thought of taking a ride.

"Where you headed?" he asked, looking sideways at my bloodshot eyes, two-day beard, and then down to my leather jacket, wrinkled blue jeans and boots.

I got the message and handed him two twenties. "Just drive me around."

We drove out of downtown and were somewhere in the suburbs when I yelled, "Stop—take me over there." A U-turn and short backtrack later, he dropped me in the parking lot of Bob Hagestad Porsche, thrilled no doubt with forty bucks for a short fare. I walked through the glass doors and directly to the object of my eye (and now heart) a gorgeous Diamond Black Targa 911, opened the door and slipped into the driver's seat. In seconds, I was flying down a twisting road in that beauty when interrupted by a tapping at the window. A trim middle-aged man with slicked-back gray hair and a pencil thin mustache wearing a three-piece suit glared at me a moment before opening the door and spoke in a voice chillier than the Rocky Mountain winter day.

"May I help you? Could we speak outside the car please?"

Instead, I pulled the door closed and located the electric switch and rolled the window down.

"I'd like to test drive this car. Can you go with me?" I asked but really demanded.

"Sir, I would be happy to schedule a test drive for you. We have openings the day after tomorrow."

Knowing pure bullshit when I heard it and being a bit short-tempered in my somewhat debilitated state, I opened the door forcefully banging the condescending prick in the knees, climbed out of the car, and brushed by him on my way down a hall that seemed like it would lead to offices. And it did. I poked my head in the second door. A guy that looked about my age was bent over his desk focusing on a sheet of paper, his long, blond hair covering his entire face.

"Excuse me," I said, "could you arrange for me to test drive one of your cars?"

He looked up, eyes crinkling under parted hair and surrounded by bushy sideburns and a whopping moustache that covered his upper lip, revealing a mischievous face badly sunburned to a bright red, except for a band of extremely white skin exactly the shape of ski goggles around his eyes.

"Can you afford one?" he asked in a patient drawl.

"I can," I said. "And I have fallen in love with that Targa." Not very good negotiating talk,

I knew, but I was captured by full-bore car lust.

He stood and, reaching out his hand, said, "I'm Jimmy. My dad owns this place."

Throwing on a heavy leather coat while wrapping a scarf around his neck, he said, "Let's roll."

We took his car, a metallic ice Targa with caramel leather interior. He drove, roaring out of the dealership and back onto the freeway, accelerating to seventy in four heartbeats and three shifts. It was my first ride in a Porsche, and I instantly understood the addiction—the ride was even more heart-stopping than the incredible, distinctive lines of the car. I didn't think that was possible.

I found myself admiring Jimmy's driving. He sat straight up in the seat, eyes constantly searching down the roadway, both hands on the wheel except when he moved his right hand to the shifter and smoothly sliced through the pattern, talking to me all the while about the car. He explained the gear pattern as he shifted, pointing out the RPM points on the tachometer for each shift. Then, with no warning, he downshifted from fifth to third and then second, the car straining while the engine behind us screamed violently. Braking to a stop, he smiled at me and said, "Your turn."

We changed places and just before I pushed in the clutch to take off, he said, "Just one more thing..." and then explained to me the 911's idiosyncrasies created by the engine weight being positioned **behind** the rear wheels.

"She'll try to sling her butt in front of you if you don't watch her. Never, never, never lift your foot from the accelerator in a curve."

I nodded like I understood and began the drive I will never forget. I was shocked at the noise from the engine, surprised that the ride was rough compared to American cars, amazed at the precision making turns, and totally in love with a driving experience that I never could have imagined. A few minutes later, we pulled into the dealership; I handed Jimmy a check for $19,262 after getting assurance that he was going to get the commission. He called my banker, and I drove my new love out of Hagestad Porsche and right by the crestfallen salesman in the blue suit.

That's not the end of the story--not by a long shot. I got up early the next morning and blasted south out of Denver toward Santa Fe. The car amazed me. It could accelerate on a steep hill in fifth gear! I was having an absolute ball when, just before the New Mexico border, the radio began to buzz in waves of static. I was checking the on/off switch (it was off) when the dashboard lights flashed on, then off, then on again. And before I could think more about this amazing phenomenon, the sound of an explosion like a giant firecracker erupted from the front of the car followed by smoke. Within seconds, the engine died. I steered the poor, powerless creature off the road and opened the front bonnet. What a mess. The battery had exploded spouting acid which covered my luggage. So where's Da Jewel, now?

While I was still staring into the front compartment not knowing what to do next, a tow truck coming from the other direction pulled up. In minutes, I was in the front seat of Manny Garcia's tow truck headed back into San Luis, Colorado with the Targa being towed behind in its shame. Manny informed me that I was incredibly lucky because there was only one bus a day to Santa Fe, and I would make it by fifteen minutes.

His prediction was correct. I bought a ticket from San Luis to Santa Fe and climbed aboard the Greyhound, the first time in my life I had been on a bus. It was crowded, with only one seat left, so I took it. As if I hadn't already had a challenging day, my seatmate by the window had wild, curly long hair; a full, totally unkempt beard; and was drinking wine out of a jug and eating Oreos. I didn't think my mood could be any worse as the bus pulled slowly out of the grocery store/bus station until I saw my Porsche sitting in front of Manny's.

The hairball next to me came alive. "Vhat a gorgeous Targa. Vhat is it doing in dis place?" he asked in a heavy German accent.

"Gorgeous! Gorgeous, my ass," I replied crossing my arms and wishing to be anywhere other than where I was.

A few minutes passed as we rolled into the desert night when the Germanic voice came out of the darkness. "Vould you like some vine? It's really not all that bad, especially with Oreos." I couldn't help myself—the absurdity of it all, I suppose—I laughed and said, "why the hell not".

Over the next four hours, Hermann Klaus explained to me that he was a college student in Germany and that he brought Mercedes and Porsches to the U.S. as a way to pay for his exploration of America. He had seen twenty-seven states already and would add twenty-eight tonight with New Mexico.

"Do you still want a Porsche?" he asked.

"Yeah...yeah, of course I do. I think this is just a fluke," I said.

"It is, "he replied. "They a-r-r-r-re vundervul machines." Pulling a pad of paper, a pencil and a flashlight out of the backpack, he proceeded to write detailed instructions for me on how to buy a Porsche in Germany for U.S. delivery, completing the instructions with the address of his family home in Munich and an invitation to come stay with them when I came over to pick up my car.

I called Bob Hagestad from Santa Fe the first thing in the morning. The Denver dealer was kind enough to offer to do almost anything reasonable to make me happy, but in the end, he understood my disappointment, and tore up my check. I then followed Hermann's instructions to the letter, concluding with picking up Black Beauty II in Munich last July and driving it around

Europe for two weeks. Unfortunately (or not), Hermann had committed to a car delivery to

Florida and was not available. However, his twin sister, a medical student in Berlin home for the summer joined me as tour guide and much more over for the duration of my stay in Europe. She had legs as long as the Rhine and a very European attitude toward sex. As a gentleman, I won't say more. Now, how's that for Da Jewel?!

ᧁ

I am at my absolutely favorite place in the entire world—reclined on a chaise lounge on the east deck of the top floor of my home in Telluride. I just took the day's first sip of the espresso that Marta brought me, the combination of coffee and burnt rubber smacking my taste buds and brain fully awake after a night, as I have explained, that provided no opportunity for sleep. Daybreak is also my absolutely favorite time of day. While it would be full morning in the flatlands, here the sun has just spun itself behind Bridal Veil Peak and is probing its rigid tentacles out from either side of the mountain, poking holes in the lingering morning clouds wherever possible. The mist left over from last night's rain serves as a translucent three-dimensional projector for the rays. A few have struck their intended targets—trees, grassy hillsides, rooftops, and roads, creating dazzling bursts of brightness and contrast where all around is wet and dank. The irony is rich. When I was in school, I always thought Odysseus carrying on about the rosy fingers of dawn was corny...but now I get it, at least my version of it.

Above all else, the morning mountain aroma steals the show from all other senses. As the day warms, still-standing pine, fir, and spruce pump out deliciously scented sap, which blends with the smoky fragrance of fallen comrades burning in fireplaces throughout the valley. I am immediately transported to long-ago camping trips with my family and then, later with Beto Maldanado and Andy Trost. They will be here later today—Beto and Andy...and Paul Kistler.

"Another espresso, boss?" Marta just cannot get comfortable calling me Darren and I won't tolerate Mr. Jacobs.

"No, Marta, not just yet. I am still working on this one. You have become a master barista, Marta."

She says, "Thanks, boss" and goes back in the house. She understands me well and knows my time alone here is sacred. What a find she has been. I was standing on the hill over there watching the cranes put the last trusses in place when I saw this woman striding up the street. There was something about her purposefulness and a can-do face that struck me. She strode up the slope. Shoulders squared, chin out, she asked, "Mr. Jacobs, will you be needing a housekeeper? If so, I would like to apply." She was wearing what she always wears: a pair of crisply--pressed blue jeans, sparkling white gym shoes, a golf shirt and windbreaker, which seemed to be the perfect ensemble for her stocky, athletic build. Her dark hair was pulled back into a ponytail, and she wore not a speck of makeup.

Until that moment, I was debating who I might bring up from Santa Fe, but she settled that issue quickly. Though I am big on gut feelings, I am not sure that I had ever, or have ever since, had such a strong intuition about a person. I hired her on the spot.

She takes incredible care of my house. This is important, because I love my house. My long-time buddy and architect, Hilton, and I spent a year in design making sure that we got it

exactly right. Our frequent trips to Vail and Aspen to "steal" ideas (*cherettes* was the term he taught me) often resulted in all-night sessions with him sketching clear beautiful lines on sheets of paper that we taped on the walls of the hotel room. The nights passed with us standing back quietly looking at the sketches, exchanging ideas, and, of course, drinking Jack Daniels. And, if I do say so myself, we got it right.

"How about that espresso now?"

"You know, Marta. I think I am having a reaction to the adrenalin high since my elk herd adventure. All of a sudden, I am so tired I can hardly move. I'm going to try to snooze right here. Wake me in two hours if I drift off."

"You got it. I'll have lunch ready when the guys get here."

༄

I remember closing my eyes and nothing else until I was jarred awake, free-falling into black space. I hate that dreadful slice of time when we are barely conscious and can't figure out whether we are in a dream or life. When I opened my eyes, the sun was up, and seeing Bridal Veil Falls quickly anchored me in time and place. I wanted to explore the dream, so I lay back and tried to remember. I caught just the inkling of a vision of staring up the side of a huge steel cliff that soared skyward out of murkiness, higher than a New York skyscraper. I grabbed on to that thought and, in a moment, the rest of the dream unfolded. Somehow, I was in two places at the same time—standing on the ground by the side of the steel wall watching a huge jet above me and, at the same moment, I was alone in the cabin of the jet trying to land it on a tiny ledge on top of the wall. When the landing gear first touched down, I was thrown out of the window of the cockpit and into the metal canyon, falling and spinning so that I would see the shiny metal face on each rotation, but otherwise, nothing but pure blackness. I guess that's when I jolted awake.

The dream knocked the wind out of me a bit, but a shower and shave put me right. I am really excited to see Andy, Beto and Paul. We have all been running in different directions lately, particularly me. Things have just been nutso, so when it quiets down for a minute, I realize how much I miss them. There's a lot to be said for "the good old days" when we saw each other a couple times a week. But life has moved on, or to be more accurate, I have forced life on—on into a form aptly described by the metaphor "a three-ringed circus". So, I have no one to blame but me.

Today, we are having a board of directors meeting for Cerberus. That will take us late into the night, but I told the guys to clear their calendars for the next few days for a surprise. All three of them have been bugging me to tell them more about it, but I absolutely will not. I'm having too much fun picturing the looks on their faces when I do finally break the news. Even now, I find myself grinning ear to ear. It's good to be King.

Marta knocks on the bedroom door. "Boss, the fellows are here."

"Be right down, Marta."

One final check in the mirror before I make my entrance. The familiar image looking back is of an average guy of average height with brown hair—longer this year than ever before—decked out in blue jeans with a razor crease (thanks to Marta), the slightly bell-bottomed legs pulled over a pair of dark alligator boots. And, a white dress shirt perfectly pressed but with two buttons opened at the collar and sleeves rolled up exactly twice. Handsome is not the first adjective one would use to describe him, yet there is something about him. He has a broad face that appears to have always been tanned. "Darren darling, a classic isn't determined by the cover—it's what's on the inside," I remind myself of my mother's words. I am practicing a barely discernable smile when the image's eyes startle me. They don't blink. They don't look away. They are without a doubt my strongest weapon.

∽

I didn't design the staircase with dramatic entrances in mind, but it unquestionably provides a stage--a wide, curving arch descending as if supported by air from the second-floor landing into the great room. And a "great" room it is. From the floor to the peak of the beamed ceiling is a full three stories. The two exterior walls are set in thinly quarried stone from over near Mancos and flank the *piece de resistance,* a solid wall of glass, twenty feet wide floor to ceiling, and around which the entire house was designed. You see, long before we started actual designing, Hilton and I engaged in an exercise to ensure that the view of Bridal Veil Falls and its host peak was positioned to its greatest advantage. We spent days with a crew of carpenters erecting and tearing down and re-erecting a two-by-six structure that represented the outer frame of the glass wall. Then, once we had finally determined the exact location of the window, we took the entire next day from before sunup until the last rays of sunset, pacing in what is now the center of the great room floor. Throughout the day, the view changed in dramatically different ways but always remained breathtaking. We staked out the entrance hall and walked into the room that-was-to-be over and over, knowing that we had created a first impression that would drop jaws as long as the house stood.

The magic of the great room was working, as always. Beto, Andy and Paul were all standing by the window, eyes fixed on the giant water cascade, mesmerized.

"Hey, guys," I said about halfway down the stairs. "Welcome to paradise."

I shook hands (I'm not a hugger) and shared greetings with the three men I trust my life with, intentionally capturing and holding each one's eyes for a few seconds longer than is traditionally comfortable in America. This is a trait I perfected as a young man once I learned that it earned vast amounts of trust instantly, not only with people like my comrades where the feeling was genuine, but also folks that really shouldn't rely on the genuineness they let themselves feel.

"How was the trip up?" I asked.

"Piece of cake," Beto said. He always drives as he is naturally gifted and formally trained.

I relayed my experience with the elk herd. They listened wide-eyed--they know I don't bullshit them--with occasional interruptions of "no shit", "you gotta be kidding," and whistles.

Andy put me in a soft headlock and said, "B-b-b-b-oss, don't try that, again. Da-da-da jewel shouldn't be over, uh, tested". We all laughed but I had to turn around and put on a game face quickly to hide the emotions that snuck up on me. Nobody gets to me like Andy.

"You guys ready to get to work?" I asked, walking back up the stairs with them following.

We filed into my conference room on the second floor. I put a lot of thought into this room. It's a windowless space twenty-five feet long and twenty wide. Plush gold carpet covers the floor. The walls are covered with recessed panels of dark polished mahogany that put on display the simple beauty of expertly crafted woodworking. A teak and mahogany conference table that Hilton designed sits in the middle of the room, surrounded by eight high-backed and heavily stuffed chairs covered in tobacco-colored leather. A contrast to the dark woods, the top half of the front wall is covered by a shiny whiteboard cleaned to perfection. Along the wall sits a credenza that matches the table. Marta's sandwiches, coffee and a variety of snacks and drinks are arrayed along the length of the credenza.

"Dig in to Marta's smorgasbord," I announced. "Then we'll get started."

Once they all had collected their eats and gotten seated, I announced as officially as a publicly traded company board meeting, "The quarterly board meeting of Cerberus Distribution Partnership will come to order. Roll call. Beto."

"Here."

"Andy."

"Here."

"And Paul."

"Present."

I knew they all think this formality is a bit over the top, but I like the order. "All board members are present. Paul, will you start us off with financial and operating results for the past quarter?"

Paul stared at me unmoving for a few seconds...and then more than a few seconds, before jumping up abruptly with a black marker gripped in his hand. In four quick strides, he was in the front of the room. He paused momentarily with his hands crossed behind his back staring at the blank board. Then he took one step forward, and in swift, confident strokes wrote headings across the top and line descriptions down the left side of the board, all from his memory. This was no problem for Paul as he had explained; he saw the schedule as clearly in his head as if it was typed and printed.

Our operating structure is straightforward. For internal control, we have established a pyramid management system with accountability at each tier--primitive but damned effective. This meeting, held quarterly, is the only time that all of the pieces are pulled together, and no written record of this meeting will ever exist.

Paul printed five headings across the top of the board: Albuquerque, Santa Fe, Phoenix and Tucson with a Total column to the far right. In a frenzy-like trance, Paul spread Arabic figures, each formed identically, across the board, precisely aligned opposite description lines and descending in perfect columns. Despite the incredible speed with which he posted the information, the board took on the look of a computer printout, each figure precisely drawn. As Paul moved across the board and back, Beto, Andy and I leaned left and right unable to keep up reading the information as fast as it was written. After almost ten minutes of unbroken writing, Paul stepped back and scanned the material. With a nod of his head, he reached out and placed a single line under each column, entered totals and then double lines to indicate completion.

Andy and Beto smiled at each other shaking their heads. Although they had seen this performance many times, it always amazed. I finished tapping away at my calculator. "Not that I doubted it, but every line cross-foots and every column foots. I'll catch you in a bust someday, Paul," I said laughing.

Paul's eyebrows arched in a shocked look. "That is not possible. Now, let's go through the numbers—I'll round to hundred thousand's if that's okay--and later provide detailed analysis. Total profit for the quarter was $3.8 million on revenue of $11.2 million." Paul grabbed a green marker and inserted two numbers with percentages. "Revenue was up 17% over last quarter and profit increased 26%." He then pulled a red marker out of the tray and inserted numbers followed by ampersands adjacent to the revenue numbers for all five columns. "In total we moved over four hundred pounds during the quarter. You can see the distribution by district. As always, Albuquerque leads, but Phoenix is gaining. All have nice increases except Santa Fe and we need to talk about that."

For the next two hours, we diagnosed and discussed the numbers in depth. We had slightly exceeded our gross profit target, fifty percent, which is a legacy holdover from the first days of the business when for simplicity's sake we "keystoned", or doubled our cost, to determine the projected retail sales price. Expenses were analyzed in depth including rising transportation costs and payments in all four regions for "political contributions and support to police organizations". We were all pleased with the results except for Santa Fe. I deferred that issue, "Let's talk about what to do with that kettle of fish later." All nodded agreement.

Paul returned to the board and began a new presentation. At the top of the board, he wrote two columns labeled "Pounds" and "$'s". He entered line items: "Beginning Inventory", "Purchases", "Sales" and "Ending Inventory" and slotted the numbers in the adjacent columns. Then, he pointed at the bottom numbers. "Our ending inventory is 426 pounds at a cost of $11,600,000 with a market value of over $23 million."

Beneath the inventory calculations, Paul entered four line items: "Beginning Cash", "Plus Profit", "Inventory Change", and "Ending Cash". "After allocating approximately $500,000 of profits to increased inventory, we have a net cash increase for the quarter of $3.3 million. Ending Cash is $21,372,000." Though we all knew about where things stood, seeing the actual amount of value for the inventory and cash on hand brought a sudden stillness to the room.

I broke the silence. "As always, thanks, Paul, for your efforts... all of you, for that matter. We continue to produce amazing results. So much so that I have planned what I think will be a pleasant surprise for you tomorrow. So, as has been our custom from the first quarterly meeting, we will now retire to the vault to count inventory and cash."

Beto jumped up. "You can't just tell us you have a surprise and not tell us anything else. Come on, man, I won't sleep a wink tonight."

I shrugged. "You'll live. Let's go. We have a lot of work ahead of us."

Leaving Beto sputtering, we all rose and headed two floors down to physically count hundreds of bundles of cash that would total more than twenty million dollars and carefully weigh almost two hundred thousand grams of uncut cocaine.

CHAPTER 2

SATURDAY, MAY 20

Andy, Beto and Paul were in their regular spots around the breakfast table when I walked in. Beto was up like a shot when he saw me. "So, what's the big surprise?"

Three pair of eyes looked at me inquisitively. They were finishing up waffles with crème fraiche and strawberries, one of Marta's specialties. We had worked until after seven last night finishing up the cash and inventory counts. To celebrate the completion of the ritual, I grilled steaks which we ate outside overlooking the village lights of Telluride while keeping warm around the fire pit. Marta added baked potatoes and salad; and I threw in two bottles of Chateau Mouton Rothschild cabernet sauvignon and four Cuban Cohiba Supremos.

"Can't I at least have a cup of coffee, Beto?" I asked, having difficulty controlling my desire to grin.

"Come on, man, you're fucking killing me." Beto's impatience was legendary.

I finally relented. "Well, let me just say that I am sure you will find it both pleasurable and profitable. I have a Lear waiting for us down at the airport. We're headed to Nassau, Bahamas, for a few days."

Beto reacted in his typical "understated" style. "What the hell?! Ain't this a little short notice, man?"

"Yeah, it is short notice. So what? And don't worry about clothes—we'll get what we need down there to last us a couple of days...they don't dress much, anyway—and as for passports, those aren't required, either."

I had their attention now. "For over two years now, we have been building significant cash reserves in the vault downstairs and talking about how we have to do something about it. Paul and I have been investigating offshore accounts, ostensibly on behalf of one of my clients, for the past few months. I've indicated the amounts needing to be placed exceed ten million dollars. Wednesday, I got a call from a banker in Nassau, Karl Van der Berg, who is affiliated with a Swiss bank. As luck would have it, they are having a series of meetings in Nassau over the next few days. Karl invited me down as his special guest to meet his fellow bankers and learn more about the wonderful world of Swiss banks. I accepted on the condition that my three closest associates be allowed to accompany me. 'But, of course,' he said."

By this time, Beto was on his feet. "Hot shit, if we ain't choppin' in tall cotton? Jet to Nassau for the weekend. How much is that going to set us back?"

"Don't worry, we can afford it. Actually, Karl offered to send a 'company plane' as he put it, but I didn't like the idea of our travel being controlled by someone I haven't even met yet. I set us up with a charter out of Denver that is quite familiar with flying into Nassau. Evidently, a good many of the oil and gas folks from Denver make the trip frequently."

"Do these fat cats work weekends?" Beto asked.

I laughed. "From what I understand, Beto, these guys will work anytime there's a chance they can make a buck."

I noticed that Paul was staring at the ground quietly. "Paul, what's up?"

"Oh, nothing, no nothing, Darren. I'm just a little stunned about the timing. As you know,

I think this is something we really need to do. We badly need to get all that cash out of the country and someplace safe. I studied international banking a bit at Harvard, but it was at the theoretical level. This is a phenomenal opportunity to learn about it at the real-world level."

"From some of the best professors on the planet, as well," I added.

"Let's make like sheep and get the flock out of here," Beto said, his boyish excitement bubbling over.

∽

An hour later, Beto pulled my black Land Cruiser into the area reserved for private jets at the Telluride Airport. We were all gob-smacked by the sight of the sleek, white Lear 28 waiting on the pad for us. A fuel truck was tethered to the port wing by its fueling hose. A pilot, I presumed, outfitted in a black leather cap and matching leather jacket, white shirt, and thin, black tie walked around the plane holding a clipboard in one hand and pen in the other, checking as he went. I pointed to a door marked "Private-Customer Lounge" and we all entered but not before we each took one more peek at the sculpture with wings.

The lounge was formed by a ring of couches that sectioned off a corner area. Two televisions hung on the walls, and a carafe of coffee and soft drinks on ice sat along a counter. Before I could ask for further direction, a compact, athletic-looking man approached walking at a brisk pace with ramrod-straight posture.

"Are you the Jacobs group?"

I held out my hand, "I'm Darren Jacobs."

"Captain Dave Richardson" he replied, as I shook his hand, then introduced him to my bunch.

"We're finishing refueling and preflight. Should be done in just a few minutes. There are restrooms over there"--indicating with a nod--"but we have a head in the back, so no problem. We'll be about three hours to Houston Hobby for a quick refuel and then on to Nassau. Anything else I can tell you?"

"I think we're all ready. We're traveling light, just a duffel bag each and a couple of briefcases," I said looking the captain over. He radiated confidence, not cockiness, and I immediately became comfortable with the premise of putting my life in his hands.

The man we had seen outside inspecting the plane approached and handed the clipboard to the captain. "All ready, sir, all looks good."

"Gentlemen, meet co-pilot Tom Hanson."

Hanson doffed his cap and shook hands around as we each introduced ourselves. He was a full head taller than Richardson and much younger looking. The captain had short, steel-gray hair and looked to be in his late forties, while Hanson was prematurely balding with just a blond fringe but looked to be no more than thirty.

The captain looked over the checklist and, nodding his head, said, "If you gentlemen are ready, your carriage awaits."

Beto poked Andy in the ribs. "Some fucking carriage for a couple of Albuquerque Valley Rats."

Richardson and Hanson marched to the fold-down stairway extended from the gorgeous jet with the four of us following single file. Richardson stepped briskly in the plane, while Hanson stopped at the stairs insisting on carrying our duffels aboard. "Just part of the service, sirs."

Ducking to enter the cabin, I must say I was under-whelmed. This was my first time in a private jet, and I was stunned that the cabin seemed so cramped, with its low ceiling and oval walls that tapered in at the top and bottom. Five rows of single seats lined each side of a narrow aisle that ran down the middle of the cabin, ending at a small door at the back over which hung a lighted "Lavatory" sign. Though the seats were deep buckets with tall backs, they were closely sequenced, and leg room was limited. Each row was bracketed with porthole windows in the fuselage.

Hanson poked his head in the cabin. "If you gentlemen don't mind, two of you please sit on each side of the aisle, but it doesn't matter which of the seats aft to forward...front to back...that you choose. Please buckle up for takeoff as indicated by this sign. When we hit cruising altitude, the sign will go off and you can unbuckle your belt if you wish. However, we recommend keeping the belt on while seated. We expect a few bumps on the climb out, but not much else on the way down to Houston. I'll be back once we get level and serve drinks. I know I'm not much to look at, stewardess--wise, but I'm all you got."

I chuckled inwardly at Hanson's self-deprecating humor and settled into my seat in the middle row of the cabin. Paul sat across from me and Andy across from Beto one row back. From the starboard side of the plane came a high-pitched electric motor buzz followed quickly by the rising whine of the jet engine. Identical sounds came from the port side and, with both engines screaming, little could be heard in the cabin over the din. A squeak signaled the release of the brakes, and I felt the forward motion as the jet taxied. I looked out the porthole and down the runway, a somewhat unnerving view, as the runway was not level, rising dramatically the last two thousand feet of tarmac.

The plane turned left and was lined up down the runway. The jets revved, whining louder and louder; and then, like a cable holding the tail had been released, the Lear jumped forward, the acceleration pushing me back in my seat. Even Black Beauty II could not match the Lear's g- force creation. The ground rushed by in a blur and, somewhere long before the end of the runway, the force created by the lift of the wings gently separated the landing gear from the runway. For just a moment I felt that I was riding on a magic carpet as the jet glided smoothly. Then, the pilot shoved the nose up in a forty-five-degree climb, and I was forcefully pushed back into my seat. I turned to look at my gang, even Paul grinning broadly. I liked that all four of us were experiencing our first high-speed climb out together. We are experienced commercial travelers; but this was a completely different experience. I settled back into my seat and found myself unwittingly grinning from ear to ear like a kid pretending that he was being propelled skyward in a rocket ship to outer space.

As the plane reached altitude and the captain pulled the nose back to level flight, Beto, in his inimitable style, caught the moment. "Mother, was that an E-ticket ride!"

We had a short stop in Houston for refueling and a quick lunch and then plunged eastward from bright sunlight into quickly descending darkness. I must have dozed at some point and when I opened my eyes, the black of the ocean was broken only by a small island of lights, our intended target I presumed. Moments later, we touched down smoothly on the Nassau runway and taxied to a remote pad. Headlights from some kind of vehicle chased the plane to a stop and then pull alongside the plane while the turbines were still whirring. The driver's door of a long, black limousine opened. A monstrous mountain of a man of uncertain but clearly mixed racial heritage in a dark suit, white shirt, black tie, and chauffeur's cap emerged. His shaved head, the size and shape of a basketball, shone with mahogany skin.

Tom lowered the stairs and led us to the tarmac. The giant took my hand, which completely disappeared into his fist.

"Mr. Jacobs, my name is Tuso. On behalf of First Swiss Bank, welcome to Nassau."

If his appearance had me a little off-balanced, his voice totally bowled me over. He spoke in a rumbling voice with an impeccable Oxford English accent. "I am to take you to your quarters for the evening. Mr. Van der Berg sends his regrets that he was unable to meet you tonight but looks forward to seeing you at brunch in the morning."

Tuso picked up our duffel bags—they looked like four purses on him –and put them into the trunk of the limo, while we said our goodbyes with the pilot and his colleague.

"So, what do you guys do until Monday morning?" I asked Dave.

"Ah," came Richardson's reply, "one of the benefits of flying jet charters. We are going on a sport fishing charter tomorrow. We would love to scuba dive--these are some of the best waters in the world—but we're on too short a turnaround. You can't pilot a craft within 24 hours of diving."

"Now I would never have thought of that," I said.

"Bends are the risk. But the sport fishing is great this time of year, so it's not a bad second place."

"Tough life you lazy butts have," Beto said, getting a laugh from all.

And, with that, my three cohorts and I piled into the limousine and Tuso drove us into Nassau, stopping in the curving drive of a pink, two-story mansion. Before our limo had come to a complete stop, the double doors of the house opened, and a regal man with a coal black face encircled by silver beard and clipped hair stepped out.

"Gentlemen, this is Devon," said Tuso. "He is the manager of our guest house which we reserve for visiting customers and dignitaries. Your wish will be his command."

CHAPTER 3

SUNDAY, MAY 21

D o you ever wake up and can't remember where you are? It took me a while, but looking around, I slowly began to sort things out. I had no idea about the time, other than I knew it was daytime because sunlight was trying to fight its way through the windows which were protected by heavy curtains. The walls and ceiling were a soft white, a strong contrast to the plush turquoise carpet. The décor was tropical with matching bright blues, pinks and tangerines in the bedding and artwork. The furniture was white wicker. "Ah, yes, I am in Nassau." I lay back in bed trying to get oriented. The previous day's flight seemed almost like a dream.

Eventually, I stood and separated the curtains, revealing a pair of Arcadia doors that opened to a private deck overlooking Nassau harbor and the brilliant azure sea that stretched beyond. A breeze moved the palm tree fronds akimbo and brought in the fresh smell of sea air. The thick, almost oozing warmth poured over me and I thought how different it was from the crisp, pine-scented coolness I had left behind in Telluride. Yet, I find both exhilarating. I like variety.

I had showered and was shaving when I caught myself smiling, thinking about how I had surprised everybody yesterday. Then the phone rang.

"Good morning, Darren. This is Karl. I trust you slept well?"

"Absolutely," I said, looking around for a clock, "what time is it?"

"Just after nine. We have planned a brunch on the veranda here at the house. Would eleven work?"

"Sure. I'll get my crew together and look forward to seeing you then. By the way, we don't have much in the way of clothes since this was such short notice."

"In Nassau, that is no problem. Show up for brunch in whatever you have, and I will have

Tuso run you over to a haberdashery for some island garb, if you wish." "See you at eleven," I said.

I studied the phone a bit but was unable to figure out how to call the troops, so I punched "O". Immediately, an official sounding female voice answered with an European accent I couldn't quite place. "Yes, Mr. Jacobs, how may we help you?"

"Good morning. How do I call my associates' rooms?"

First, I called the kitchen and ordered coffee service for four to be delivered to my room so that we could gather around ten-thirty, have coffee and chat a bit before heading to the brunch en masse. Then, I rang Andy, Beto and Paul.

∽

A few blocks away, Hans Wittler and Karl Van der Berg were holding a meeting around a small round table in Hans's office.

"Everything we know about our four visitors is in these files," Karl said sliding a stack of manila folders across the table to Hans.

Opening the top file, Hans asked, "So Darren Jacobs is clearly the leader of the pack?" "Yes," Karl said. "No question about that."

"So... let's start with him then. What should I know about our Mr. Jacobs?"

"He's a conundrum, Hans. Outwardly, he's a golden boy. Harvard lawyer, member of the New Mexico legislature, and fourth generation scion of New Mexico's first family.

Incredible wealth. But his personal life--he tries to keep very private. Two of his entourage that you will meet later, Andy Trost and Beto Maldanado, have been his best friends since childhood. They even called themselves the Three Musketeers. These two guys barely made in through high school and, from what we can tell, the Jacob's family may have covered up a bunch of police trouble.

Marriage doesn't seem to be even a remote possibility..." "Is he homosexual?" Hans interrupted.

"Oh, god no. Far from it. He always has a gorgeous woman on his arm, and they say his Santa Fe house has revolving doors for a regular stream that come to see him. Talking to some of our friends in the Democratic Party, they would love to see him settle down so they can run him for national office, but he, supposedly, is having no part of that. He doesn't want the spotlight or the requirement to 'clean up his act' as they put it." "So...what was the source of the family wealth?" Hans asked.

"His great-grandfather was an industrialist; invented some type of farm implement that became ubiquitous and made a fortune; which his son used to buy huge tracts of land in New Mexico. With the World War Two boom, the land became extremely valuable. The family trusts are huge."

A deeper reading of the file would have revealed far more about Darren's story. He was born and raised in New Mexico, the great-grandson of Knut Jacobs who began relocating from the Midwest to New Mexico in the late 1800's. Knut had made his fortune by inventing and manufacturing plows that became the standard all over the farming belt of the United States. By 1900, he was among the 100 wealthiest men in America. On a hunting trip to Colorado and New Mexico, he had fallen in love with the Rio Grande Valley around Albuquerque. In the years that followed, he sent his agents secretly into the area with instructions to acquire what became holdings of raw land measured in square miles, not acres. He built a beautiful adobe *ranchito* in the *bosque* along the Rio Grande where he spent increasing blocks of time until his final move to New Mexico at retirement. By 1925, he had liquidated all of his stock holdings to buy more land in New Mexico.

As with many powerful families in that era, the core wealth created by an invention was multiplied many times by ensuing investments. The future Jacobs generations saw the value of their land holdings escalate dramatically as Albuquerque and the surrounding areas flourished. World War II was the ultimate game-changer as the military presence in New Mexico mushroomed.

Kirtland Air Force Base trained bomber crews for missions in Europe, many of the crews returning to Albuquerque after the war to become civic leaders. The Manhattan Project had forever put New Mexico on the map while spawning the Los Alamos and Sandia Laboratories. And the wealth that was created by the growth established New Mexico's "first family".

Darren was the only son of the third-generation descendants of Knut. As with his father and grandfather, he was educated at Harvard. He had deviated, however. Both his immediate fore bearers had studied medicine and became physicians, while Darren gravitated to political science and law.

The wild streak that marked Darren's youth seemed to somewhat lessen with maturity.

He had left such a mark in his early teen years that he was shipped off to New Mexico Military Institute to finish his last two years of high school. Rumor had it that his transfer to NMMI was part of a deal his father cut with a local judge to avoid potential felony issues. While the rigidity and structure of the military reined him in to some extent, he continued to be New Mexico's most watched "bad boy". His red Corvette convertible was so notorious that the New Mexico Highway Patrol kept track of its whereabouts on a regular basis. Alcohol and girls rounded out his favorite activities and kept the family in an uproar. All breathed a sigh of relief the day he left for Harvard. At least in Boston his escapades wouldn't be quite so visible.

But as time wore on, Darren trained his substantial intellectual capabilities on his studies so that he graduated respectably in both his undergraduate and law school classes. With his family connections, he was a welcome prize for several competing law firms anticipating his return to New Mexico. As a result of his father's longstanding friendship with the senior partner, Darren chose Stevenson and Marshall. He worked hard and learned well at the tutelage of his mentor, Brian Stevenson. His frequent involvement with matters of state government opened the door to a political future, through which he strolled. His star rose quickly and by the mid- seventies, he had become a powerful member of the state legislature.

Just as Karl described, he would have been a perfect candidate for national office except that the Democratic Party leaders could not get him to fall into the proper mold in his personal life. Never married, Darren dated a long string of beauties; most he had met during his frequent weekend trips to Las Vegas and Los Angeles. He inherited and remodeled an elegant adobe compound on Canyon Road in Santa Fe, which he fully staffed with a housekeeper, cook and gardener. When not traveling, Darren was known to host private parties that combined political big wigs, lobbyists and "fascinating" women visiting Santa Fe as Darren's guests. Although the occasional scandal surfaced, the Jacobs' family connections bolstered by the Stevenson support staff quickly swept any unsightly sediment out of view.

Additionally, Darren fervently maintained his leadership role in "The Three Musketeers", along with Andy and Beto. The three, friends since grade school, had dubbed themselves The Three Musketeers in a finger-slicing, blood-sharing ritual along the Rio Grande the summer before junior high school. Their early shenanigans were now stories of lore in New Mexico, including tying a teacher to the flagpole in front of school one morning and streaking an assembly long before streaking became a fad. Although Darren's stint at NMMI split them up during the school year, their high school summers began right where the previous year's high jinks left off without missing a beat. Much to Darren's family and political supporters' chagrin, the three were still thought of as a unit; The Three Musketeers were alive and well as adults.

~

"So...why is Mr. Jacobs coming to avail himself of our services? If they have such wealth, they must have advisors to handle all of that? Could this be, as he has alluded to you, for a client?"

"Good questions, Hans. It may be, as he has suggested, for a client. Certainly, he has clients with wealth in Santa Fe. However, there are rumblings around New Mexico that he and his cohorts may be generating some ill-gotten gain"

"Drugs?" "Possibly."

"So...that could explain some of the Dr. Jekyll and Mr. Hyde you described, eh Karl?" "Yes. Just so."

⌒

After leading a quick strategy huddle, we walked down the hall toward the center of the sprawling house in what we guessed was the direction of the meeting place. After a misstep or two, we finally ran into Devon who directed us to a large, living area with sunken seating. Accordion-hinged panels had been pushed back against both apposing walls, opening the movable wall to the veranda where a large round table draped with a white linen tablecloth and set with silver and porcelain was completely shaded by a cantilevered umbrella. Two men were seated at the table in conversation. As we approached, they rose.

"Darren?" asked the first man coming forward and betting correctly that I would lead the group (or does he already have pictures of me in his file?). "Karl Van der Berg, so good to finally meet you face to face. May I introduce the head of our international banking group, Hans Wittler."

I suppressed a laugh as *Mutt and Jeff* automatically popped into my head as the two men approached. Karl, a blonde giant, ushered Hans toward me. Both men were dressed casually but elegantly in well-pressed cotton slacks, linen shirts, and Italian slip-ons. Hans's face was bright red, with thinning gray hair combed straight back from the forehead. Though shorter than me, his blue, flashing eyes commanded my attention. This is not someone to underrate.

"Good to meet both of you, and thank you for your kind hospitality," I said.

Introductions followed all around and we took our seats, gently directed by Karl. With the practiced skills of diplomats, the two bankers easily led the conversation, asking cautious questions of each which generated limited snippets of our individual stories as they shared equally benign pieces of their own. I got a kick out of the charade. You *old foxes, I'll bet a dollar against a donut hole you have a complete file on us—just like the one I have on you.*

Karl gave a brief summary of the history of Swiss banking in the Caribbean, as we all listened carefully. Paul asked thoughtful questions. While we talked, three servers in livery quietly took our breakfast orders, suggesting omelets and waffles and various meats while assuring us that anything we wished would be prepared. Soon, plates of beautifully presented breakfast food were delivered, and the conversation slowed and became sporadic, catch as catch can between bites.

Hans turned to me. "We have a friend in common, Darren. Thomas McCorkle." "You know Corkie?" I asked.

"Yes, quite. He represents many clients who bank with us. You two were in the same law class at Harvard, am I correct?"

"We were. And got to know each other pretty well. We were in the same study group first year. Corkie's great. I haven't talked to him in a while ("a while" being day before yesterday when we talked at length about these guys). He's still in Manhattan?"

"Oh, yes, he's a diehard New Yorker now. We very much enjoy working with his firm. I am certain that we will have an equally enjoyable and mutually profitable relationship with your firm, Darren. We are excited to present our program this afternoon. Hopefully, this will be the beginning of a long friendship," Hans said.

The introductory pleasantries continued for an hour more, breaking up with the mutual understanding that we would get down to business in the afternoon session.

Hans and Karl returned to the patio.

"Well, Corkie certainly wasn't exaggerating when he said that Darren Jacobs was a cat of a different breed," Hans said.

"Entirely so. I can remember only a handful of men in all of my career that had his kind of je ne sais quoi. Authority with charm. But something more," Karl replied. "On the one hand he seems mature beyond his years; on the other; a kind of boyish delinquency lurks. It almost makes you want to sign up for whatever he has going."

The two bankers had just had an experience similar to most when first coming in contact with Darren. People were indescribably drawn to him. His eyes had the inescapable power to look over a room and somehow create the feeling in every person in the room that he had looked only at them. People used words like "presence" and "gravitas" to try to define his power, but they were not really helpful in characterizing the undefinable way that he had of interacting with his fellow human beings.

Whether at a cocktail party, a conclave of politicos or a men's night on the town, Darren somehow always ended up in the middle of the action. But it wasn't as though he aspired, or even sought, to be the leader of the pack. To the contrary, when in a group of people, Darren engaged one person at a time, focusing on a single conversation, listening intently, asking questions, always responding to what he had just heard, and, finally, smoothly disengaging to move to his next post, leaving his most recent chatee totally charmed. This dance took place over and over until Darren quietly possessed the entire audience.

The overarching impression that people took away from Darren was one of solidness. He seemed old beyond his years, a young man who stood steadily with one leg in the previous generation and the other in his. The rumors and stories of his wild ways as a young man seemed incongruent with his current form. And, yet, under the surface, something always seemed to boil and occasionally vent in the form of a wickedly humorous and sarcastic remark accompanied with a sparkle in his eyes previously unrevealed. Careful observers were compelled to question their original assessments and consider the possibility of a more complex Darren Jacobs.

Hans summarized. "I believe we will enjoy doing business with him. And, even more, I believe it will be very interesting,"

⌇

We convened at three on the "Special Client Group" floor of the bank's offices, meeting in a conference room with a board table that could seat twenty comfortably. Andy, Beto, Paul and I sat on one side of the table, huddled at the end. Hans and Karl sat opposite us on the other side of the table. The large room was tastefully decorated but not extravagant. I liked the décor—modern, sleek teak furniture and beige fabrics. Framed, enclosed shadowboxes were affixed to the walls at both ends of the conference table.

I looked around the room and nearly laughed out loud. We were all dressed in similar garb--tropical casual clothes. Tuso had escorted the four of us to a high-end men's clothing store, where we each picked up a couple of days' clothing consisting of light weight slacks and shirts. Hans and Karl looked as though they were dressed with clothes from the same store. Tuso tried to have the bill sent to the bank, but I insisted on paying.

"Gentlemen," Hans advised, "please help yourselves to water, soft drinks or coffee." He pointed to a low table with the refreshments, his English perfect but still with a trace of a Germanic lilt.

"Let's get straight to it." With a nod of his head toward the shadow box on the front wall, he said, "Karl, please."

Karl rose, pulling a key out of his pocket that he inserted into a silver keyhole in the corner of the wall-mounted unit. He twisted the key, and the hum of a hidden electric motor started as the face of the unit slid open revealing a white board. Written on the board were four headings: "Security", "Privacy", "Legality", and "Procedures". Under each heading was a box diagram of three descending levels.

Hans rose and stood by the board, speaking. "These are the areas that we would like to cover today. We prefer for this learning process to be an exchange, not a lecture, so do not hesitate to ask questions, please. As many times as we have made this presentation, I am sometimes surprised by a question that has not been asked before...and sometimes, I am stumped." He smiled humbly, but I wasn't buying.

"Let's begin with Security. Your clients' funds, or their derivatives which we shall discuss later, will be held at our facility in Zurich. In our nearly century-old history, a client has never lost a penny that has been placed with us. This includes two world wars. As you are aware, Switzerland has maintained a unique safe haven environment for business leaders from around the world to interact, no matter the political disruption that may be in place at the time. Swiss banks are a critical piece of that process, both regulated and strongly supported by the Swiss government. In short, there is no safer place on earth to provide your clients with peace of mind that their wealth is secure. Questions? Paul."

"Yes, Hans, is there any insurance protection, such as the FDIC or FSLIC in the U.S.?" "No. I would say this—we are so strong that we could sell such protection to other world banks but choose not to. Consequently, it does not make sense for us to insure with an insurer less strong than ourselves. At the risk of being redundant, I remind you that no client of ours has ever lost a penny."

Hans looked and at Paul and me. We seemed satisfied so he moved on. It occurred to me that Paul's presence was easily understood, but not so much that of Andy and Beto. We had concocted an explanation ahead of the meeting if asked, but it was becoming clear that the bankers were very careful and limited when questioning us. Perhaps the bankers thought Andy and Beto are my bodyguards, which would be an easy conclusion to draw, and if I need bodyguards, well, it is no business of theirs.

"The hallmark of the Swiss bank account, in addition to safety, is privacy. We Swiss are rabid about this issue and our bank, likewise. We will not disclose our clients or their holdings. Period. End of discussion. To this end, we will--have--spent millions of dollars in legal fees to protect the privacy of a single client. Even, as you may have read, certain World War Two situations that are becoming somewhat high-profile require our utmost defense. While we may have sentiments with the litigants in equity, we cannot allow for our principles to be eroded by one grain of sand. You will direct how you wish to interact with our bank, and we will respond.

If you...your clients...prefer not to have written reports, a bank officer of the highest level will provide telephonic reports on secure land lines. You will be provided dial-in numbers. If ever you wish to visit us here in Nassau or in Zurich, we will accommodate your visit with the level of visibility that you wish as we have private, secure entrances in both banks. Additionally, your account creates the privilege of safety deposit boxes at either location; again, with access dictated by your needs. You may think of your and your clients' privacy as an inviolate right."

Hans looked from face to face as if searching for questions, and then back to me. I gave him a simple nod of satisfaction.

"So, I have held the floor enough. Karl, in addition to being a brilliant banker, is an international lawyer, and will take over to discuss legality and procedures."

Hans returned to his seat as Karl rose and began speaking. "Gentlemen, thank you. As Hans mentioned, the banks of Switzerland are viewed as a national treasure. Swiss law is extremely strong protecting the rights of foreigners to place their assets in Switzerland for safekeeping with the knowledge that when a client needs access to those assets, they shall always be available. For example, there is an absolute bar under Swiss law that prohibits a foreign government from appropriating one of its citizens assets held in our banks. Further, Swiss law will not recognize any restriction on the transfer of those assets other than at the client's direction, nor disclose the transfer even under a foreign government order. Also, as Hans mentioned, foreign government orders requesting disclosure have no standing in Switzerland and will not be recognized. We will not allow our castle walls to be penetrated by any government or individual.

"Our clients put their assets in Swiss banks for a myriad of legitimate reasons, over and above the pure banking benefits. Over the history of the bank, our services have been used by our clients to avoid political persecution, illegal actions by corrupt governments and a range of situations too broad to even imagine. For that reason, we make no judgment as to a client's motivation. Swiss law is based on this high-minded principle...it is the core of our bank's culture. Gentlemen, we have covered much ground in a short while. Shall we take a break for refreshment?"

The meeting resumed in exactly fifteen minutes with Karl explaining the legal structure of the various banking and investment entities outlined on the board. More out of curiosity than concern, Paul and I asked many questions seeking to understand and learn their motivations. Then, the discussion moved to an overview of procedures, including methods of deposit, wire transfers and the various investment opportunities that the bank could make available. Hans emphasized that all funds could be held as liquid cash or invested in a wide array of choices made available by the bank's investment arm. The discussion turned to specifics as Paul homed in on processes that we could use.

"So, here is a not-so-theoretical question," I prompted. "What if our client holds significant amounts of cash that it would like to deposit into your bank? How exactly would that work?"

Hans looked at Karl holding his hands open and outstretched.

"That is very simple. For example, your jet could have been the carrier for large amounts of cash. Rather than having Tuso meet you at the plane, we would have a bank officer and an armored car arranged ahead of time. The funds would be counted, deposit documentation provided, and the cash loaded into the armored vehicle for transport to the Nassau bank branch and subsequent transfer to Zurich. It is that simple."

A pause in the conversation ensued, broken by Paul. "That explanation is very straightforward and clear. I still have a good number of procedural questions about what goes on in Zurich but I'm sure we don't need to deal with them today."

"Paul," Hans said, "please feel free to come to Zurich anytime. We would welcome your visit."

Paul pulled me aside. "What would you think if I went to Zurich now?"

It hadn't occurred to me, but it should have. "Paul, I think that's a great idea. Let's get this thing buttoned up. We've been procrastinating way too long."

Paul turned to Hans. "Would it be possible for me to fly back to Zurich with you,

Hans? Our client is under some time pressure so we would like to respond to its needs."

Hans appeared a little surprised but recovered his diplomatic exterior quickly.

"But, of course. It would be our pleasure. I am actually flying back tonight, so you are welcome to join me. I will make all necessary arrangements for you to meet with the appropriate people tomorrow morning in Zurich."

I stepped around the table and shook hands with Hans, and then Karl. "Gentlemen, thank you for your time. I can speak for all of us when I say that we are quite comfortable that this relationship will work well for our client. We look forward to working together."

With that, Karl hit a buzzer on the phone and in just seconds, a drop-dead gorgeous black woman dressed in a tan suit with a skirt that revealed long, perfect legs pushing a cart in front of her carrying several bottles of Dom Perignon champagne and six fluted glasses.

Bloomfield, New Mexico

The silver van, a Dodge with a pop-top, skidded into a dark corner of the parking lot, kicking up gravel that quickly fell to the ground and a cloud of dust that floated away disappearing into the darkness. The front doors of the van swung open in unison as the side door slid along the track and banged into the stop. A quick burst of Allman Brothers music blasted into the night and abruptly died away. Fragrant, gray smoke drifted through the doors and away into the New Mexico night as three long-haired young men sprang from the portals and intently walked toward the lighted structure.

A rectangular concrete block building sat in the middle of the lot, surrounded by half a dozen pick-ups and a few cars. A glass storefront exposed the brilliantly lit interior. Chairs—actually modified school desks--with white Formica dining tops lined the glass, several occupied by customers, some eating—some waiting. A counter bisected the width of the building. Behind it, two men and two women in bright white uniforms topped with boat-shaped caps worked feverishly as smoke drizzled upward form the grill. Above the building, the white shape of a huge sign that looked like a dirigible tethered to the roof floated over the structure, proclaiming in bright red and blue neon letters "Blake's LotaBurger," the New Mexico icon that had come to define delectable cheeseburgers loaded with culinary fire in the form of Hatch green chile.

"God I'm starved," the tallest of the men, Ricky Gydeson, announced striding in front of the other two.

"That bag of chips and package of Oreos didn't last very long," Bruce Talbot said.

Marc Martin chimed in. "Once again, we have proven that 'munchies' is just an urban myth," breaking the three up into laughter Locals waiting for late dinners eyed the men suspiciously and wondered what was so funny as they filed in and lined up under the "Order Here" sign.

"How may I help you?" asked the chunky, grandmotherly lady with her hair in a net and a red, white and blue badge pinned on her white dress straight out of the Thirties that indicated she was "Ruby Cardenas, Assistant Manager." She reminded Marc of the cafeteria ladies from his grade school days.

He stepped to the counter. "Three Lotaburgers with cheese and green chile, three large fries, and...you guys want shakes?" "Chocolate?" "Chocolate...and three chocolate shakes".

Ruby echoed back: "that's three Lotaburgers with cheese and green chile, three large fries, and three chocolate shakes...eleven twenty-seven." All three dug into jeans pockets and threw bills and coins on the counter. Marc tallied the money and pushed it across the stainless- steel counter. "There you go."

Ruby counted. "This is only ten seventy-seven." This sent the other two travelers into a giggling fit. "And he's an accountant!" Ricky said, followed by more giggling. Marc held out some more change sheepishly and Ruby picked out the balance of coins needed.

The cook, a tall Hispanic teenage boy, tossed three ready-made paddies on the grill setting off a loud sizzle while Ruby dropped three orders of fries into the hot fryer. After a flurry of well- rehearsed activity, the cook placed mounds of diced Hatch green chile on the grill, releasing an aroma that was as close to heaven as real New Mexicans could imagine—acrid, smoky, and sweet all roiling together in the spirits rising from the grill. Skillfully, the cook swept up each pile with a single, serpentine swipe of the spatula and deposited the chile on the waiting burger. Then, bracketing slightly browned buns around meat, cheese, lettuce, onions, tomatoes—the all- important green chile—and mustard, all were wrapped in paper and placed in Lotaburger sacks with fries and condiments. The men grabbed the food and headed out the same door they had entered only minutes before, every eye in the place warily following the interlopers.

As the three filed out, the plate glass door shook with a loud bang. The man in the middle grabbed his head and yelled "Owwww". Marc, bringing up the rear, jerked back startled. "Oh, geeze, Bruce, I am so sorry. I just pushed the door. I, I..." Unable to hold their laughter any longer, the first two doubled over laughing until they could hardly get their breath. As the inside diners watched through the storefront, the two clowns demonstrated to the victim their well- choreographed stunt that relied on the perfect timing of the front man kicking the door at the bottom just as the next guy through grabbed his head. "You are children," Marc snorted as all three dissolved into laughter, heading back to the waiting "Silver Goose" with their treasures.

CHAPTER 4

MONDAY, MAY 22

Nassau International Airport, Bahamas

W ow, those guys are beet red!
"Good morning, Captain. Looks like you and Tom got more than a little sun." "Yes, we did, but in the process, we hooked into some great fish. Tom latched on to a blue marlin that he fought for an hour. We had quite an experience."

"I'm glad it worked out well for you. We may not have had as much fun as you guys, but we fully accomplished our business objectives, so I guess that counts for something," I said.

"Did you lose one of your troops?" Tom queried.

"Paul hopped on a flight to Zurich last night, so it will just be the three of us. I hope that doesn't cause a problem weight-wise or whatever."

"Oh no, no problem," the captain said. "Shall we get underway?"

With that, Tom took our duffels and led us up the stairway and into the plane while the captain completed the on-ground paperwork.

Soon, we were lined up on the taxiway. The co-pilot came back to the cabin to check that our seat belts were fastened and all else was well. Moments later the Lear began its rollout down the runway. Although I was now a "seasoned" jetsetter with two previous take-offs under my belt, the exhilaration was undiminished. I watched out of my window as the plane literally jumped off the ground and headed skyward. Within moments, Nassau was a green and brown fleck in a giant blue ocean behind us.

I settled into my seat while my thoughts ranged back over the last few days. What a whirlwind! But it had been fun, and more importantly, brought me a lot of comfort about the future. *Things are falling into place nicely* I thought and closed my eyes.

I may have just dozed off when a huge BOOM shook the plane, the blast exploding with a shudder down the port side of the jet. I looked back to see Andy and Beto violently thrust forward as the plane seemed to stop in midair. A second later, I let out a scream of pain as my head struck the seatback in front of me with a "splat". The plane dropped like a rock. We were attached to the craft only by our seat belts.

Andy was screaming a piercing war cry. Beto was frozen, his hands gripping the armrests in a white-knuckle death grip. The cabin rolled to the right like a carnival ride. I remember holding my nose as blood ran from an open gash, and again, I felt as though time had slowed. I looked across at my cabin-mates, Andy with his face locked in a scream; Bato's, a bloodless mask. Through the aircraft windows I could see nothing but ocean. It seemed to me that the wing pointed to our ultimate destination.

Just as suddenly, the jet rolled wildly to the left. I saw flames pour from the port engine. The roll slowed but sickeningly continued until we were upside down and then on over until the right wing was again pointed straight toward the water below. I saw Beto retch, spewing a stream of barf into the air that seemed to float weightlessly there.

The cabin then righted in its rolling motion but still pointed downward at a dizzying angle.

"Shit. Fucking shit, Darren," I heard Andy yell. The craft was screaming in a high- pitched whine, gathering speed as it dove. The rolling began again, though less drastic, first left and then right in a sickening roller-coaster like motion of weightlessness followed by a huge force jamming me into my seat. Soon, we were all puking violently, slimy projectiles floating then splashing about the cabin, combined with the blood that continued to spurt from my face. Oxygen masks had fallen from the ceiling and swung menacingly over our heads.

The violent swinging was replaced by a hard, driving bank to the left with the craft seeming to gather even more speed, painfully pushing the arm rests into my ribs. I looked out the window. I could barely see the horizon and, directly below, I could now see the form of waves.

The diving turn seemed to last an eternity, taking the ship through two, then three, complete three-hundred- and sixty-degree rolls. The entire cabin was shaking as though being driven on the crossties of a railroad track. I could see the individual wave tops clearly visible as the plane dropped relentlessly, losing altitude at a horrifying pace.

Ever so slowly, I felt the nose of the plane rise, though the craft continued in a hard, banked turn. It looked to me that we were within a couple hundred meters of the water when the craft's dive slowed then leveled. The screaming whine stopped, and I heard only the soft sound of air flowing around the craft. I sat quietly trying to compose myself.

"Andy, Andy, are you okay? How's Beto?" I asked.

Andy wiped mucous from his face with his hand. "I'm fine. Beto? Beto?" Beto's frozen visage was unmoved, his eyes unfocused.

"Darren, you're bleeding," Andy said.

For the first time, it dawned on me that blood covered my clothes and hands. I reached to the pain on the bridge of my nose, as the cabin door opened, and a clearly rattled Tom Hanson poked his head through. His first attempt at words produced only gusts of air. Finally, walking unsteadily into the cabin he asked, "how are you guys? Mr. Jacobs, you're bleeding. Andy? Beto?"

Andy had regained his battlefield composure. "We're okay. Darren's gash looks worse than it is. Beto's taking a bit of trip on us, right now."

Tom looked over to see Beto's blank expression, punctuated by vacant eyes that conveyed nothing. Anticipating the worst, he had brought a first aid kit. He handed a bandage to Andy. "Stick that on Darren's wound if you can. The port engine is gone. We're flying on the starboard engine. Pull your life vests from under your seats and get them on."

Andy grabbed a vest and put it over Beto's head, struggling to get it snapped around Beto's unmoving body. He and I then put on our own vests.

Looking out the window, I could see damage to the wing, part of the aluminum skin pulled open and blackened.

Tom went on. "Listen, guys, I'm not going to shit you. We aren't out of this yet. The captain did an unbelievable job of keeping us out of the drink, but we are literally flying on a wing and a prayer right now. We're going to divert to Miami International. Captain is radioing ahead to prepare for us. We will fly at this altitude, hopefully, all the way there. I'm going to go back up now. I'll come back and give you instructions before we set down...unless I don't get the chance. If we have to ditch, I'll give you as much warning as I can, but it may not be much. Just lean forward and grab your ankles. The captain and I will get you out of the plane."

With those instructions, Tom returned to the cockpit leaving the cabin door open. I leaned into the aisle, but all I could see was Richardson's right hand resting on the controls.

"Andy, we've got to see if we can get Beto back. He may need to have all his faculties before this is over with," I said.

Andy leaned in and started talking in Beto's ear, though I couldn't actually hear the words. Minutes went by as Andy continued to speak to Beto, then Beto turned his head and looked at Andy as if coming out of sleep. "Andy, what's going on? Where are we?"

Their whispered conversation continued for some time. Beto began to move a little and look around the cabin, finally settling his eyes on me. "Darren, you're hurt, man."

Andy turned his face to me, and I was shocked, yet again. Tears were streaming down his face faster than he could wipe them away. Since he was twelve years old, I have never seen him cry.

"Beto, I'm okay. Just a gash. We're in a bit of a pickle, but it's all going to be okay," I said.

Beto nodded slowly as color returned to his face and recognition to his eyes. Looking out the window, he finally spoke. "I don't think we're supposed to fly this low. Do you think we are going to get into trouble?"

I threw a troubled glance at Andy just before Beto turned to look at us, his typically perpetual trademark smile having returned to his face causing all three of to laugh in relief.

For forty-five minutes, the jet rumbled just over the water. Not a word was spoken. I guess we were each lost in our thoughts, and I found myself thinking back to the first time I saw Andy and Beto--the summer before sixth grade. That's the first year— after many years of begging--that my parents allowed me to ride my bike on the dirt paths through the Bosque--forest in English--along the Rio Grande River behind our farm. I was beside myself ecstatic at this new freedom and tore through the sandy river bottom populated by old cottonwoods as fast as I could pedal. About a half an hour into my ride, I flew around a corner to find two boys walking with fishing poles on the path directly in front of me. There was no way I could stop before hitting them, so I slammed the rear brake hard and laid the bike down into a slide, smacking into both of them with the tires. Before I could get out from under my bike, the Hispanic kid was on top of me with his fist cocked. I was relieved, but only for a minute, when the larger Anglo kid grabbed him.

"Beto, no way. The rich kid's mine."

I remember feeling like a gladiator in the arena waiting while the two emperors argued over which one was going to kill me. Worse, they had hold of my bike and were surely not going to let go of it.

"Let's flip a coin to see who gets him first," the Anglo kid said. "Fair's fair."

He then flipped the coin, Beto called "heads" and won. Well, I wasn't going down without a fight, so I squared up with my fists raised to box—as I had been taught men do—when Beto tackled me, knocking the breath out of me when I hit the ground. As I crawled around, trying to get my breath back, the two of them laughing so hard they were nearly breathless something came over me and the next thing I knew, I was on top of Beto pounding him with my fists and the big kid was trying to pull me off.

Somehow, we all three ended up sitting on the ground, completely exhausted, eyeing each other, trying to decide who was going to do what next.

"I'm Darren."

The big kid said, "Hi, I'm Andy," and looked at Beto in inquiry.

That's the first time I saw Beto's award-winning smile, and I remember being very, very happy to see it.

"Hey, Darren, I'm Beto. You're about half tough—for a rich kid, you know."

We spent the rest of the afternoon, and then the rest of the summer, taking turns riding my bike, having mud fights in the flats by the Rio Grande, and becoming the very best of friends.

And I spent the summer, evading my parents. "What in the world do you do down there, Darren? You're not getting into any trouble, are you?"

"Oh, no, I have become quite the bird-watcher," I lied. Every day that I could get away, I rode off on my bicycle with a backpack loaded with my binoculars, a birding book, and enough food for three guys. Andy, Beto and I had a meeting place where I kept some old clothes hidden. As soon as I arrived, I would replace my slacks, golf shirt and clean tennis shoes with a ratty pair of jeans, a white tee shirt, and an old pair of Converse All Stars; of course, reversing the process prior to returning home. Sometimes, we would even make up notes for my birding book which I would show Mom and Dad at night. They were thrilled with my interest in ornithology.

One day, Andy said, "School starts in two weeks. Can you believe it?"

My stomach got queasy. The summer had so captivated me that I hadn't even thought of school starting, but when I did, I realized that I did not want to go back to the private school where I had been my entire school career. I had found my buds, and I did not want to give them up. I broached the subject with Mom and Dad that night, only to be met with a resounding "No". Our family had a hand in founding the school, and the thought of a Jacobs not attending was "sheer folly". But I persisted with daily pleadings, arguing about wanting to know regular kids, not just rich kids. I knew this would have a punch since my parents were, I now realize, what would be called liberals. The winning argument, however, was my promise to bring home straight "A's" if I could go to public school. Mom, Dad and I had had many discussions about my laziness at school and how they could not understand that I could be perfectly "okay" with underperforming.

I rode like the wind to our meeting place that day, yelling to Andy and Beto as soon as I saw them, "I'M GOING TO SCHOOL WITH YOU. I'M GOING TO SCHOOL WITH YOU." It was that day that the three of us, in a finger-slicing, blood-exchanging ritual along the Rio Grande, pledged our loyalty to one another for all times and dubbed ourselves The Three Musketeers. Thinking back, I think Andy and Beto were first stunned, and then impressed, that I would give up my fancy school "in the Heights" to be with them. *And now, we may all die together in this shiny tin can.*

༄

Their early shenanigans are now lore in New Mexico, including tying a teacher to the flagpole in front of school one morning and streaking an assembly long before streaking became a fad. After high school graduation, Andy and Beto had gone a very different direction from

Darren's blueblood route to Boston. A bar fight in Belen one night left three railroad workers badly injured and Andy and Beto in the local jail. Hauled before a magistrate for the fourth or fifth time, Hector Martinez had had all of the two he wanted. "I'm going to give you two another night to sit in your stinking cell and think about this offer and make a choice. On the one hand, you can choose to visit *mi amigo,* Don Reynolds the local Army recruiter, or, on the other hand, I am going to throw the book at you. Those boys are hurt more than a little, and you are going to be looking at felony charges. And, need I remind you? your rich *compadre* is no longer around to bail your sorry asses out of this mess. So, you go think tonight and come back tomorrow morning with an answer."

So, Andy and Beto joined the Army. Both excellent athletes in high school, they signed up for Special Forces training when it became available on the condition that they be allowed to stay together. Easily completing requirements as two of the best candidates to ever go through the rigorous program, they were immediately shipped off to the rapidly spinning-out-of-control mess in Vietnam. There, they spent two tours of duty, mostly in Cambodia and Laos in operations that didn't exist as far as the U.S. government was concerned. They decided not to re-up for a third gig just about the time that things really started to go badly in Vietnam. Back in Albuquerque, they read about the Tet Offensive that marked 1968 and were particularly glad not to be in the middle of it.

"Hey, *pendejo,* when you going to get your white-ass down here for a serious blowout?" Darren's answering machine in Boston announced Andy and Beto's return to the States. "If you're not too snooty, that is. We'll be hanging at El Patio all night. Eddie's on duty. He'll find the least damaged one of us to talk to ya'."

I didn't call, however. Though it was the middle of the fall semester of the second year of law school, Ie got the next flight out of Boston for Albuquerque, traveled all night and took a cab straight to the El Patio on the highly likely chance that the other two-thirds of the Three Musketeers would be seated at the bar working off the previous night's hangover. "Sure as shit, I knew I would find you low-lifes here." And, thus, began two straight days and nights of partying as old friends reunited and the distance of the two years that had passed since they had last met in Hawaii quickly faded. The Three Musketeers were back!

As sobriety slowly started sneaking its way back on the afternoon of the third day, Andy, Beto and I finally sat down for what passed as serious discussion among them. I began the conversation in a straightforward manner. "Other than creating mayhem, what are you two scumbags good for?" Andy and Beto feigned hurt. I rushed on, "Seriously, what are you two going to do now?"

After a brainstorming session that offered up and then discarded ideas including a motorcycle shop, filming porn movies, and doing something with turquoise jewelry, I stopped as if jolted and looked up. "Let's buy the El Patio from Eddie. He's always bitching about running the damned place, and you two know as much about bars as anybody."

"That may be true," offered Beto, "but our knowledge don't extend past this side of the bar. We don't have a friggin' clue what happens in the kitchen or behind the bar. And, besides that, the goddamned liquor license is probably worth two hundred thousand these days. Eddie's had it forever."

Eddie was summoned and I point-blank asked him, "You wanna sell this son of a bitch, for real Eddie?"

Eddie's one-word response: "abso-fucking-lutely."

Before heading back to Boston, I stopped by and saw my somewhat shocked father and told him about the deal I proposed.

"I need to borrow the money out of my trust, and I still needed Caleb Jacob's signature," which his father grudgingly provided. And, thus it was, that Beto and Andy became bar owners and managers. The Jacobs family lawyers set up a three-way partnership at my instructions, even splits all the way around. The name was, of course, El Tres Musketeers, Limited.

Beto and Andy surprised everybody by treating the El Patio as if it were a military mission. Eddie stuck around long enough to show them the ins and outs of running the place, including the critical lessons of how to make sure the help and vendors didn't steal every damned penny of profit. They started having promotions like "Girl's Nights Out" and bringing in live music. In no time, the college crowd and young professionals had made El Patio the place to be. With my approval, they wrangled an SBA business loan to add on room for a real dance floor and a covered patio to handle the overflowing crowds. A couple of really talented brothers from Los Alamitos, the Burnhams, put together a house band that played five nights a week. Lawyers, Guns, and Money was a hit from day one. By the time I got home for summer break, Beto and Andy had amassed a chunk of cash for splitting three ways.

"Here's you a little taste of reward for your entrepreneurial vision that saw the potential of a couple of worthless assholes like Andy and me," said Beto as he handed me a check for twenty thousand dollars, one-third of the first six months' profits. Beto and Andy had the bookkeeper draw similar checks for themselves. I was dumbfounded. I knew they were doing okay, but this was unbelievable. Looking around the dumpy little office in the back of the bar, I could hardly believe what a gold mine I had invested in.

"And here's the icing on the cake." Andy handed me a bundle of bills with a five- thousand-dollar band around them. "This here is tax-free *dinero*, partner. It doesn't exactly come from the bar."

Puzzled, I asked, "then where the hell does it come from?"

"Look," interjected Beto, "when we were in 'Nam, we sort of learned how to make a little spending money from, ahem, let's say a distribution business. Here, want to try a little of the merchandise?" Beto rolled an Acapulco Gold fatty across the table to me.

I sat stunned for a minute and then couldn't hold back a wide grin. "You crazy bastards. Nothing you do should surprise me." i lit up the doobie, expertly placed it between my lips and inhaled deeply. "Good shit, no doubt."

"Only the best," replied Andy and Beto in unison, smiling.

∽

Tom yelled back from the cockpit. "All right, gentlemen, please get ready for arrival at Miami International. We are going to make a wheels-up landing, so you won't hear the landing gear deploy. We're going to be a little busy up here, so this is your last announcement. Hang on tight, fellows."

With that, he pulled the cockpit door closed. I could see the Florida shoreline appearing out the port side of the plane. My first thought was that wave skimming in a jet would be pretty cool under other conditions. Like if I weren't so scared that I couldn't summon any saliva into my mouth. For the first time in my life, I felt real heart-pounding, palm-sweating fear—the primal fear of not surviving. And I can tell you, I didn't like the feeling at all.

I looked back and, for the first time ever, I saw panic in Andy's eyes. "Don't sweat it, brothers. This cat knows what he's doing." I said it emphatically...but it wasn't what I was feeling.

~

Vallecito Lake, Colorado

After searching around the cabin successfully, Marc threw on his jeans and sweatshirt from the night before. Although it was mid-May, at nearly nine thousand feet, it was damned cold. Trudging to the kitchen, he scrounged around in the cabinet and pulled out a drip coffee maker and filters and got it set up on the counter. They had stopped in Bloomfield the night before and picked up essentials for the morning. He dug the Folgers out of the bottom of a paper grocery bag and, using the key provided on the lid, spun the metal strap around the top finally releasing a gust of coffee aroma with a whoosh. He measured the coffee directly from the can into the filter and after opening a gallon jug of water picked up the night before, filled the reservoir to the brim. They wouldn't get the well cranked up until later in the day so bringing drinking water was a priority. Marc hit the start button and the coffee began to make. First mission accomplished.

Marc had been a visitor to Ricky's cabin many times over the past two years. As always, the first view from the deck in the morning literally took Marc's breath away. Sprawled below was the pristine blue body of water, Vallecito Lake, twinkling as though covered with sparkling diamonds reflecting the morning sun. The lake was surrounded on all sides by pine-covered hills that arose from grass meadows now yellow with dandelions. Incredible peaks set the backdrop above the lake and surrounding green basin, rugged rocky crags shooting jaggedly into the sky and still covered with most of the snow from the winter's fall. Marc became hypnotized moving his focus to and from the three planes in his view—the blue of the water closest, a solid green and yellow panorama in the midfield, and most transfixing of all, the contrasting field of dark gray shapes interspersed with blindingly white, mixed geometric forms in the distance.

Unconsciously, Marc started humming "Rocky Mountain High" which was soon interrupted by the obnoxious buzzer announcing the coffee's readiness.

Marc was on his second cup of coffee when his peace was shattered by Bruce's morning ritual, a noisy stretch accompanied by growls, yelps and groaning that issued forth from the kitchen and seemed to go on forever. Finally, Bruce stepped outside wearing gray, beat-to-hell sweats and sipping coffee out of a huge, turquoise mug with the orange and black image of Tigger wrapped around its perimeter. "Hey, man."

"Morning, Bruce. You okay?"

"Yeah, if warmed over shit is okay. Based on how I'm feeling, I'd say you were pretty smart to limit your intake of those goddamned tequila shooters last night." His always deep voice was more of a growl.

Marc just laughed, thinking to himself that Bruce had an "off/on" switch. He had a tendency to run full tilt when he was partying, working, or studying. But when he was just relaxing, no one could do it better. He crawled into the hammock slung diagonally across the corner railings where he might not visibly move for an hour.

In a few minutes, Ricky emerged in his standard issue cabin garb; old blue jeans faded to the palest of blues, running shoes, an undershirt and blue and gray Pendleton plaid overshirt. At six foot four, he still had the build of the serious basketball player that he had been; his lean frame a regular fixture running his five-mile circuit around the old nine-hole golf course by the law school.

"Hey, Bruce, you gonna live?" Ricky chided.

"I'm debating. Right now, I would say the effects of a terminal, fucking hangover are likely to win."

"Let's walk over to the Shoreline and get us some breakfast and a bit of the hair of the dog. That'll cure what ails ya'," Ricky said.

With that, Bruce miraculously propelled himself out of the hammock in spirited gymnastic form landing squarely on his two feet, and the three set out the half-mile walk to the Shoreline.

☙

Precariously perched alongside the Vallecito Lake Road, the Shoreline was built in a style known locally as "backwoods trashy" with barn red vertical siding, white trim, and a tin roof. Out in front, it sported a chalk board with the daily specials.

Marc read aloud, "Today's Special -- Homemade Biscuits and Gravy with Two Eggs—$2.25."

Inside, the interior décor was no improvement over the exterior. But it didn't matter because the entire back wall of the restaurant was glass that framed a spectacular view of Vallecito Lake, backdropped by the snow-covered mountains. The tacky plastic plaid tablecloths and linoleum floor were hardly even noticed by the diners, as all eyes focused on the scenery, glancing down only when necessary to take in a bite of food or slug of coffee.

The three marched straight through the dining room, out the back door and down a flight of steps to the outdoor deck that sat one level below the main floor. A few other locals were already at tables in various stages of eating, sipping coffee, or reading *The Durango Times*. Hummingbird feeders were hung all around the railing and the early morning round of aerial warfare had already begun. A male Ruby Redthroat as big as a finch was driving off the competition.

"Hey, Ricky," hollered one of the old-timers, "you out for the summer?"

While Marc and Bruce sat down at a table along the rail, Ricky sauntered over to where the old gentleman was sitting. The table they picked was not popular with those sufferers of heights as the forest floor was at least a hundred feet below. The view, however, was unbeatable.

After a few minutes, Ricky returned to the table. "That guy used to practice law with my dad. He pretty much naps all day now, but we fished with him a lot when I was a kid." Ricky's family was part of the original settlers at Vallecito, building a cabin on the lake in 1946 as the water was still backing up behind the dam to create the lake. The Gydeson family relocated to Vallecito in the summers, though Ricky's dad commuted to his law offices during the week. The summer population around the lake had grown to several thousand, but everyone except the greenest newcomers knew Ricky and his family.

"Good morning, gents, glad to see you survived the year," said a beaming Addie Carson, a local cowgirl that Ricky had known all his life and Bruce and Marc had gotten to know the past few years. Addie lived with a no-account cowboy who they did not like. He worked cattle in the summer but the rest of the year, he drank up Addie's earnings and chased skirts while she was working night shifts. "What can I get for you this morning? My guess would be three Bloody Mary's to start."

"You guessed right, Addie. And when you get time, three specials to boot," Ricky replied. "God, Addie, you look great. Did you get a new 'do or what?"

"Ahhh, you sweet talker," she said over her shoulder as she sashayed off with a coffee pot expertly refilling coffee cups while gliding effortlessly between the tables. Marc was reminded of highly efficient truck stop waitresses he had watched with admiration.

Addie delivered the Bloody Mary's breaking the silence that had fallen over all three as they were each lost in their own thoughts staring out over the lake.

"Don't tell me. The first thing we have to do is go back to the cabin and fix the shitty pump," offered Bruce with a grimace.

"Yep," Ricky said, "that's always the first order of business in the summer. At least the water table is up this year, so I don't think pulling enough water is going to be an issue."

"Does that mean we don't have to put up that, obnoxious sign this year?" asked Marc. "And we can live somewhat civilized?"

The previous summer had been a particularly dry year and water rationing was in effect at the cabin, which meant the institution of a rule codified by a sign on the only bathroom door: "If it's yellow, let it mellow. If it's brown, flush it down." It wasn't much of an imposition on the fellows who just periodically wandered off into the woods, but female visitors were particularly grossed out.

"Yeah, with the table way up and all that snow still in the pack, we'll be fine. And look at that little falls squirting out of the cliff over there." Ricky pointed to a spot across the valley. "That's a sure sign that the pressure on the whole aquifer is good."

Addie reappeared with three plates heaping with biscuits, gravy, and eggs. All conversation ceased as the young men ate with gusto the way young men can. With expert timing, Addie returned to the table with three mugs of coffee, which she sat down before clearing the table. The sun was fully on the deck now and warming with the intensity only a mountain sun can provide. At almost nine thousand feet altitude, the rays bore down with little atmosphere to protect the sun worshipers.

Bruce lit a cigarette, a vice he had no ambivalence about no matter the pressure from his friends. He fended off every criticism with a politically incorrect, "Go fuck yourself."

Marc looked at Ricky. "What time are the girls supposed to show up tonight?"

"Oh, shit, I forgot to tell you, guys. We're going to meet them in Durango about eight. Nancy and Barb talked to Donna and they're going to pick her up at the hospital when they hit town and then swing over to the Solid Muldoon."

"So that means, once we get the pump going, we have the rest of the day to just plunk our lazy asses by the lake?" Bruce queried.

"Well, not completely," Ricky said. "We need to spend time today getting our gear ready and checked out."

"Oh, ma-a-a-an, we've got till Friday," Bruce whined.

"Yeah, but none of us are going to want to spend time messing with camping gear once the girls get here. Am I right?"

Bruce reluctantly agreed, and with that, each threw a pile of bills on the table, saying goodbye to Addie on the way out.

Miami

The descent was surprisingly smooth, what there was of it. I jumped when the jet bumped softly as it connected with the foam-soaked runway, the cabin gliding just above the ground. It seemed to me that, other than not hearing the sound of the landing-gear mechanics and the low-rider feeling from sliding along on the plane's belly, the landing was typical and uneventful. But outside, I could see a platoon of fire and rescue vehicles racing along on both sides of us. The plane slowed and, finally, the left wing touched the ground, spinning the jet softly to stillness as though we were skiing to a perfect telemark stop.

Tom raced out of the cockpit and threw open the exit door. Deploying the emergency slide was not necessary; with the fuselage on the runway, the bottom of the exit door was nearly at ground level. "Let's go, gentlemen, out we go," Tom said in a cheerful, almost giddy voice.

I undid my seat belt and stood. My legs were shaky, and I had to steady myself a minute before stepping into the aisle. I felt Andy's big paw on my back. "How...how...ya' doin'...Dare?"

I turned and smiled at Andy and Beto as they filed out behind me. When I reached the exit, emergency personnel fully robed in fireproof garb were waiting for us. They helped me to the ground first and then Beto and Andy. The foam-soaked runway was slippery, so each of us was escorted by a firefighter on each side who delivered us to the waiting emergency vehicle, its back doors open. Two EMTs helped us into the back and immediately started working on my head. When they finished with me and were checking Andy and Beto, I looked out the back doors. The jet was lying crippled, its blackened fuselage, wing and engine were made even more dramatic by the contrast with the rest of the gleaming white jet.

"Andy, good thing we had Dare with us today. The fucking mojo of Da Jewel was in full force. If it had been just you and me, we'd be fish food now," Beto said. "Right, Dare?"

"Maybe Da Jewel some, Beto, but mostly one of the best pilots that ever flew a plane, I think." Possibly it was because I was still shaky from the near crash, but for the first time in my life, I wasn't so sure Da Jewel was still protecting me.

The captain exited the Lear looking as though he had been on a buggy ride around Central Park instead of one of the most harrowing experiences imaginable. They packed Tom and him into an airport security van behind our ambulance and hurried us all away from the plane. While there was no indication of fire, I guess they were taking no chances.

When the ambulance stopped and the back doors were opened, there stood Captain Richardson in full-out "take charge" mode.

"Gentlemen, I can't tell you how badly I feel about what just occurred. We will, I promise you, get to the bottom of what caused it. The FAA will be all over it, but I take this personally and will know what happened or there will be hell to pay. Tom Hanson, just so you know, responded brilliantly to the crisis, not at all a surprise to me."

Tom, still obviously shaken but the consummate professional, just nodded.

"They are going to run you all over to an emergency facility for check-ups and treatment. Standard procedure. Tom and I will catch up with you later."

Despite the EMTs attempts to corral me, I climbed out of the truck followed by Andy and Beto and I immediately grabbed Richardson in a bear hug. "Man, you guys saved our bacon. I don't know beans about flying, but I am sure what you and Tom just did was phenomenal." The captain mumbled something about just doing their jobs, as all we manly-men hugged one another. The thought struck me that, by a happenstance of fate, the five of us would have this experience as a common bond for the rest of our lives.

Vallecito Lake, Colorado

Ricky yelled from the back of the cabin, "Marc, go ahead and turn the power back on." Marc threw the switch, and the hum of the electric motor and pump began. An outside faucet was open and, in a few seconds, water began to gush, first in spurts and then steadily, from the spout.

"Perfect job," Bruce said as Marc sauntered back to the pump. "We are getting better at this shit. It only took an hour and a half this year. And son of a bitch, do you know what time it is?" Bruce asked.

"Beer thirty," Marc said smiling as the three raced for the refrigerator like children after a Popsicle truck.

∽

The three had just completed their second year at the University of New Mexico Law School. Finals had wrapped up two days before, with the day after dedicated to serious partying. And today was the first day of a two-week Colorado vacation before the three would return to Albuquerque. Ricky and Bruce had positions clerking with local firms waiting, and Marc had committed to a stint with the public defender's office for clinical law.

As they sat on the back porch drinking cans of Coors, Marc thought back to the first time the three of them met at a mixer during the two-week orientation before first-year classes started. Marc remembered reading with some trepidation the announcements posted all over the commons at the law school. On the one hand, he was anxious to meet his classmates. On the other, they were so damned young. Having been out of undergraduate school for five years, made him feel like he was almost a full generation removed from the typical twenty-two- year-old first-year student.

He took some comfort, however, that the mixer was at Bruce Talbot's house, which happened to be just a few blocks from the law school. Bruce had made quite an impression on the entire class the second day of orientation, Marc particularly noting that Bruce appeared older.

At the conclusion of the second-day orientation session, the professor asked if there were any questions and Bruce had raised his hand and stood in an easy posture that showed a lot more confidence than his fellow classmates were feeling.

"Professor, I want to see if I have this straight if that is okay?" His voice fairly rolled in a low octave.

Professor Baumgartner replied, "Certainly, that was the point of my asking if there were questions."

Marc remembered that not only would he not have stood up and asked a question, but the professor's response would have flustered him to the point that he would have likely sat down. Bruce, however, seemed undaunted.

"My understanding of the finding of the case that we just studied is that because the State of Mississippi spent so much money caring for the patients at the state-run mental institution, that Mississippi had a vested interest and, therefore, the right to sterilize long-term patients to prevent the perpetration of the burden on the state with another generation." The incoming class had been using this case as a means to understand legal process and get comfortable with the library resources over the past two days.

"That is essentially correct, though not particularly well worded. Did I hear a question in there?"

Bruce pressed on. "No, I'm getting to that. And did I understand from the dean's incoming address that the State of New Mexico is paying over $10,000 per year for the cost of the legal education of each student in this room?" "That's correct, but I fail to see the relevance."

Again, Bruce undaunted pressed on further. "Could I see a show of hands of the number of students in this room who have one or more parents who are lawyers?"

As he looked around the room, hands began to be raised until considerably more than half the room had their hands in the air.

Bruce turned to Professor Baumgartner. "That seals it. The entire class must report to the commons for mandatory sterilization."

Baumgartner smiled, despite himself, having seen the cleverness of what was coming before the class, who then broke out in first laughter and then applause for Bruce's performance.

"Dismissed," Baumgartner said shaking his head.

Marc remembered thinking that he definitely wanted to meet this guy. *Well, what better chance than the mixer?*

Having vacillated all day as to whether he would really go or not, he finally threw on a windbreaker and, heading out the door, said out loud to nobody, "Screw it. How bad can it be?"

He followed the directions on the map and found the house easily. Getting out of his car, he heard typical party noises coming from behind the house—loud voices talking over Mungo Jerry's "In the Summertime" punctuated by the occasional laugh. Following a path around the side of the house, he found himself rounding the corner to a backyard filled with people paired off in twos, threes, and groups, most with plastic cups in their hands. His first reaction was to turn around before anyone saw him and head back to the car. What the hell was he doing here with these kids? Before he could act, though, he found himself the object of Bruce's invitation.

"Come in, man, how about a beer? Bruce Talbot," he said extending his right hand.

Marc found himself looking up at Bruce, who was, he guessed, just over six feet tall and something north of 200 pounds. Interesting coloring, blond curly hair that draped over his collar but dark skin and brown eyes.

"Marc Martin," he replied, shaking Bruce's hand at the same time.

"Glad to have another babysitter for these kids and their shitty diapers," Bruce said, swinging his arm around to indicate the cluster of guests.

One of the nearby bystanders who heard Bruce's comment looked up grinning, "Fuck you, Grandpa."

Bruce laughed while leading Marc to the keg. Soon, they were refilling their cups, totally engaged in conversation.

"So, how come you are so old?" Bruce asked, laughing and punching Marc's arm.

"I've been working for the past five years," Marc answered. "How about you?" "Yeah, same drill, but four years. Banking. And you?"

"CPA. Arthur Andersen in Denver."

"No, shit, a real live CPA?" Bruce said. "So, what's got you to law school? And why UNM?"

"Sort of a long story. I was a pre-law student at the University of Texas. Texas had this deal where you could finish pre-law in three years and go straight into law school. After law school, you got a JD and BS at the same time. Well, first semester of my junior year the Texas Legislature, in their wisdom, decided to get rid of the three-year program. I freaked since I was completely out of money and did the dumbest thing you could do--went to a counselor."

Bruce laughed at that. "And what brilliant advice did you get from that fucking font of knowledge?"

"He said, 'you've got to get a major' and pulled out a sheet of paper with all the majors alphabetically listed on them. 'Accounting. You any good at math?'"

"I told him I was, he handed me a form, and I became an accounting major," Marc said, shaking his head.

"Right," Bruce said, "but that doesn't explain how you got here."

"No it doesn't. I went on into the accounting program and almost had my accounting degree when I got accepted to UT Law School and, sort of as a lark, interviewed Arthur Andersen. They were on campus and needing folks for Denver. Well, about that time I picked up The Paper Chase...have you read it?"

"No, but I saw the movie," Bruce said.

"That book scared the hell out of me."

Bruce pulled on his jaw. "Look at the person to your left," he spoke slowly with perfect elocution. "...and now at the person on your right. At the end of this year, only one of you will be left."

"Exactly, that was the speech that did it for me. I turned down the UT Law School and took Arthur's offer."

"But now you're here?" Bruce asked.

"Yeah, you know, I really liked my time as a CPA, but I never could get the idea of being a lawyer out of my head. I started researching about law schools a couple years ago and became intrigued with UNM. So, I threw caution to the wind in May, accepted my invitation to UNM and resigned from Arthur. Everybody I worked with thought I had lost my mind. I don't know. Maybe I have. But here I am. You must have had a similar story?"

Bruce laughed shaking his head. "Sort of. I got into banking to get rich and found out that the only rich bankers were pricks who had inherited their banks from their daddies. I didn't particularly like the people or the work, started looking around at how guys made a lot of money starting from scratch, and saw a bunch of lawyer clients at the bank doing really well." "Where were you a banker?"

"Here. I'm an Indiana boy, born and raised. Went to Indiana U. and then followed that little red head over there out here to Albuquerque. "

Bruce pointed in the direction of a woman on the other side of the yard. Even with her back to Marc, he didn't have to watch but a moment to sense the energy. A group of women, most of them a head taller, were gathered around her. She was obviously the center of attention, her arms in constant motion and dark auburn hair bouncing in long curly ringlets.

"Ricky, glad you made it," Bruce said to a new arrival just coming into the backyard.

"Have you met Marc yet?"

"No, hey, Ricky Gydeson." He turned to Marc and held out his hand. "Marc Martin," Marc said shaking hands.

"Welcome, man, we have now officially convened the old farts club," Bruce said. "Marc and I were just telling each other how we got here in our advanced and declining states. I figure you have to be part of the group."

This was the first time Marc saw the Ricky Gydeson smile, more with his eyes than his mouth, which was mostly covered with a bushy mustache. Ricky conveyed warmth that Marc, and everyone who met him, found immediately disarming.

He spoke softly. "You're right, Bruce. Just turned a doddering old twenty-eight. UNM undergraduate in journalism. The last six years in Window Rock."

Marc was intrigued. Window Rock was the head of the Navajo Nation. "My gosh, what did you do there?"

"*Navajo Times,* editor the last four years."

"That had to be interesting, especially with all that's been going on in the tribal politics," Marc said.

Ricky shrugged. "Tribal politics is how I got to law school, but that's a story for another day. I could sure use a brew."

The three spent the next couple of hours emptying and refilling beer cups, talking comfortably as though they had long been friends, with occasional bathroom breaks and time- outs for Bruce to slip away to change the music. Linda Ronstadt and the Stone Ponies, Kenny Rogers and the First Edition, Three Dog Night and Paul Simon. Marc liked music and especially liked Bruce's picks.

Marc was telling Ricky and Bruce about a crazy client in Denver who had put air-to- ground rockets on his helicopter, when he sensed that he had lost their attention and noticed everyone looking behind him. When he turned, the reason for all the commotion became clear—the most striking woman he had ever seen had walked into the backyard. She had ridiculously long legs exposed below a navy-blue skirt that ended at least a foot above her knees while riding on stiletto high heels. A matching navy-blue jacket hung slightly lower than the skirt and covered most of a light blue shirt unbuttoned sufficiently to reveal a well-tanned chest with mounds left and right separated by strong cleavage. Her face was darkly tanned with cheekbones Katherine Hepburn would have envied, foundations for the largest, lightest blue eyes Marc ever remembered seeing. Long, straight black hair framed the diamond face and hung over one shoulder and behind the other. Completing the effect, her smile revealed perfectly white teeth surrounded by luscious, pouty lips.

"Barb!" Ricky raised his hand. She smiled and nodded in recognition, striding toward them. She and Ricky grabbed each other in a quick hug and then separated and smiled while looking into each other's eyes as though no one else in the world existed.

"Let me introduce you to some new friends and fellow ancient classmates. Barb, this is Bruce, our host... and Marc. Barb and I are...um, married. All of two months."

Barb took Bruce's hand in both of hers and looking him squarely in the eye said, "Barb O'Brien. Thanks for having this *soirée*...sorry to be so late, but duty called."

Marc noticed that Bruce was more flustered than he had been adlibbing in front of the whole class but was able to say graciously, "Just glad you could make it."

She then turned to Marc and, with the same direct smile and look, shook his hand and said, "I'm sure we are all going to be great friends over these next three years."

Marc, not having a great response, just met her look and said, "—nice to meet you, Barb. I'm sure you are right."

What a couple, he thought. Ricky was six four and, with the heels on, Barb was only an inch or two shorter. With long dark hair and the full mustache, Ricky could be mistaken for a rock star, particularly Marc thought, with this beauty on his arm.

"So, what duty kept you away from a beer bust today?" Marc surprised himself by asking.

"Oh, geez, I had a client presentation all day today that my boss scheduled but made me present." Marc was surprised that there was nothing of the "beautiful woman" attitude in her talk or manner. Instead, she was warm and charming.

"That's because he couldn't do the lecture. Barb won't tell you, so I will. She is a software developer for IBM assigned to Sandia Labs," Rick said.

Raising their eyebrows in unison, Marc and Bruce looked at one another, Bruce saying what they were both thinking. "Beauty and brains, Ricky, how did you get so lucky?" "Oh, posh," Barb said, and put her hand on Bruce's arm.

This evidently jangled Bruce's memory. "Come over and let me introduce you to the fireball."

The four of them shuffled across the backyard, stopping while Barb expertly pulled a draft from the keg. Walking toward the redhead's group, Marc thought that she hadn't slowed down a peg in the past hours.

Bruce tapped her on the shoulder.

"Yeah, yeah, yeah...hold on," came the response in a tiny, high-pitched voice that didn't match the intensity of its speaker. Not bothering to turn around, she pounded home her final point to her captive audience before spinning quickly, pulling Bruce's head down by the neck, and kissing him smack on the lips.

"Hi, Sweets, I've missed you. Did you make some new little friends?"

Before Bruce could speak, she stepped toward Barb, hand extended. "I'm Nancy Arrigoni."

"Barb O'Brien. Really nice to meet you." "Wow, you are really tall."

Barb threw her head back and laughed. "Wow, you are really redheaded."

Marc and Ricky barely had time to introduce themselves before Nancy, reaching up, put her arm around Barb's waist and dragged her off. "Let's go sit over here so we can talk about these guys without hurting their feelings."

Barb waved at Ricky, shrugging as Nancy towed the much larger woman across the yard, the beginning of what was to become a true friendship.

"That's quite a force of nature," Ricky offered to Bruce.

"You don't know the half of it. She set her fucking hook in me within an hour of meeting at a fraternity party and we've been together ever since."

"You don't look like you're trying too hard to get away," Marc said grinning.

"I guess not. I am the one who hauled my ass two thousand miles to be with her. "

"Does she have family here?"

"Does she! Italian Catholic. Five brothers and three sisters. If you haven't heard of the family business yet, you will—Arrigoni Real Estate. And most of the family works in one area of the business or another. Nancy was New Mexico Broker of the year last year and the year before, and probably will be again this year."

"So, you two have been together quite a while?" Ricky asked fishing.

"Eight years," he said picking up the drift of Ricky's question. "Her family is shitting bricks that we aren't married and adding to the Arrigoni grandkid pile, but..." his voice trailing off. "We don't do well living together. You'll see. How about you and Barb. What's your story?"

"We met last year and haven't spent a day without each other, since."

"I could see how you wouldn't want to let her get away. She's quite a package," Bruce said.

"What about you, Marc, did you bring someone with you from Denver?" Bruce asked, never one to be shy.

"No, I'm solo. I was dating a woman in Denver, but when I thought about asking her to come down here, it was just too much commitment. So, we said 'adios'."

The afternoon rolled away easily with lots of talk, laughter, keg beer and the origin of great friendships.

Thinking back to that afternoon, Marc was glad that he had summoned up the courage to go to the mixer. Since then, their friendships had become incredibly important to him. It wasn't just sharing law school pain, though certainly that created a bond, but more the way their personalities clicked. Ricky and Bruce had become confidants, and Marc thought the world of both Barb and Nancy. And, now he had Donna, and she had become one of the group.

Miami

We were taken to the emergency room at Miami Memorial. I got seven stitches to close up a diagonal gash on the bridge of my nose. They threw a collar brace on Andy for his injured neck.

"You guys are going to be sore tomorrow in places you didn't know you had," the emergency room doctor said to us. "But other than that, we've checked you out. No broken bones. Mr. Jacobs, you will need to get your stitches out in about a week. Your personal physician can do that. And, Mr. Trost, wearing that neck brace for a few days will just help support the head. You have no spinal injury, just badly damaged tissue."

I had a limo pick us up at the hospital and take us to Miami federal offices, where we were scheduled to meet with FAA investigators in the afternoon. As we came out of the hospital, we were swarmed by waiting news crews with cameras running, shoving microphones in our faces. I motioned to Andy and Beto to stand down; I knew they were getting ready to bowl through the reporters and cameramen, which they were certainly capable of doing. Both had been First Team All-State Football and they would have opened up a hole for me big enough to drive a tank through. I certainly didn't want to deal with the aftermath of that.

I am always saying that Andy and Beto are very different—and also very much alike.

Physically, Andy is the prototypical high school lineman: six foot one, two hundred and fifteen pounds; Beto, the consummate running back: five foot nine, one hundred seventy-five pounds.

Andy's hair is coarse and black and he has always cut it closely to his head. It looks like a tight black cap. Beto, on the other hand, is coiffed right out of "West Side Story". He combs his straight black hair back on the sides to a ducktail and is constantly fiddling with it. To cover an early receding hairline (which I tease him about unmercifully), he combs the top over in a flap which he frequently and unknowingly checks by layering it between his pointer and fore fingers and then weaving all of fingers back along the side of his head. And, while a day of sun will turn Andy's light skin a bright shade of red, Beto is impervious to it.

"You were just involved in a crash that nearly cost your lives. Can you tell us what happened? How do you feel?" the most aggressive bleached blonde reporter yelled as three microphones were thrust at me.

I'm accustomed to television interviews from years of being in the public, so this was no big deal. I fixed my most casual smile on my face. "That's a bit of an overstatement. As you can see, our injuries are minor and the plane will be back in the air shortly, I am sure."

"You are Representative Jacobs from New Mexico, is that correct?" "Yes, that is right."

"Can you tell us if this was an official visit? We understand you started this morning in Nassau?"

"No, my colleagues and I were vacationing. We just wanted to get away for a few days."

"Can you tell us what happened? Why the jet crashed?"

"The jet certainly did not crash. In fact, the landing was quite smooth, though, as you know, we did not lower the landing gear. There was some sort of malfunction and that is about all we know. If you will excuse us, we are off to speak to FAA officials about the incident," and with that I moved forward flanked by Andy and Beto. We swiftly sliced through the group with questions continuing to be shouted—and left unanswered. I instinctively wanted to minimize the press reports consistent with my philosophy of staying below the radar wherever possible.

ꜱ

At the FAA offices, Andy, Beto, and I were escorted through the lobby and down a hallway, where they separated us into three separate waiting offices. I spotted the backs of Dave Richardson and Tom Hanson through a half-glass wall, locked in conversation with three men in white shirts and ties, FAA guys I supposed.

I was questioned for about an hour and then led to a conference room, where Andy and Beto along with the captain and co-pilot were waiting with two of the three FAA guys. After brief introductions, the questioning and discussion continued for over another hour.

"Gentlemen, thank you so much for your time and willingness to share the details of your experience with us, particularly after such an, er, interesting flight," said the senior investigator. "We have your contact information in New Mexico. Thank you for that. This investigation will likely take up to six months. We move cautiously, so don't expect immediate findings. However, we will keep you apprised as we go."

The five of us caught the waiting elevator to the lobby. Dave put his hand out as if to shake hands goodbye. I put my arm around his shoulder. "You aren't going anywhere, Captain. You and Tom are our guests tonight. We're all staying at the Doral. I won't take no for an answer."

Tom smiled, "Captain, that's a much better offer than the Holiday Inn. What do you say?"

The captain looked down and pulled on his chin silently for a bit. "Gentlemen, we would be honored. We have to wait around for the CEO of our company to get here tomorrow. We'll give him a heart attack and tell him we stayed in suites at the Doral and charged it to the company. He'll get a kick out of that, the old tightwad."

We all laughed, shocked by the captain joking, and then we crammed into the limousine. "The Doral, James," I instructed in my most proper British accent, continuing the joyously light mood we were all feeling. *Life is good.*

～

As I had arranged, we all gathered for dinner at eight. I waved the menus away and ordered oysters and calamari for appetizers, Caesar salad, chateaubriand, lobster, an assortment of vegetables, and, of course, Dom Perignon. We ate and drank and talked and laughed like men who had just survived a death sentence—which we had. I was determined to draw the taciturn captain out, which, I was surprised, was not necessary. He and Beto took turns telling stories. His were hilarious stories from his Navy pilot days, while Beto told story after story at my expense, stories that were part of the fabric of the Three Musketeers, but new to Richardson and Hanson. At times, the laughter was so riotous from the table that we drew glares from the surrounding dinner guests. However, word had spread through the restaurant, that we were the famous five who survived the Lear crash landing earlier in the day.

Understanding was the order of the evening as staff and diners alike just smiled at the celebration of life in progress.

Afterward, we retired to the Men's Lounge for "cognac and cigars". We had just settled into the cushy leather chairs in the paneled smoking room and gave our drink orders, when a television set built into the wall flashed my face. There I was smiling behind microphones. Andy's and Beto's steely visages were in the background. As we watched the screen flash shots of the stricken jet on the tarmac surrounded by emergencies vehicles, the reality of today's events returned, and the levity fled.

I looked at Dave Richardson with a raised eyebrow, "Was it as bad as we rookies thought it was? Did you ever doubt that you guys would get us out of it?"

"Well, truthfully, I didn't have time for doubts. I was totally engaged doing everything I knew to keep us out of the drink. And, if you thought we almost bit it today, then, yes, it was for sure that bad."

Tom jumped in. "Despite Captain Richardson's kind words about my performance earlier, I'm here to tell you that what I witnessed in that cockpit today was nothing short of miraculous. I watched the captain tap rudder controls and pull ailerons in ways I could not understand, nor even imagine. And it wasn't just getting us out of the dive, the aircraft was so damaged that the flying skill that it took to keep us steady, much less put us down on a runway in

Miami was...just unbelievable." The hero worship was clear as Tom showered Richardson with respect.

"Well, I've had some experience that most haven't had," the Captain spoke humbly. "I was in Nam, flew F-4s and am damned lucky to be sitting here today. I can't even tell you how many missions I flew but I can tell you that more than half a dozen times I got back to the carrier in a shot up plane. You see, I was sort of a chicken shit; I hate parachutes and ejecting. I'm one of those pilots who would rather ride it down." Chuckling, he added, "I guess in a way my fear of parachutes may have had something to do with us all sitting around here tonight. I was thinking today that I had two crash landings in F-4s that were so badly shot up that the controls barely worked at all. In one, the cockpit filled up with smoke on approach, but it was too late to bail even if I wanted to, so I just rode her down. Thanks to ground crews that got fire retardant on me as soon as that fighter stopped sliding, I was barely burned at all. Anyway, what I did today was not genius; it was enough experience in tight situations that I just barely had the skill needed to get us down. Tom, you did everything you should have. You were a rock."

I was thinking, and I felt Beto and Andy must be having the same thoughts, that if we had any other pilot than Captain Richardson today, we probably wouldn't be around to sip brandy tonight...and that act of fate seems an amazing phenomenon. Maybe Da Jewel is still working its magic?

"Did you guys learn anything about...about...what caused the engine to, uh, blow up like that, today?" Andy asked.

"Yes, we did. There is an access panel that sits right under the cockpit on the port side. It seems the access door came loose... either didn't lock properly, malfunctioned, who knows...and was sucked straight into the jet engine. That's almost for sure what caused the engine to blow. The rest of the damage was caused by shrapnel from the engine letting go. In that respect, we were damned lucky. Engine parts could have come through the fuselage or taken off the horizontal or vertical stabilizer and then we really would have been done for."

"Have there been other cases of this, Captain?" Andy continued.

"With other planes, for sure. Usually, unclosed luggage compartment doors coming loose. But there are only a handful of Lear 28's flying now and no experience, so far as I know, with any other crafts."

A tanned, slender young man in a blue suit approached the group looking from face to face. "Mr. Jacobs? Mr. Darren Jacobs?"

I raised my hand.

"Mr. Jacobs, you have a telephone call, sir. A Mr. Paul Kistler, sir. He said you would want to take the call."

I nodded and followed the page to a private phone in the lobby.

"Hello."

"God, Darren, is it good to hear your voice! Are you guys okay?"

"Yes, Paul, we're fine, but it was a close one. We're sitting around talking to the pilots who saved our lives right now. How did you find me?"

"One of the bankers I was working with today tracked me down at my hotel here in Zurich and told me the story. He also said you had called and left the hotel number, so I just rang back. The staff was great tracking you down. I can't tell you how relieved I am that you guys are okay. And feeling a little guilty that I wasn't with you."

"Paul, you can't feel that way. We're fine and that's all that counts."

∽

We chatted a while and I returned to the group. "That was Paul mother-henning us. He said to send his best to you two and his everlasting regard for you, Captain, and you, Tom. He's pretty shook, but he's going to get on the first plane he can find to New York and meet us at Stapleton in Denver tomorrow. I reserved us a

Suburban, and we'll just drive down to Telluride. I'm not sure any of us are ready to get on a puddle-jumper just yet," I said smiling.

"No shit, Sherlock," Beto added in his inimitable style.

∽

Always intrigued by what makes people tick, I engaged the captain in a lengthy and serious conversation. We moved off to the corner of the room not even noticing when our younger cohorts got tired and drifted away. Richardson said that he had talked more openly about flying and Viet Nam with me than with any other civilian— ever. I, in turn, found myself sharing stories of growing up the first son of the first family in New Mexico and the pressure that went with it. "Not complaining," I said, "but there were times I wished I was just a good old boy from the Valley".

"So, did you live vicariously through Andy and Beto?" the captain asked me.

"Ahh, very perceptive, Sensei, and probably right on. I was attracted and fascinated by the two. At first, they were skeptical of the 'rich kid' but that went away after I passed a few loyalty tests."

"Well, it doesn't take but a few minutes to see how dedicated the two of them are to you," Dave said.

"They are a very interesting pair. Their surface personalities are close to opposites. Andy is serious, sincere, even a bit ponderous. His movements and responses are always controlled and measured. Beto, on the other hand, is the master of lightness, always a quip to charm his way through every situation. As you have seen, he is almost always smiling—only the size of the smile varies. And we tease him about being so antsy. He has to always be moving—channeling his abundant energy.

But at heart, they are very similar. Uppermost, they are intensely loyal to one another. They can't even remember a time they weren't friends and inseparable. In the Valley, there was a common understanding that if you made an enemy of one, you made an enemy of other. Both came from tough family situations on the wrong side of the track. And, yet they kept one another out of any serious legal difficulties, while most of their neighbors went to the reformatory and then on to more serious institutions. And they are not stupid. They did a lot better at schoolwork than they let on. As for athletics, they neither held anything back. They were the first on the practice field and the last to leave.

And they are fearless. As kids, they often took on bigger opponents—sometimes winning, sometimes losing, but they never backed down. And, Dave, you would have loved to see them on the football field. They both put their helmets down and ran over anybody that got in their way. So, no one in Albuquerque was surprised when the stories of their exploits in Southeast Asia got reported in the newspapers along with the announcements of the medals they were awarded."

"Darren, I'd say you are a lucky man to have such friends," Dave said.

"And you'd be right, Captain. Geez, look at the time. We wore the kids out, but I guess we'd better get a couple of hours of shut-eye."

We hugged goodbye warmly. For just a moment, my silver tongue was replaced with a lump in my throat, unable to get out the words of gratefulness I really wanted to say.

∽

Culiacan, Sinaloa, Mexico

"What happened?" Esco Cortez glared at Jorge Guzman.

"Our *hombre* says it was nothing short of a miracle. How the pilot got the plane to Miami, no one can understand. Esco, even on the news they are saying that, by all rights, that jet should have crashed."

Cortez's facial expression didn't soften; his black eyes flashed with fire.

"We are already moving under our original plan, Esco. We had an unexpected opportunity with the plane trip, but we are no worse off than if we hadn't tried. We will get the job done."

Standing up slowly and walking around his desk, he stood within inches of Guzman, staring straight into his face, "You're goddamned right you will. Now, get the fuck out of here."

The two were meeting in the private offices of Grupo Cortez, the Cortez family holding company for a diverse conglomerate of businesses held in Western Mexico. The offices were located on the top floor of an unobtrusive building in the downtown area, just off the plaza. The physical structure appeared to be like any office complex that could exist in Boise, Idaho, or Mobile, Alabama. There the similarities ended, however. Four heavily armed guards sat or stood behind a curved counter protecting the elevator bank. In each corner of the lobby area, video cameras rotated through their programmed ranges sending images to the security offices in the basement. Vehicle access to the underground parking was provided by an off-street drive that dove directly into the basement. There, too, armed guards stood in front of a heavy steel door that could only be opened by one of their electronic keys. Cortez and all high-ranking officers in his company entered the building through the underground parking and all arrived in professionally chauffeured Chevrolet Suburbans with bulletproof glass and armor. All of these precautions were carefully planned and executed. And necessary for the survival of Grupo Cortez.

Esco's father, Gustav, was the founder of the business. He had been one of the early vegetable growers to begin exporting large volumes of cucumbers, tomatoes, peppers and other mixed vegetables to U.S. grocery chains. Once dams and irrigation canals and water delivery systems were constructed in Sinaloa, the growers became huge agri-business complexes covering thousands of hectares. USDA inspection stations were moved directly into Mexico and eventually, the "Mexican Winter Veg Deal" provided almost all of the vegetables for the area west of the Mississippi during the months from November through April when California production dropped. Profits became massive.

Esco grew up as a Mexican prince. He attended private schools in Mexico City during his teen years, after which he went to the University of Arizona in Tucson receiving a degree in agriculture. At his father's insistence, he got an MBA at Yale.

"You are going to be running a complicated business someday, son, and will need every edge to compete."

Gustav died suddenly and unexpectedly of a heart attack the year after Esco returned to Culiacan to work with his father in the business. Thanks to Gustav's strong lieutenants, Esco had support, which gave him time to grow into the role of *hefe*. For the past decade, Esco had diversified into a wide range of businesses. Trucking was natural as a vertical integration to move

Sinaloa crops to the border. Then, truck dealerships were added and car dealerships, and insurance companies. And finally, cocaine distribution.

Esco had met Jorge Guzman at school in Mexico. The Guzman family was involved in scores of successful businesses in Guadalajara. Jorge was bright, aggressive, and ambitious. Unfortunately, he was the youngest of six brothers. Jorge's prospects to succeed in the family business were nil. And, yet he always seemed to have a lot more money to spend than his brothers. Always with a gorgeous woman in tow, he was seen nightly on the town in Guadalajara, driving a Mercedes on which Mexican taxes were more than the cost of the car.

A few years back, Jorge called Esco. They weren't close but had stayed in touch over the years. "Esco, would you mind if I came to Culiacan to discuss a business proposition with you? I need some help. I am making good money, now, but the potential is beyond belief."

Esco was even more intrigued by Jorge's refusal to discuss even the nature of the business over the phone and invited him to come stay the weekend at his compound in Culiacan. Though Esco was now married with two young children, he and Jorge could talk privately in the "business wing" of the sprawling hacienda. It was during these discussions that Jorge revealed that he had made connections with cocaine producers in Colombia and was turning significant profits providing coke to rich Mexican kids.

"But, Esco, coke is just hitting the States and it is **going** crazy. Someone is going to make untold fortunes getting coke from Colombia to the States and it might as well be you and me. You have the resources and I have the connections and know how to run the business."

"Let me sleep on it," was Esco's only reply.

The next morning with a simple "I'm in" Esco started the ball rolling and the two began discussing their business plan. It was a partnership made in heaven, or hell, depending on your point of view; Jorge's street smarts coupled with Esco's methodical, MBA-trained approach to a start-up business. After two long sessions, the foundation for what was to become one of the largest cocaine distribution networks in the Western Hemisphere was laid.

⌒

Cocaine, technically cocaine benzoylmethylecgonine, got its pharmaceutical name from the combination of "coca", the plant from which it is extracted, and "ine", its alkaloid suffix from the language of chemistry. Slang names are more colorful, such as "coke", "blow", "marching powder", and "toot".

Its use originated in what are now Bolivia, Peru and Colombia. Indigenous peoples chewed the leaves for its euphoric feeling and as a painkiller. When first introduced to the Spanish, the priests declared it a work of the devil, but in time, its benefits became evident to the conquistadores and it was legalized and taxed.

The cocaine alkaloid was first isolated by the German chemist Friedrich Gaedcke in 1855. Gaedcke named the alkaloid "erythroxyline", and published a description in the journal *Archiv der Pharmazie.*

Sigmund Freud published his work *Über Coca,* in which he wrote:

...cocaine causes exhilaration and lasting euphoria, which in no way differs from the normal euphoria of the healthy person.

You perceive an increase of self- control and possess more vitality and capacity for work. In other words, you are simply normal, and it is soon hard to believe you are under the influence of any drug. Long intensive physical work is performed without any fatigue. This result is enjoyed without any of the unpleasant after-effects that follow exhilaration brought about by alcohol. Absolutely no craving for the further use of cocaine appears after the first, or even after repeated taking of the drug.

The cocaine from Colombian cartels originates with coca crops grown by small farmers on tiny plots well hidden by the jungle. The growing and processing at the farm level, which has changed little in a century, creates a product known as "pasta". Leaves are harvested six times each year, sun dried for a day and then minced with a trimmer and sprinkled with cement. Several hundred pounds of the resultant mixture are then soaked in gasoline for another day. The leaves are removed and the remaining liquid mixed with battery acid. Powdered soda is then added and the blend filtrated through a cloth which creates the pasta. At this point, the product is forty to sixty percent pure cocaine and sold to cartel laboratories.

The laboratories are processing centers tucked into the protective vegetation of the deepest, darkest reaches of the Colombian jungle. At the laboratories, the pasta goes through repeated recrystallization from solvents creating an interim compound, "pasta lavada". Solvents are applied and then drawn from the pasta lavada numerous times—the final result, pure crystalline cocaine or freebase.

Cocaine gained acceptance in society in the late eighteenth century. Pope Leo XIII purportedly carried a hipflask of the coca-treated wine, Vin Mariani, with him, and awarded a Vatican gold medal to its creator, Angelo Mariani. From Coca Cola's initial founding in 1886, its formula included a pinch of extract of coca leaves. Various laws were passed in the twentieth century banning the use of cocaine but were generally not enforced until it became specifically named in the Controlled Substance Act of 1970.

In the mid-seventies, its debut with rich partiers in Los Angeles was explosive. Within weeks, its popularity as the drug of choice for the "seen and be seen" crowd was firmly established. Demand far outpaced supply as the white powder could not be shipped from its origin in Columbia through Mexican cartels fast enough. Prices escalated wildly to five hundred dollars a gram for a while as only the most flush of California's party crowd could afford the luxury.

In time, Columbian production soared in response to the huge gold pot at the end of the United States rainbow. California demand could be sated and opportunities for new markets could be addressed. Bi-coastal partiers had introduced the New York club scene to cocaine brought back from LA, but it was more than a year before significant quantities of coke could be delivered to an almost desperate audience. Denver, via Vail and Aspen, became the third high- demand market, as skiers and penny-stock brokers flush with bucks from a crazy local stock market snorted their way through grams and then ounces and then pounds of the white powder. "Coke" was here to stay.

CHAPTER 5

TUESDAY, MAY 23

Durango, Colorado

"Hey, you, get your lazy fanny out of bed. I don't intend to spend one of my rare days off watching you sleep", Donna Graham yelled from her kitchen.

Marc rolled over and eyed the clock—a few minutes after seven. He closed his eyes with a groan and marveled at the woman. Donna had worked a twelve-hour shift at the hospital the day before, danced his legs off at the Solid Muldoon until after midnight and brought him to her apartment, where she practically ripped his clothes off and climbed on top of him for some extended and badly needed sexual relief for both of them. Then, sometime in the middle of the night he was awakened by a hand massaging Mr. Dick followed by another rousing sexual romp. And now she was showered, dressed, packed, and looking like a million dollars at seven o'clock.

"Here, baby, here's some of that black magic elixir guaranteed to get you cranking." She set a steaming mug of dark roast coffee on the night table. Marc sat up and took a sip, the strong taste shocking his senses back to life. "Hop in the shower. As a committed relationship partner, I bought you some Jockeys and socks and your very own toothbrush. Let's go, let's go."

With that, Marc rolled out of bed without a stitch on and headed for the bathroom. Donna was right. The shower was heaven and soon he was singing a John Denver medley in what he believed to be perfect pitch.

"Donna, you genius, you had a good idea staying here in Durango last night. I was not looking forward to that drive to the lake and it was nice having a night of privacy here at your place, not that I would have been self-conscious, anyway, the shape I was in last night."

"We needed that. Two months of abstinence is no fun, but the cure is pretty wonderful."

"I am not cured yet, Donna, not by a long shot."

"Good thing, cause I see several more treatments in your near future."

Marc and Donna piled into her Blazer and headed for Vallecito, stopping at the French Bakery for croissants and coffee to go. In just a few minutes, they were out of the little town and cruising up Flórida Road, Marc happy that Donna drove so he was free to just enjoy the scenery. On the right, The Flórida River ran alongside the highway, winding in tandem with hairpin turns and flowing under bridges at country road intersections ever so often. In breaks in the dense vegetation, Marc could see white water rushing over river rocks in some places and deep, quiet pools in others. Occasionally, a fly fisherman would be standing in the river in hip-high water with a rod flicking overhead.

The drive took about an hour. The walls of the Flórida Canyon expanded and contracted finally opening into a wide meadow where the Flórida Road teed into Vallecito Lake Road. The Vallecito Road ran along the west side of a vast valley carved by the Pine River, its path now parallel to the mountains rising out of the east side. Checker-boarded with wheat and alfalfa fields, the valley was more than a mile across.

Donna shoved the floor shift into second to climb the last bit of Vallecito Road to get to the top of the dam, a structure built in 1940 to form the reservoir. As they peaked at the dam pinnacle, the spectacular view of Lake Vallecito spread for miles to the north, surrounded by meadows and giant pine trees, backed by white peaks, many nearing "fourteeners". So they could just sit and look for a minute, Donna pulled off on the dam road.

"I tried to imagine this view ever since we left in the autumn, but you just have to be here to get it," Donna said. "Looking at it now, it's hard to grasp that for most of the time since we were here last, no one could get up here because of the snow. Especially this year. Wow, what a winter."

"I know what you mean. When I got up yesterday morning and walked out on the deck, I about halfway expected to be disappointed, that my memory had stored something that couldn't possibly be real, you know, a Paul Simon 'Kodachrome' kind of thing, but instead, it was more incredible than I remembered."

The two stared across the lake until, finally, Marc said, "I guess we'd better get up to Rickey's. They'll be wondering about us."

Donna pulled out onto the highway and had driven only a few hundred yards when the Silver Goose appeared headed in their direction. Both drivers stopped in the middle of the road while rolling their windows down.

"You kids doing okay this morning?" Ricky smiled a wry smile.

Donna didn't blink. "I'm okay," and thumbing at me, "he's worn out. Where are you two headed?"

"City Market in Bayfield. Marc, you feel up to going with us?"

Marc conferred with Donna, kissed her cheek and ran to the Silver Goose. Donna waved and took off upland.

ᔋ

Denver, Colorado

"Stop! There he is," I commanded as Beto pulled the rented Suburban to the curb. I hopped out of the shotgun seat and headed toward Paul. Shielding his eyes, he was looking left and right as he stepped through the automatic doors at Stapleton Field.

I think of him as the personification of a Polish count teleported into the twentieth century. His thin frame is always maintained ramrod straight, his head held high. Except for a cowlick on the crown that continuously rebels, his thin blond hair streams back from his pink forehead. His deep-set pale blue eyes, positioned a bit closely together, are split by the perfectly straight ridge of a long, thin nose. His protruding upper lip is countered by a receding chin.

Adding to his weird European appearance, Paul is stuck in a fashion time warp. He established his style of dress at prep school in Switzerland and never changed: pegged thin-leg pants, high-heeled boots that zip on the sides, and slim, solid-colored ties. His slacks and jackets often combine plaids with distinct patterns and unique color combinations.

Today is no exception. There Paul stands, stiffly erect clad in a blue, yellow, and green madras jacket with dark blue and white vertically striped pants. He is oblivious to the people gawking around him.

"Hey, Paul, over here."

He looked up, stared at me a moment before a controlled smile spread across his face. I bear hugged him and pounded his back in hale-fellow-well-met form, while passengers streamed around us, before leading him to the waiting vehicle.

"I didn't think I would ever say it, but damned if I'm not glad to see you two ruffians," Paul said settling into the back seat and shaking hands with Andy. Beto flipped him off from the driver's seat without looking back.

I was glad to see Paul's attempt at humor. Generous people meeting Paul call him reserved; others, cold. His intelligence attracts the strong and bludgeons the insecure. When asked a question, Paul often appear to freeze, staring at the questioner (Andy called it the "fish eye") for an uncomfortably long period of time before answering precisely, often using perfectly crafted paragraphs that begin with topic and end with closing sentences.

And, yet, when Paul chooses to turn on the charm, he can be frightfully disarming, pairing his quick wit with a litany of stories and off-the-wall facts to become the consummate entertainer. An avid reader, he can discuss Shakespeare or LeCarre, in English,

French, German or Spanish. And he genuinely loves sports. He follows American and European football, professional baseball and basketball and uses his total recall of statistics to impress the most fanatical of sports fans.

Beto pulled into traffic. "You guys want to eat something before we get on the road?" "I'm good, they fed us about an hour ago over Kansas," Paul said.

"Let's drive for a while, if that's okay with everybody?" I asked. No objections came.

Soon the traffic thinned, and we were out of Denver headed south through the mountains. It was uncharacteristically quiet in the car when Paul said, "Darren, I heard the news reports, but they were sparse, and I don't usually find them trustworthy anyway. Could you please tell me exactly what happened? I would very much appreciate whatever details you care to share."

The words poured out of me for the next half hour without stop or interruption--except for the occasional "is it possible?" or "can that be? Oh my god" from Paul-- describing the scene in the jet from the time of the explosion to touchdown in Miami and then all that occurred afterward.

"I'm telling you, man, if we hadn't had Dave Richardson at the controls, I am fairly sure you would be planning funerals for us today. It's funny how fate works out, the good and the bad," I concluded.

"Have they identified the cause of the explosion?" Paul asked.

"Just that a service door on the pilot's side of the plane came loose and got sucked into the port-side jet. It will take them a while to figure out how the malfunction occurred. That ball is in the FAA court, so you know how long it could be before anything is likely to come out of there."

Reliving the event had an unexpected result. The atmosphere in the Suburban became heavy with silence.

Finally, Paul spoke up. "I should have been with you guys. I feel terrible."

"Here, y-y-you can wear this for penance," said Andy, ripping off his neck brace and wrapping it around Paul's neck. "I sure as hell don't n-n-need it."

I turned to the back seat to look at Paul while I spoke. "Look, Paul, we all survived, and we are fine. Maybe a little more screwed up in the *cabesas* than we used to be, but only marginally worse. You can't have survivor guilt when everybody survived, so stow that crap. You were doing the best thing for all of us in Switzerland. No more discussion on this issue."

"Fuck that, Dare, I think the little wimp ought to buy lunch today," Beto fired, lightening the mood Beto-style.

～

The miles rolled by as my mates began to relax, chatting comfortably and enjoying the Rocky Mountain scenery. We stopped in Buena Vista for a pit stop. After some great green chile chicken enchiladas at Dos Hermana's and a gas up, we were back on the road.

I thought back to times when I didn't know if this day would ever come to pass—whether Andy and Beto would ever accept another member of the tribe.

I had run into Paul while representing a wealthy Manhattan client, Jacob Bernstein, who had bought a second home in Santa Fe. Bernstein, a banker, started to spend more and more time in Santa Fe. Ultimately, he leased office space just off the Plaza in Santa Fe to open a family office for his personal investments. After completing his MBA at Harvard, Paul became the first employee of the banker's family office. At first, he commuted from New York with Bernstein, but as the investment holdings of the family office grew and staff was added, he began staying in Santa Fe fulltime. We worked together almost every week.

Paul seemed to become a New Mexican at heart very quickly. Despite his East Coast and European upbringing and education, he liked the exotic surroundings and bohemian lifestyle. I also helped with his transition as we often worked together during the day and, at night, I would include Paul so that he soon became a fixture with my Santa Fe entourage.

I was taken with Paul's skills, skills that I could use. I gradually began formulating a plan to bring him into Cerberus. After including Paul at several small get-togethers where Andy and Beto were present, I began dropping hints that Paul might make a good addition to the team. At first, Andy and Beto were adamantly opposed, and I backed off. But I continued to point out how much money we had accumulated and were making and, yet, we had no talent for financial management in the group.

"So, Darren, what happens if you lay out our business plan to Paul and he freaks? It's one thing to do a little coke at night. It's another to become part of a coke dealing ring?" Andy asked. "Trust me. He's going to love it." If there's one thing I know, it's people. And...I had a plan.

Zozobra, Santa Fe's biggest party every year, was coming up the following weekend. This is more fun for me than Christmas, so I had been at work for a month planning my usual soiree. I say "usual", but in fact I try to outdo last year's every year. The Burning of Zozobra is an age- old pagan ritual in Santa Fe; Zozobra, Old Man Gloom, is burned and with him all of the evils of the past year.

I kicked off the shindig with cocktails (and maybe a smattering of less legal substances) for about thirty at my compound on Old Canyon Road. The crowd was a mix of political cronies, old school buddies, family friends, wives and girlfriends (never both) and some interesting women that came in from Los Angeles. I had limos lined up out front which took all my revelers to the park where the Burning of Zozobra was held. When we arrived, an area had been "reserved" by some of Beto's associates, all very intimidating gentlemen, and blankets spread over the area. I had arranged for a light supper which was waiting in picnic baskets tended by the caterers costumed in Hopi wedding dress. In the middle of our area set a large washtub full of ice and dozens of magnums of Dom Perignon.

I tell people that the Burning of Zozobra is simply unimaginable until you have actually witnessed it. The giant figure, six stories tall, hovers menacingly over the crowd. It is dressed in white garb, actually from the local Native American culture but it creates the impression of an Asian martial arts ninja. Lit by spotlights, the giant white creature presents a drastic contrast with the pitch-black sky. Its giant block-shaped head is as big as a hot-air balloon and white with black features including eyes that roll and a mouth that opens and shuts. Zozobra's arms wave akimbo, operated by unseen puppet masters using techniques handed down for generations.

While the visual imagery is surrealistically frightening, sound provides the ultimate sensory impact. As the ritual begins, Zozobra waves its arms and moves its mouth in unison. Huge hidden speakers emit ground-shaking growls and roars. Some guess they were recorded African lions; others argue, Grizzly bears. At Zozobra's feet, mounds of gathered kindling are lit on fire. Zozobra's gigantic white surface acts as a screen, projecting flame and shadow across the monster's visage as the fires grow. Zozobra's pace quickens as the flames leap upward. Its arms flail at the rising smoke.

As Zozobra's roars reach a frantic pace, attendants light torches with the flames from the burning piles and race toward the manic figure, igniting the bottom of his clothing simultaneously. Flames shoot skyward as the flammable clothing catches. Zozobra's roars change to screams of pain and agony as the inferno engulfs his head. His arms swat at the flames in King Kong fashion as his head swivels in agony, his mouth hideously open as spine-chilling screeches split the night. Then, the giant head bursts into flames and the black eyes roll back into his head. The gaping mouth opens and closes with the horrible cacophony of sounds, which continue as Zozobra dies his horrible death, marked by the inevitable collapse of the flaming giant.

I enjoyed sneaking a glance of Paul's face as he experienced the spectacle for the first time, his features highlighted by the flames reflecting on him. As with all first-time participants in the death of Old Man Gloom, Paul was totally mesmerized. How could anyone witness the spectacle without being overtaken by primal emotions?

As the last of the death cries rolled over the crowd, I asked, "So, Paul, did that get your juices going a bit?"

Sensing the time was perfect, I put my arm around his shoulders and with a bottle of champagne in tow, walked him to a quiet place in the park where we sat on the grass and talked intently for nearly an hour. I could feel the curious glances of my fellow partiers; they would just have to wait. Finally, we rose and rejoined the group where I announced, "back to the casa to celebrate. Paul has graciously agreed to join us in our business endeavors." Paul clicked his heels and bowed to the applause of all.

I remember seeing Andy and Beto smile a knowing smile to one another that I interpreted to mean, with some pride, "he always gets his way". Which, it occurred to me, was pretty much true.

～

"Okay, we have a little time here; shall we discuss what's going on with the biz in Santa Fe?" I asked halfway turning toward the backseat. "And, more importantly, what exactly are we going to do about it?"

Paul related the Santa Fe numbers, again, from memory.

"Andy, this is your territory. What's your take?"

Andy pulled on his jaw judiciously. "Salazar is, uh, cutting the product and st-st-st-sticking the extra coin in his jeans."

"Damned, those are pretty strong words. What makes you so sure, Andy?" Paul asked. "Mystery shoppers, uh, Paul, mys-mystery shoppers."

Paul screwed his face up quizzically. "Eh?"

Andy looked at me as if to say "you're the pitchman—you take this". Speeches are not his forte. So I jumped in.

"We sell great blow. That's our rep on the street, and we always want it to be that way.

The fastest way to lose that rep, and a lot of cash, is to have a 'Poundman' or even an 'Ounceman' cutting the good stuff by adding crap and keeping the extra dough. Since we first started in the coke game, we felt like two things would keep our guys straight. First, they are making a ton of bread. Second, they are scared shitless of Andy's enforcers."

"As well they should be," Beto chimed in. "Those are some mean mothers you have cultivated over the years, Andro. Real junk yard dogs. "

"Yeah, but, ummm, you can never underestimate the power of greed. S-S-Salazar is a great example."

"But, Andy, I still don't understand how you are so sure. What is this about mystery shoppers?" Paul inquired.

"Well...I have a group of customers. I, uh, I'm the only one who knows who they are. I give them some bread and they buy our blow off, uh, off the street—regularly-- and bring it to me. I, ummm, assay it. If it has been stepped on since we let go of it, I, you know, have them by, uh, the short curlies...so to speak."

Andy continued. "In the Santa Fe area—are you still with me? I found our product cut twenty-five to thirty percent, using my, you know, umm, secret shopper network. We went upstream, and every single ounce had been cut." There was now an edge in Andy's voice.

"So what happens now?" Paul asked.

"We have no choice, Paul. We have to act," I said. "Andy, take care of it."

"What does that mean?" Paul asked.

"That's my...my, umm, call, Paulito, and you don't want to know more." Andy stared grimly out the window as the Suburban and subdued occupants rolled toward Telluride. As we neared Bayfield, it occurred to me that Marta would appreciate it if we picked up some groceries.

"Beto, pull into City Market, please. I am going to call Marta and get a shopping list."

∽

I rang Marta from the parking lot pay phone and, as I suspected, Marta appreciated the call and came up with an extensive list. Beto was pushing the cart as the three of us loitered along trying to locate the items. It was clear to the greenest housewife in the store that none of us knew what we were doing. We rounded a corner and bumped squarely into a cart.

"Mr. Jacobs, what in the world are you doing here?" Bruce Talbot exclaimed in genuine surprise. Trailing him were two other young men.

"Hi, Bruce, we were just headed back to Telluride, and are now trying to replenish our pantry at my housekeeper's direction," I said.

After a brief awkward pause, we executed introductions all around. Bruce, who was clerking for Billy, had met my crew, but we were all meeting Bruce's classmates, Marc Martin and Ricky Gydeson, for the first time.

"So, what are you three up to?" I asked. "Semester just over, I suppose."

"Yes, sir," Bruce answered. "Ricky has a cabin up the other side of Vallecito Lake, and we are grooving, er, relaxing up there. At least for a couple of days. On Thursday, we take off for our annual wilderness hike for the next week. That will end the relaxation for a while."

We loosely joined up and wandered around the store together, except for Paul who got bored and returned to the car. Andy seemed intrigued about the wilderness trip, and Ricky was happy to explain the route he had lined out and all the places they planned to hit along the way.

We completed our shopping and left Bruce and his crew in the store divvying up their bill. I guess I dozed a bit in the car and woke up nearing Telluride. Ballard Mountain dazzled our eyes as the last of the day's sunlight cast lit it up, in stark contrast to the rising bank of gray clouds rolling into the valley behind it. Each of us seemed lost in our own musings as we drove by the Telluride Airport that we had left just a few days before.

A genuine downer had set in. The talk about the mess in Santa Fe had created a sour, ominous mood and, somehow, passing the airport and being so palpably reminded of the near-death experience, took the blade of the funk and sharpened it. The monster storm rolling in wasn't helping, pulling down the barometric pressure and spirits with it. I decided that I needed to act to turn things around.

"When I talked to Marta, gentlemen, well, let me put it this way--tonight we are going to be dining on Marta's famous pot roast dinner. My mouth is watering just thinking about it."

As I hoped, Beto picked up the vibe. "Oh, man, are we in for a treat. You did remember to request the biscuits?"

"Ha, oh sure, I couldn't forget Marta's Best Biscuits. No way, Jose. Those are required to sop up the gravy."

The mood lightened with each mile as we rolled through Telluride past the old Victorian two-storied beauties of the mining glory days, taking a left up Oak toward Tomboy Road... and, finally to home. As we alighted from the car and stretched and loosened up our bodies, long tired from being cramped in the Suburban, a zephyr hit us, and we were wrapped in a flood of pine-scented air. We all stood and looked out over the valley where the lights of the good Telluride citizens were blinking on, while in the sky the white etchings of lightning shot overhead followed by the fully expected but still startling crack of thunder. Deep rumblings echoed up the canyons, shaking the earth rhythmically as only the natural amplifiers of the Rocky Mountains can. I was totally surprised when my eyes, as if in someone else's body, filled with tears. For just a moment, life was so good that I was overcome.

～

I got this one right! Marta's dinner worked the desired magic on all of us as we consumed pot roast, potatoes, and carrots cooked in her secret herbs. We had shaken off the road dust from a long day starting in Miami with a quick run through Telluride and up the canyon a ways. When we got back home, Marta had dinner ready. In unspoken deference, Beto, Andy and Paul waited for me to sit at the head of the table before each found his chair, defined by custom as clearly as if name tags had been set at each place.

The Scandinavian teak table sat in the center of the slightly elevated dining area that overlooked the great room. I felt immense satisfaction as I surveyed the feast Marta had set on the table; the faces of my closest friends and associates; and, behind them, the great vaulted room with its stylish leather and teak furniture set off by splashes of color from the artworks created by Taos masters on the walls. None, however, compared to the beauty of the mountains, forests and clouds framed in the two-story wall of glass.

"Don't Bogart those biscuits, Andy, send 'em this way," Beto said. Smiling with satisfaction, Marta pulled the third dozen of biscuits out of the oven. As we sat around the dining room table, our eating slowed with second and third helpings, I watched their frayed nerves disappear, the atmosphere becoming mellow, comfortable and warm. I opened a third bottle of a meaty cabernet, a 1965 Charles Krug Vineyards, then poured refills all around while thinking that this was a great wine that should stay cellared for years. *Oh, what the hell.*

A pine fire blazed in the fireplace, its quiet roar comforting until pockets of pitch would ignite and explode as loud as pistol shots. The lights dimmed and blinked sporadically as the local power supply was hammered by the elements.

The mountain storm had rolled into Telluride Valley and hung among the peaks.

Heralding the deluge's arrival, hail beat the metal roof in unremitting rage for fifteen minutes, creating a roar that made our conversation impossible. When the hail quit, the ground was covered with white pellets, short-lived as the warmer rain followed in layered, ghost-like sheets sweeping away the white and creating pools joined by rivulets of swiftly moving water and hail. The sky flashed white every few seconds, outlining the surrounding mountains, followed by a period of inky blackout from which cracks and rumbles erupted, rattling the plate glass windows as if a hungry bear were pounding them in rage.

The rain slowed. The frequency between flashes of lightning and bolts of thunder lengthened. After consuming a baked dish of peach cobbler and a half gallon of ice cream, we migrated to the great room, easing into comfy plush leather chairs with moans and groans attributable to classic over-eating.

"This is going to be a soaker," I predicted staring out the giant window into the darkness. "Once a storm like this gets hung in this box canyon, it just has to rain itself out. Outside is not fit for man nor beast."

"Did you hear what the Maggie, that's a female Aggie now that they let girls in Texas A & M, told the doctor when he informed her she was pregnant?" Beto asked.

Silence. "No? She told the doctor she was pretty sure it wasn't hers." Beto laughed by himself.

"'Young lady', the doctor said sternly, 'who is the cadet responsible for this? He will do the right thing.'"

"'I'm not sure, Doctor, it was either the band or the football team.'"

"'Hmmm, must have been the band. The football team hasn't scored all year.'" Darren and Andy smiled weakly at one another, while Paul gave him a good-natured finger as Beto dissolved into raucous laughter.

In an instant, we all turned facing the front of the house. The sound of screeching tires shrieked over the storm, followed by the explosion of glass and metal. Andy was on his feet and running to the front door in an instant, followed by Beto and Paul. As Andy jerked the door open, a crack of lightning shook the house striking the ground nearby. The lights went out instantly, leaving behind total darkness and the residual, tangy smell of ozone. Another flash of lightening revealed a white pick-up truck crashed into the cut bank on the far side of the street, tilted precariously on two wheels.

I grabbed two electric torches out of the hall closet and handed one to Paul. The angled lights peppered with raindrops flashed across the scene. The driver was slowly extricating himself from the cab while two motionless bodies lay sprawled in the street. Andy touched the shoulder of the first body he ran to.

"You okay?" he asked as he gently tried to turn his head to the side.

Both bodies suddenly came to life, springing to their feet and, in the same motion, swinging pistols out of their jackets, the barrels zeroed in on the four would-be rescuers. The driver advanced toward me with his gun drawn.

"All of you. Stand still and put your hands out. No heroics, *hombres,* we're all going inside where it is nice and dry. Hand the light over." He motioned to me, and I gave him the flashlight.

One of the attackers grabbed the light from Paul's hand and backed through the front door, while the other waved his gun, splitting off Andy and Beto and following them into the house. Paul and I followed, the driver poking me in the back with the nose of the pistol. As we entered the house, the power returned as quickly as it had gone off, the inside now well-lit. Quickly surveying the house, Marta was nowhere in sight and I hoped like hell she had followed instructions and locked herself in the vault.

My eyes met Andy's.

"Ahh, ahh, ah. Don't do anything stupid." The apparent leader of the invaders waved the gun between Andy and me.

The admonition was not required. Well-schooled by Andy and Beto, I had already assessed that these were professionals; the way they held their weapons, how they had split the group apart and shepherded them into the house, all of their movements were methodical and balanced, athletic—their eyes constantly shifting, missing nothing. The staged wreck had been executed perfectly. No doubt about it, these guys knew what they were doing. And they didn't seem concerned about hiding their appearances. *Not a good sign* I thought.

My mind raced, seeking to gather and sort facts. All three were Hispanic. The driver was maybe in his thirties, the other two mid-twenties. All wore jeans, athletic shoes and rain jackets. The driver was clearly the *hefe*—six-two, over two hundred pounds, but with the quick movements of a much smaller man. His skin was light-colored shaded by a two-day growth of heavy, dark beard and a full mustache covering his entire upper lip, his forehead exposed by a prematurely receding hairline.

The other two both looked like typical South American footballers, one nearing six feet and the other not much over five-seven. Both were wiry, the taller man with a burr haircut; the other, long black hair swept behind his ears and a four-inch scar running down the right side of his face.

In Spanish, the leader directed his men to search us. The smaller of the two patted-down Andy first, while the other two captors held their weapons trained on Beto. It occurred to me that they must have known ahead of time whom they would have to deal with in a physical confrontation. And then, how interesting it was that the weapon search was done using FBI- developed processes, taught to police forces around the world. Andy's leg sheath was quickly found and his nine-inch hunting knife removed and tossed across the room.

"Now lie down, facedown with your hands clasped behind your head. You know the drill." Andy complied, and the process was repeated with Beto with the same result—his knife found, removed and pitched aside. Paul and I were given similar searches but, of course, we had no weapons.

With all four of us spread on the floor of the great room with our hands cuffed behind us, the *hefe* picked up the telephone and punched the numbers in the handset.

"We're in. All four of them are disabled. No casualties." He listened for a moment. "Mr. Jacobs, you're wanted on the phone. Please rise and walk very slowly over here. Tell your associates to be smart."

He removed my cuffs so that I could hold the phone. I spoke into the mouthpiece,

"Darren Jacobs."

"Darren, good to hear your voice. I am glad you were not hurt."

It took a moment for me to recognize Jorge Guzman's voice. "What the fuck's going on, Jorge?"

I was immediately irritated at myself for showing a lack of control in my speech.

"Let me phrase it in your lingo, Darren. There is going to be a change-of-control in your business. You and your boys have had a good run and you've been good associos, but your run is over. Effective tonight, we are taking control of your distribution networks. And to make the transition seamless—is that how you would say it?—we are going to have a physical transfer of cash and inventory."

I was momentarily dizzy as my mind spun. Not once had it ever occurred to me that my Mexican cartel partners would turn on me like this. As some order formed out of the chaos, a hopeful thought sprang into my consciousness.

"You back-stabbing"--I paused with mother fucker on my tongue but, wanting something more insulting--"spic. You cannot possibly believe that I am just going to let you get away with this. The four of us are not the only people you have to deal with."

"Darren, we are very thorough in our preparations. You must know that about us by now. I am fully aware that you have had allies in the law enforcement arena that have supported your efforts, particularly here in Telluride. However, note that I say 'have had', past-tense. Would you like confirmation from Sheriff Lang? He is standing right here next to me."

I struggled to keep a poker face, but despite my best efforts, my face crumbled, and my hands trembled as the desperation of the situation forced its way into my reality. This was Pearl Harbor in Telluride.

"No? You don't wish to talk to the sheriff, Darren? Has the *gato* got your *lingua*? Okay, let me make it clear what is going to happen. I am on my way up. When I get there, you are going to take us down to your little 'wine cellar'. You are going to disarm the alarms and open the vault. We are going to do a wealth transfer. No hundreds of pages of legal documents and negotiations over 'whereas' versus 'therefore'. We are going to take possession of the company's assets that we have just acquired and reallocate them to our custody. Then we are going to quietly drive off. We will leave you with your precious wine collection, and you and your buddies can sit and drink cabernet, smoke Cohibas and talk about the good old days. Is this claro, Darren? This is our definition of a hostile takeover, and you have no wiggle room. See you in ten."

And with that, the phone clicked in my ear.

I stared out into the blackness. When the full impact hit me, it nearly buckled my knees.

I had never felt real fear in my entire life—now I have been scared out of my wits twice in the span of a few days. And then, the sixty-four-thousand-dollar question hit me—*were the two events connected?*

༄

Culiacan, Mexico

"Senor Cortez, Senor Guzman is on the phone," the young woman announced from the middle of the spacious office in clear English with only a touch of a Latina accent. A large window spanned the wall behind the desk revealing a view of the city, lights starting to come on down below. She stood still looking at Ciudad Culiacan through the window, awaiting a response. Her announcement was addressed to the only other occupant of the room, his light brown hair hanging over his forehead, his head bent to his desk moving slightly left to right as his eyes tracked across a paper on his desk. Moments passed this way. The secretary shifted and a few more moments passed. Finally, the head rose slowly revealing a pleasant smile.

"Thank you, Mita. Please close the door behind you," he said in a soft voice and with perfect Nebraska English.

"Diga mi, Jorge," he said after punching the speaker phone.

"Everything went as planned, hefe. I am leaving now to go to Darren's house."

"*Bueno,* call me once you have secured everything."

"Yes, sir. It shouldn't take longer than an hour."

Vallecito Lake, Colorado

"Geez, I'm freezing," Barb shivered. The cold mountain rain had chilled her to the bone. "Here, babe, put this around you," and with that Ricky threw an old army blanket over Barb's soaking clothes.

The three couples were huddled around the fireplace of Ricky's cabin as Bruce and Marc worked on getting a fire going. Marc supplied materials as Bruce carefully laid in the fire, placing a layer of dry kindling on the grate along with three small split pine logs followed by wadded newspaper stuffed under the grate. Bruce had just grabbed the box of kitchen matches when Ricky yelled out, "Shit, Bruce, don't forget to open the flue."

"Good catch, shitbird. This may be the first time I haven't smoked up the place making the first fire."

Flames grew quickly with the paper exploding and the kindling quickly catching. The sounds of cracking and popping accompanied the roar from the flames as the pine logs caught. After Bruce added two logs perpendicular to the first layer of logs, Marc watched the fireplace burst into leaping points of yellows and oranges, the heat spilling into the room, the warmth baking his face.

Soon, all six soaking refugees from the violent rain and hailstorm that had suddenly popped up over the mountains were crowded together getting warmed. They had spent a gorgeous late spring day in the meadow by Vallecito Lake. As it was before Memorial Day, the summer season hadn't started yet, so they pretty much had the lake to themselves. A lot of just lying around was interspersed with horseshoes and Frisbee throwing and, on the few occasions that energy levels reached sufficient levels, games of volleyball. Ricky had brought his Hobie Cat sailboat down to the meadow, and the couples took turns sailing across the lake and back, the yellow, orange and deep purple striped sail adding a bright splash of color to the blues of the water and greens of the forest. The water levels were high, up into the meadow, so the skippers could aim the prow at the shore and glide the plastic hulls right up on the grass, uncleating the sails and, thus, releasing the wind in preparation for the next riders.

Marc and Donna were heading back to shore from the middle of the lake when Marc felt the airs go from soft to strong in a matter of seconds. A lazy cruise turned into a white-water, wave-jumping thrill ride. Before the Hobie could regain shore, pea-sized hail started pelting the water in an advancing wall that marched invincibly down the canyon toward the lake. Fully exposed on the catamaran's trampoline, Marc tried to protect Donna from the hail but to no avail as the ice shards pelted their skin in stinging, biting licks.

In the meadow, Ricky raised the alarm, getting Bruce, Nancy, and Barb to start grabbing the group's assortment of lounge chairs, towels, food, and games and stowing them in the Silver Goose. The race was lost, however, as the ice-cold shards of hale struck, evoking howls of pain before the four could reach the protection of the van. Though Marc had loosed the sails, the Hobie was flying across the waves and slid twenty yards ashore on the wet grass. Donna leaped off the trampoline deck before the boat came to a complete stop, running for the van with Marc on her heels.

～

"Ooom, fire good. Now man need beer," said Bruce, heading for the refrigerator. "Who else is in?"

Nancy was on her feet in a blink. "I'll get the tequila shots ready!"

Watching them kiss in the kitchen, Marc thought how much fun they were when not fighting. Their relationship was tempestuous, to say the least. Bruce had a stubborn streak and Barb a temper. Both possessed strong personalities, a wicked combination. When they fought, and that was often, it was not pretty. "The stuff of Shakespeare," Bruce would say.

But when they partied together, they were firecrackers. Their antics and outbursts created a circus. They openly bragged that they were great in bed, a fact that last year's fellow cabin occupants could readily affirm based on the experiences of being awakened a time or two every night from the sounds emanating from their room.

After a few rounds of Tecates with limes and tequila shots, the party was in full swing and, on a unanimous vote, the decision to head to Virginia's for dinner was made. Roadie beers were opened and shared, and down-filled nylon jackets thrown on for the hike to Virginia's.

∽

"Virginia's" was the only word on the carved wood sign by the road and, for those in the know, no more was needed. At the end of a twisting drive through giant pines revealing only the next turn and then the one after that, sat Virginia's, a huge log structure surrounded by a gravel parking lot that could hold several dozen cars or pickups. Between Memorial Day and Labor Day, however, overflow parking spilled out on both sides of Vallecito Road.

Stripped logs covered with shining varnish lay horizontally one on top of the other to form the walls of the square structure. Picture windows had been cut into the logs at various intervals, each revealing its own unique glimpse into Virginia's. Atop the exterior walls and extending out on all sides to form a generous overhang sat a heavily slanted tin roof, the top of its ridge line more than forty feet from the ground. Hummingbird feeders and hanging pots filled with a mixture of petunias, pansies, and red geraniums offered flashes of color. Other than that, the outside was "mountain plain" as Virginia liked to say.

"Ricky, get your skinny butt over here and give me a hug!" Virginia was parked on a stool by the bar just inside the only entrance, or exit, to the place, looking like a modern-day whorehouse madam in western wear. Fiftyish, blousy, and busty, she sported a tangled mop of coal-black obviously dyed hair and was outfitted in her cowgirl outfit *de jure*. Her huge bosom encased in a Jane Russell bra stretched to bulging out of her shiny purple cowgirl blouse with pearl white snaps on the sleeves and up the front, several of which were undone to reveal a cleavage that could pass for a butt if photographed and cropped in a certain way. The blouse was tucked into a pair of black cowgirl pants that were so tight that just getting them on must have been a real feat. The pockets of the pants were slashed in opposing L-shaped black ribbing and the legs tapered into her fancy purple cowboy boots covered with extensive stitching. Her heels were hooked into the cross-pieces on the stool.

"Virginia, you get younger every year," cooed Ricky as he hugged her like he had been hugging her most of his life.

"Well, you little shit, I see you must have got an A in Principles of Lying at law school. Looks like you got your whole crew with you. Barb, sweetie, you haven't figured out that you could do a lot better than this joker, yet?"

Barb, as if in a receiving line for royalty, cued up behind Ricky, and then, surprisingly, lunged toward Virginia with her left hand extended, thumb pushing up her wedding ring. Tears ran down Virginia's face as she laughed and cried at the same time.

"Hon, you know I was just kidding. You couldn't do no better than our Ricky." She grabbed Ricky and Barb and held them tight until she could control her crying.

Fully recovered, the queen received Nancy next, a warm hug between them. They had hit it off the first time they met, recognizing their kindred fiery souls.

Once all six had appropriately addressed Virginia, they slipped into a booth in the bar area. The big dining hall was completely open from the front wall to the back with no partitions or screens in between. Picture windows were spaced along three walls with mirrors covering the wall behind the bar. Since the log beams forming the roof structure were exposed, the place had a cavernous feel. No light could reach the highest points of the arched ridge so that a creepy feeling emanated from the darkest regions. Marc remembered Ricky telling him about being scared to death when he was a boy. His Uncle

Don having convinced him that vampire bats lived up in the topmost beams, Ricky lived in fear that they could swoop down and bite him on the neck any minute.

The bar area was set off from the dining area with a low wall providing structure for the booths and a modicum of separation between the often R-rated bar language and activities and the more family-oriented dining area. Neon signs flashed above the mirrors behind the bar: "Coors", "Pabst", "Miller High Life", and "Budweiser" taking turns as twinkling stars when their time to shine came up.

But the real character in the bar was generated by the eclectic mix of junk, antiques, and treasures hanging from the beams over the bar area. A washboard that had belonged to Virginia's grandmother. A squirrel rifle from the previous century. A coal miner's helmet with a light just above the brim. A huge pair of red satin panties that could fit a rhinoceros was nailed up, hanging down like bunting. A variety of license plates from New Mexico and Colorado from the twenties and thirties. The collection was so large, even Ricky saw something new every year.

"Time for the annual good luck ritual," Ricky announced as he climbed up on the table. There, just above his head, hung a pair of size seventeen high-top Converse All Stars that once belonged to Ricky's buddy who was an All-American forward for the Lobos. On a summer trip during college, Ricky had brought Ron along, and the first night in the bar, Virginia had begged and pleaded for his shoes, which were provided after a series of *pro bono* tequila shots. They became her favorite memento in the collection.

Ricky rubbed the shoes while chanting, "Rig-a-me-re, rog-a-me-re, kick 'em in the knee.

Rig-a-me- rog-a-me-ras, kick 'em in the...other knee". A favorite UNM, unauthorized cheer.

The six in the booth, a few locals at the bar, Ernie the Barkeep, and Virginia all cheered. The official blessing for the upcoming season was now administered. That accomplished, Ernie came over to get drink orders. He looked like a character out of the previous century with thinning hair slicked straight back, a pencil-thin mustache and a white and black pin-striped shirt held closed at the collar by a bolo tie with a huge chunk of turquoise on a silver setting.

"Welcome back, kids, what'll it be?"

A couple of rounds of tequila shots and Tecate's were accompanied by the jukebox renderings of "You Ain't Nothin' but a Hound-dog,", "Peggy Sue", "Orange Blossom Special", and "Bird Dog" from the oldies side and a variety of Eagles, Fleetwood Mac, and Cream from the newer offerings. The table buzzed with lively conversation and occasional riotous laughter as Nancy told a series of jokes that would make a whore blush.

Meanwhile, Virginia had stepped into the kitchen and whipped up six plates of chicken fried steak, mashed potatoes, and biscuits covered with gravy. Her cook called in sick, so she prepared her one and only specialty. All ate heartily with the guys cleaning up what the girls couldn't finish.

"So, let's play the 'in-a-perfect-world' game," Nancy suggested.

"What the hell is the 'in-a-perfect-world game'?" Marc asked.

"You astral-project into the future and say, 'In a perfect world, here is what my life would look like.' Bruce has volunteered to go first."

"I sure as hell did not," Bruce objected.

"Well, go first anyway. I'll reward you later." With a wink.

"Okay, in that case. This is an easy game. In a perfect world, I will be a captain of industry. I will be the CEO of ginormous publicly traded companies. I will be a Time Man of the Year and regularly quoted in the Wall Street Journal. I will have homes in Santa Fe, Manhattan and Paris and an island in the Bahamas. The President will call me before enacting any important legislation affecting business. I guess that's about it."

The table sat dumbfounded until Marc spoke. "Is anybody surprised by the size of this guy's ego?" All roared with laughter, including Bruce.

Bruce feigned insult. "Okay, smart-ass, what's your story?" He stared at Marc. "I don't have a clue."

"Seriously," Bruce challenged incredulously, "you don't have an idea. You've never day- dreamed about your Uncle Walt dying and leaving you ten million?"

"No. Never even occurred to me. All I can see is getting through next year and then getting picked up by a strong law firm. That's my in-a-perfect-world story."

"Borrrrring, borring, borring," the girls chimed in, in unison. Even Marc laughed.

"Well, unlike Marc, I have a vivid vision of my future," Nancy piped in. "I am going to be the second richest woman in the world behind the Queen."

"Oh, pray tell," Barb dramatized, "and exactly how do you propose to do that? I hope you aren't counting on your womanly charms. Good as they are, they aren't going to take you there."

Nancy prominently displayed her middle digit. "Screw you and the horse you rode in on. I am going to own the best hotels in the world—London, Paris, New York, Berlin, Hong Kong— and hundreds of others. I am going to jet around the world and be the leader of the cool people."

Bruce hugged her. "We can meet in the most elegant of places. Ringo, Mick, and Slowhand will be our inner circle."

"When you two play In a Perfect World, you don't mess around," Ricky said, laughing. "So, Donna, what's your story?' Bruce asked. "Develop a better robotic heart and get fabulously wealthy?"

"A long way from that. My mission is to bring good health care to the Navajo Nation. In a perfect world, every Navajo baby would be born in a well-provisioned clinic with excellent medical personnel. Every family would be able to get medical care regularly."

The table grew absolutely silent. No one knew what to say. Because Donna was the newest member of the group, she was the least known. Her dream caught everybody off guard.

Nancy reached across the table, looked squarely in Donna's eyes, and touched her arm.

"That is an incredible dream. I hope you accomplish all of it."

"Hear. Hear," the rest agreed in unison. "So, Barb, your turn," Nancy said.

"Okay. I will surprise all of you. In a perfect world, I would be a stay-at-home mom with five kids."

The table broke out in pandemonium. How could this hard-charger give it all up to be a mommy?

"Ricky, did you know this?" Bruce asked.

Ricky smiled and shook his head. "I absolutely did not but somehow...I am not surprised."

Putting his arm around her, he continued, "not surprised and not the least bit unhappy."

Marc chimed in. "Okay, Ricky, what's your perfect-world story?"

"I would write America's greatest novels, in the league of Hawthorne and Twain, Pynchon and Bellow. Great novels that readers would flock to and not be able to put down once they started reading. And, finally, I would receive the Nobel Award for Literature."

None were surprised at Ricky's dream, as they all knew that leaving journalism had been difficult for him. He often spoke of his time in Windowrock. He frequently worked a full day and, after putting the paper to bed, spent half the night writing for himself. He had showed them several manuscripts of started, but unfinished, novels and short stories. But he wouldn't allow any to be read. "They need more work," is all that he would say.

Quarters came out, the jukebox played loudly and the three couples, pulling Virginia and Ernie into the mix, danced joyously. Suddenly Bruce stopped and shouted, "Wait. Stop. Turn off the jukebox," while pointing excitedly at a television.

There on the screen, Darren was speaking into a bevy of microphones, Andy and Beto behind him. Ernie turned the juke box off just as the screen switched to a Denver reporter. "Jacobs and his colleagues were slightly injured in the crash landing at Miami International Airport." The screen changed to a view of the crippled Lear resting wing-deep in foam on the runway. "Now to Julie for the weather..."

"Holy shit," Bruce said. "We saw these guys at City Market today. They didn't say a word about any plane accident. I noticed he had the cut on his face but didn't want to ask him about it."

"Isn't he one of Billy's clients?" Nancy asked.

"Yeah, what a coincidence running into him today."

The juke box was turned back on and the dancing resumed until Virginia shooed them all out some time after midnight. The brisk mountain air sobered the bunch a bit during the walk home.

Back at Ricky's cabin, they hit a couple of numbers, gobbled Oreos and Moon Pies, and, once in bed, despite their best efforts to be discreet, issued sounds of sexual enjoyment into the wee morning hours. Once, they all started laughing in the dark, but finally quieted down and went to sleep, except for Marc who, as usual, couldn't drift off. He became irritated with himself. He sensed that something threatening lurked ahead, but, having nothing but a gut feeling to go on, wrote it off to the occupants of his typical, nighttime anxiety closet.

∽

Telluride

Handcuffed again and laying face-down in my great room, I heard the door open and the voice of Jorge Guzman, who had entered my house as an intruder rather than the guest he had been so many times before. Despite a rage that I felt sure would provide me the means to choke Guzman to death, I was determined Guzman would see nothing.

"*Buenos noche*, Jorge. Please come in," I said. In Spanish, he ordered all of our cuffs removed, and two of his henchmen helped me stand.

"Thank you, Darren, for your kindness," Jorge replied echoing the sarcasm that had laced my invitation.

Hearing Jorge's voice triggered a memory of our last telephone conversation. Never giving it even a thought, I had told Jorge all about the quarterly Cerberus board meeting.

"Darren, where's your housekeeper?" Jorge asked. "My guess—she's hiding in the vault by now."

"Okay, now, we are all going to go downstairs nice and slow. You gentlemen keep your fingers laced behind your head. No sudden moves. My *pistoleros* know their stuff."

Jorge gave instructions in Spanish to his gang. Two were to escort Beto and Andy downstairs and let the other two upstairs know when it was safe to bring Paul and I down.

In a few minutes, we--the four pairs of captives and captors--stood outside the vault.

Jorge motioned to me. "Tell her to open the doors."

"Marta, we are all okay. Please open the doors just as we have discussed. Hit the open button to the right of the door."

Her muffled reply came, "Darren, is that you? I can barely hear you."

Raising my voice, "It's me, Marta. Please hit the open button and let us in."

A mechanical "clink" sounded, followed by the soft hum of electric motors. The doors parted in the middle and began the controlled roll toward their respective jambs. We had practiced this dozens of times. Once the doors were fully opened, Beto and Andy, their eyes tightly closed, sprang into action.

A blinding flash of light exploded from inside the vault, and at exactly the same moment, deafening sirens screamed from all sides. Beto spun on his heel, crushing his smaller guard with a blow to his windpipe and, circling his arms around the limp upper body, spun him around as the dying man's reflexes pulled the trigger of the Glock spraying bullets in the direction of the driver. In simpatico with Beto's motion, Andy pushed his guard's arm upward as rounds from the gun spun off into the ceiling. The gun emptied in seconds and, as the gunman swung his free fist toward Andy, Andy grabbed the attacker's head and twisting violently, broke his neck in a single move.

I dove into the vault behind Beto, who was still standing holding the limp body of his guard as a shield. Jorge pulled Paul in front of him, wrapping his arm around Paul's neck and with his free hand aimed his pistol at me. Andy was now holding a Glock that he had pulled out of a compartment by the door. Jorge's sole remaining thug moved behind him and, with Paul as a buffer, they began backing up the steps and out of view. Andy silenced the sirens. From the vault, we could hear footsteps across the great room, the front door open, and, moments later, the sound of a car roared off in the distance.

"Darren, are you all right?" Beto asked. "Marta?"

Marta was silent, pressed into a corner on her knees with her eyes closed, sobbing softly.

"Yeah, I'm fine, I think. I...I...," my voice trailing into silence. Sweat broke out on my forehead and I began to shake and breathe heavily.

"You're bleeding." Andy ripped the left sleeve off my shirt. "You got nicked, partner, but it's just a scratch. Does anything else hurt?"

I remember sitting down heavily on the floor bumping into Marta who was now sprawled there. I couldn't get my eyes to work. Beto helped Marta stand, holding her upright and whispering to her. He walked her outside the vault to the hallway and a chair and helped her sit down. She smiled and wiped her face with her hands. Her sobbing slowly subsided.

"Darren, buddy, sit up here in this chair." Once Andy had helped me to my feet, I took a few wobbly steps under my own power and plopped into a chair next to Marta.

"Are you okay, Marta? I am so sorry. I am so sorry," I said. "Believe me, I would never have..."

"I'm fine, Darren. Don't worry. Are you hurt?"

"No, no, just a scratch. I'm fine." I actually couldn't even feel it, though my other senses were finally beginning to kick in.

Andy stood and spoke to Marta and me, with no hesitation or stutter. "Listen, guys, we have to go upstairs and make sure all of the bad guys are gone."

"They took Paul," I said, almost as a half question. I wasn't sure about reality at that point.

"Yeah, I suppose they got him as a hostage. We can worry about that in a minute. First, Beto and I need to go make sure the coast is clear. I want to close you and Marta in the vault till we get back. Is that okay, Darren?"

"Do you really have to go up there? Can't we just hang down here for a while?" I asked, shakily. I did not want Andy and Beto out of my sight.

"You'll be fine here. And so will Beto and I. We just need to make sure the house is empty." I was taken with Andy's calm, forceful way.

"Yeah, sure, go do what you gotta do. We'll be fine." I was regaining some sense of composure and knew that Andy was right.

Andy and Beto dragged the two *pistoleros* bodies out of the vault and down the hall. Marta began crying again. I put my arm around her shoulder and turned her head away from the grisly scene, gently escorting her into the vault before Andy closed and secured the vault doors with us safely ensconced inside.

∽

I checked my watch every minute or so. It seemed the hands did not move at all, but after fifteen minutes that seemed like fifteen days, there was a knock on the vault door.

"All clear, man. We're okay. Open up." Beto's voice barely resonated through the heavy door, but it was the sweetest sound I could imagine.

I helped Marta up and then held her arm as she steadied herself. Neither of us was quite right but we managed to operate the mechanism to open the vault door and walk out. I could still feel my pulse pounding but not as badly, and I was beginning to feel more aware, and a calmness was returning.

"Let's go up and get some coffee," Beto suggested "and maybe something stronger."

Beto helped Marta up the stairs. I waved off Andy's arm and climbed the steps slowly but on my own power. The great room was eerily quiet, the rain now softly padding on the windows before running down the panes.

Though I would like nothing more than to go up to my room and close the door, I knew I had to be the leader once more. Then, I saw Marta's stricken face and taking charge became easy. I knew Marta needed to get busy and Beto, Andy and I needed to connect.

"Marta, do you feel up to making us some coffee? Andy and Beto and I may be up for a while. And then, go pack a bag, honey, I'm going to call Charlie over at the hotel. I want you to go down and stay with them at least tonight."

I put my arms around Andy and Beto and pulled them into a three-way hug. No words were spoken—or required. "Okay, guys, I need to go upstairs for a minute and then we'll figure out what's next."

I went into my bedroom and slid open a wall compartment over the dresser, revealing a telephone hidden inside. Two years ago, fearing my home phone could be easily tapped, I had Beto (expert in such matters) cut into the telephone box of a neighbor who only used his home a month or so in the summer, during which periods the clandestine service was removed. I use the phone sparingly, only with critical privacy calls, and always called collect. Tonight, I was certain that the sheriff had tapped my house phone and would be listening to every call. This was the closest thing I would have to a secure line.

I called my buddy, Charlie, and asked him to send a car to pick up Marta. I told him I was surprising Marta with a couple of nights in luxury and I expected his staff to treat her like royalty. And bill me. A few minutes later, a white courtesy vehicle pulled into the drive. Hovering protectively, Andy and Beto walked Marta to the car. Seeing that she was still shaky, they helped her into the front seat and put her small bag in the back. Beto handed her an envelope stuffed full of cash. "Darren asked me to give this to you."

Andy leaned into the car and spoke softly. "Hang on. We'll get you taken care of, but it may take a few days. Marta, we feel horrible that you got caught up in this. Everything is going to turn out just fine. Try to put what happened out of your mind... and try not to worry."

Marta looked at him blankly. Andy closed the door and the car disappeared into the rain and mist.

◞

From Sheriff Lang's communication trailer, Jorge Guzman placed a call to Culiacan that he knew could signal the end of his existence. "*Hefe,* we've run into a little bit of trouble. Nothing to worry about, but..."

◞

I was on the phone in the great room when Beto and Andy walked back into the house from seeing Marta off.

"Yes, I understand. That's very good of you," I said, keeping my voice controlled yet full of intentional condescension.

"We'll talk and I'll give you our answer tomorrow morning." And with that, I quietly placed the phone back in the cradle. But the calmness in the motion was not what I felt. For the first time in my life, I felt like I hated someone so much that I could kill him.

"That was our old buddy, Sheriff Lang. He promises the three of us safe passage out of Telluride---and forever more. All we have to do is leave the vault open and never, ever get back in the coke biz. Paul will be released in a few days. Isn't he a gratuitous, compassionate bastard? So, old friends, we need to talk."

"They took the wrecked pickup with them when they left. So, at least we don't have that mess lurking around outside, but we do have a couple of dead guys downstairs that we are going to need to deal with," Beto said.

"Stuff them into the walk-in refrigerator. That'll take care of them for a while anyway." Even I amazed myself at how unemotionally that came out. I was learning some very interesting things about myself now that people were trying to kill me.

"We'll take care of it, Dare," Beto said, and he and Andy disappeared downstairs.

∽

While they were busy with that grisly chore, I returned to my bedroom and, using the secret phoneline, called Billy Mercado at his home in the North Valley of Albuquerque. Another friend since childhood, Mercado is the lawyer I use for anything sensitive. I didn't bother calling collect. That little detail didn't seem so important anymore.

"This better be important," Mercado snapped, answering the private number he only gave out to a few clients.

"Billy, this is Darren. We're up in Telluride and the shit has hit the fan."

"What, are the feds making some end run around Lang?"

"No, I wish that's all it was." "Damned, it must be serious then."

"Cortez and Guzman have tried a coup. They intend to take over our business. And that fucking traitor Lang has thrown in with them—they bought him off. I guess they've decided they don't need us anymore."

"This is serious then. Wait a minute, how did you find out? This isn't the kind of thing that you send someone a registered letter?" Just as I expected, Mercado's mind quickly engaged and registered the enormity of the situation.

"Much more direct. They sent three *pistoleros* to the house. It's a long story, but the bottom line is they ambushed us and held us till that *puta* Guzman got up here. Guzman announces that not only do they plan on taking our business, but they want us to turn over all the cash and inventory in the vault, as well."

"Well, you're talking to me, so I'm assuming something didn't go according to their plan." "Correct. Andy and Beto killed two of the *penche cabrons...*"

"Holy shit!"

"And maybe wounded the other one. Guzman and his henchman used Paul as a shield and backed out of here."

"They've got Paul?"

"Yes. They say they will let him go in a few days if we'll just open the vault and leave quietly with our tails between our legs."

"Man, this is a mess. I suspect Guzman has brought professionals with him?" Mercado asked.

"Yeah, we met three of them and they are, or were, bad mothers. But, Billy, you should have seen Andy and Beto in action. They were amazing. They moved so fast—and it seemed like they knew what each other was thinking. I'll give you a blow-by-blow description when this is all over."

"So, what can I do for you?" Mercado asked.

"I don't know, man. I just thought I ought to let you know what's going on and get that brilliant mind of yours focused. The three of us probably aren't thinking too clearly right now. I told Guzman that I would tell him in the morning what we are going to do."

"Aren't you worried they may come back tonight?"

"No, they lost the element of surprise. We'll stay on our toes—the boys have an arsenal up here—but I don't expect them to do anything stupid tonight. Anyway, time is on their side. I'm sure they have bottled up the canyon." It was good talking out loud to Billy.

"Let me noodle on it, Dare. I don't have any bright ideas right off the bat but call me back if anything changes. No matter, give me a call first thing in the morning before you call Guzman."

"Okay, Billy. There isn't going to be a lot of sleeping done around here tonight, so call if you have any brainstorms."

"G'night, man. Take care."

∾

Before leaving, Marta, functioning on autopilot, had cleared the kitchen table of the supper dishes and in a daze, loaded and started the dishwasher, and made a pot of coffee. I grabbed three cups, setting them and the carafe on the table. Beto and Andy returned and sat down on either side of me. Something was irritating me, until I opened the dishwasher door to put a stop to the noise.

I jumped right into the topic. "Hard to believe we were sitting here laughing our asses off just a few hours ago with the world by the balls and nothing, I mean, really nothing significant to worry about. And, now," holding my arms out "here we are—"

"Thanks—thanks, to you, Dare. If you hadn't had the foresight to have the, uh, booby traps set up in the vault," Andy paused, "we might not be sitting here. Even knowing it was coming, you know, that flash of light and the sirens blasting in my ears—well—truthfully, nearly petrified me for a moment."

"Yeah, me too, but it was exactly what we needed when we needed it. Darren, as usual, you are just a little bit smarter than the average bear," Beto chimed in.

"Remember when we did the practice drills after the installation and you guys gave me a lot of grief about being such a worry wart? Huh? Huh?" I couldn't pass up the brief victory lap.

"Yep, but thank god you, you, you, uh, were," Andy said.

"So. Shall we talk through our alternatives? Andy, you want to take a shot?"

As usual, Andy thought a moment before speaking slowly and clearly. "Darren, if it weren't for them having Paul, it would be an easy call for me. They might, um, get our shit in the end, but we would take a lot of those—er--assholes with us. In fact, I don't think they can risk a shoot-out in Telluride. The Feds have stayed out of this place only because it's a rat's nest they haven't gotten to yet. But a g-g-gun battle would end all of that, so I don't know how they could even pull that off."

Andy paused to sip his coffee.

"But with them having Paul—that's a, uh, game-changer. They won't hesitate to kill him, and it won't be a pleasant death, which, of course, they will tell us about in great detail before they start the –uh—process. So, I'm kind of stuck."

Andy lit a cigarette, and took a long drag, a no-no in my house that I chose to overlook.

"There's an outside chance Beto and I could retrieve Paul. A little special ops Telluride-style." He arched his eyebrow first to Beto and then Darren.

Beto's face lit up. "Shit, man, now I remember why I like the cut of your jib."

I held my hands out. "Hold on, hold on, you two. Guzman has likely brought an army and they are aligned with Lang's bunch. We're not talking about some picnic with amateurs here."

Andy pulled a drag on his cigarette while Beto and I waited. "Yeah, I am not the least bit worried about Lang's 'dep-u-tees'", Andy emphasized with a roll of his eyes, "but those three tonight were pros. I'm guessing they were somehow trained in Virginia or, at least, by some of our—hmmm--operatives from Virginia--and there's likely to be more where they came from.

But...but, we would have surprise on our side. They aren't going to be expecting a counter-attack, eh, Beto?"

"Besides, Darren, what other options have we got?" Andy looked from me to Beto and back. "I could live with turning over the biz. I'm not so sure this is such a bad time, anyhow, with what's going on up in Aspen and Vail with the—uh--narcs. But I'll be corn-holed before I turn over all we've worked for these years to those—those--dorks"

"We could fight our way out over one of the passes?" Beto offered.

I took in a deep breath. "I thought of that, but you can bet that they have Imogene, Black Bear and Ophir covered. They will have picked out the best places to defend, and I don't think even you guys can win that war."

Other than the main highway that ran by the airport, only three jeep trails led out of the box canyon. Imogene, the easiest, took off from behind my house and headed up north, winding up at Ouray. Black Bear was the monster that went right through the end of the canyon over Red Mountain Pass. Ophir was the least rugged and emptied out over by Silverton, but we would have to cross enemy territory—Telluride proper—held by Lang, so it was out of the question.

"No, you're right, Dare," Andy agreed. "I c-c-can picture two or three spots on each of those trails where two dug-in defenders could wipe out an army."

We all stared dumbly at our coffee cups. It was clear that our options were extremely limited and all the talking in the world wasn't going to change that.

Finally, Beto looked up. "Dare, I'm going to ask you something and I don't want you fucking flying into one of your famous rages. We're in the shits and have to think of everything. Have you considered that Paul could have gone over to the dark side on us?"

I couldn't believe what I was hearing. "Have you lost your mind!" My voice seethed with anger. This time I had no intention of hiding that I was pissed. "He's been with us every step of the way. You know it wasn't that easy for him—for anyone—to break into this group, and he's been one of us through thick and thin. When hasn't he done everything we asked of him?"

Andy had been shifting his look between Beto and me, trying to read everything he could from the two faces he knew better than any others in the world.

"Beto, you wouldn't have asked that without some grounds. What are you seeing that maybe we aren't?" Andy asked.

"Oh, shit, you two have gone completely out of your minds. This is how paranoia blows people apart," I snapped.

Andy spoke softly but with insistence. "Beto?"

"I don't know. I thought I saw something not quite right about how Paul acted while Guzman was here. I can't put my finger on it. I've been playing the scenes back in my head and I can't quite get it. It may be nothing. It may be something."

I was primed to jump all over Beto when Andy held his hand up to quiet me. He is the only person in the world that could get away with this. "Darren, Beto and I have had more tight situations together than Butch and Sundance. I learned a long time ago--not to disregard Beto's instincts. He's got a gift, of that I am sure. I'm not saying we should—umm--convict Paul right here, but can't we at least keep an open mind? When this all blows over, the three of us will agree to never speak of this again. But for right now, can't we, uh, keep our minds open?"

"One final thought. Darren, do you remember ever telling Paul about the traps set in the vault?" Andy asked.

I paused and looked out into the darkness through the great room windows. "No, no, I am pretty sure that I didn't. It just never came up. Why, what are you thinking?"

"Well, clearly those guys weren't ready for it. If Paul had known about it and has crossed over on us, for sure he would have prepared them. But if you didn't tell him…"

"No, I'm sure I didn't. I've had it with you lunatics. I'm going to bed."

The events of the day set in. I was completely worn out. Even Andy and Beto looked exhausted. They headed downstairs to the vault, returning in minutes with two M-16's and a crate of ammunition, having decided to sleep in the great room with the armament. Just in case. I armed the alarm system and went off to my bedroom without saying another word. As if the tension of the overall situation wasn't enough, the remnants of the unpleasant discussion left a stench in the air.

CHAPTER 6

WEDNESDAY, MAY 24

I had just started downstairs when the telephone in the great room rang, jolting Beto awake. Andy was watching out the window, his rifle draped over his shoulder. Rays of sunlight were just starting to tilt across the valley, the house snuggled in the shadow created by the soaring end of the box canyon deferring daybreak until the incessant rotation of the planet finally won. I answered the phone.

"Darren, this is Dave Richardson. Sorry to wake you so early but I thought this is a conversation we should have sooner rather than later."

"No problem, Captain, I was just mustering up the energy to go make coffee. Give me your number and I'll call you right back." I hung up the line thinking *this will screw with Lang's head--waiting for the next call.*

I ran upstairs and, shifting to the secret line in my bedroom, rang back. "What can I do for you?"

"This is difficult news to deliver." Richardson took a deep breath. "I believe the access door on the Lear was intentionally loosened and the cabin warning light rendered inoperative. While there are other tests and detail studies that ought to be done to be positive, I think the FAA investigators feel the same way. They won't say so yet and probably not for a while. But I thought you ought to know."

I sat up straight and swiveled my legs over the side of the bed. "You...you...you're saying someone sabotaged the plane?"

"I'm almost positive, Darren. Maybe the rest of the investigation will shed a different light on it, but I don't think so."

"Wow, this is a bolt from the blue. I don't know what to say."

"Well, somebody wanted that plane down. I don't think they were after Tom or me. Our company is really doing great, so some sort of insurance scam doesn't make sense. It kind of comes down to a case of mistaken identity, or—"

"Or me and my boys. And that makes no sense. I've made some enemies in court in my day, but I can't imagine one of them with the inclination to do something like this."

The reality was starting to dawn on me, but I wasn't ready to even consider the possibility with Richardson. "Well, maybe something will turn up so that the conclusion isn't so sinister?" I felt bad being disingenuous with someone I respect so much.

"Darren, at some point as you know, the FAA might turn this over to the police. Oh, yeah, one more point. There were particulates in the engine from metal other than from the door. I'm thinking a small plastic explosive and shrapnel may have been tucked into the engine compartment. That seems to be the evidence that bothers the Feds the most. Well, anyway, that's all I can tell you for now, and I really shouldn't have told you this, but I feel a personal responsibility to anyone who has been a passenger on my watch, so there you are."

"Thanks, Captain. I know you probably stuck your neck out a little passing this on, and I really appreciate it. Please let me know if you hear anything else worth knowing about."

"Take care, Darren."

"You, too, Dave."

I went back downstairs and found Beto, fully dressed in crumpled clothes, yawning and trying to clear his head of an obviously crummy night's sleep on the couch. Andy was in the kitchen making coffee.

"Mornin', Andy," I grumbled. "What's doin'?"

"Ugh, what a night. Feel like sh-sh-shit and no great party memories. Doesn't sound like much of a, uh, deal, does it?"

"No, it sure doesn't. I think I bought the same package," I said.

"Who was on the phone?" Beto asked entering with a carafe of coffee in one hand and mugs in the other. He set them down on the coffee table.

"Mornin', Beto, how are you?" "Hey, Dare, partly shitty to shittier."

We all sat, and I poured dark roast black coffee into the mugs. After a first thoughtful sip, I shared what I had learned. "That was Captain Richardson on the phone. He thinks our little Lear episode was no accident; that someone rigged the plane to bring us down. I guess after yesterday we don't have to scratch our heads too hard to figure out who that might be."

"Fuck, fuck, fuck...those mother fuckers!" Beto jumped straight out of his chair, pumping his fists furiously.

Andy just sat quietly staring into his coffee cup as if he could summon some genie out of the mug to make this nightmare go away.

"The captain said the FAA is not near ready to come to that conclusion yet, but he just wanted us to have the benefit of his thinking early. It may take those morons months before they actually reveal anything."

"What is he b-b-basing his thinking on, Darren?" Andy asked.

"It looks as though the access door was tampered with as well as the idiot light that would have indicated it wasn't closed. Plus--and this is the kicker--it seems some metal pieces were jammed in the compartment, for insurance. Dave said there were foreign metal sources in the engine that couldn't be airplane parts. He said that the investigation was going to continue for a while with all sorts of laboratory tests and so on and so forth, but it would take something drastically different than he had seen so far to change his mind."

I stood and walked to the window, looking down over the roofs of Telluride, watching the sunlight advancing relentlessly one block and then another. No one said anything for several minutes, the power of the unspoken sucking all of the air out of the room. Finally, Beto spoke. "Paul wasn't with us on that plane. That sort of puts a whole new light on our discussion from last night."

For the first time, I permitted myself to think about the possibility of Paul's disloyalty. My bowels churned and I wanted to scream. Instead, I assumed my best courtroom demeanor. "I would say it differently. It's another piece of evidence that is problematic. Saying it 'puts a whole new light' on the issue is overly strong. Unlike you two, I am not ready to write Paul off yet."

"Darren, that's not fair. Beto and I are, you know, not trying to throw Paul under the bus. We're just saying that we need, ummm, to keep an open mind and be prepared for all—any-- possibilities."

"Well, let me ask you this, Andy. What if it was you down there being held captive by those cut-throats, and I was sitting up here leading a debating society about whether you were a traitor or not? How would you feel about that, mister?" I couldn't stop myself. "This isn't getting us anywhere. I'm gonna call Billy and see if someone not sitting in this boiling pot can figure a way out."

Having spoken my mind, I poured another mug of coffee and began to walk back to my bedroom leaving the Three Musketeers seriously at odds with one another for this first time in a very long history. Over my shoulder, I saw Beto look at Andy, his face tired and tormented. He just slowly shook his head, out of sadness and disbelief, I suppose.

～

"Billy, this is Darren. Sorry to bother you so early."

"Oh, man, don't sweat that. I didn't sleep more than a few winks last night anyway."

"So, any great ideas while you were cogitating on our predicament?" I asked.

"No, not yet. But I'm not sure I have the full picture, either. Darren, go over for me where you think things stand."

"Okay, sure. Guzman and Lang have thrown in together, no doubt about that. As you know, Lang has six deputies that are as dirty as he is. We should know—we've had them on our payroll for years. They aren't anything to sneeze at, but Guzman brought his posse from Mexico, probably a bunch of them, and they are bad muthuhs. The worst combination possible: no compunction about killing and the skills to back up the attitude.

Together, they have us bottled up. I'm sure Lang has his boys well positioned along the Airport Road, the only paved way in or out. Also--we talked about this last night--the three Jeep trails are the only other way in or out of this place and we're sure they have all been covered. Even Andy and Beto don't want to take on trying to bust through one of them, so that tells you how well they probably have them fortified.

And, of course, they have Paul. Oh, by the way, just to make things a little more interesting, the pilot of our Lear called this morning and said he is certain the plane was sabotaged. Andy and Beto and I have been knocking heads together because they're suspicious of Paul."

"Oh shit, oh dear, the plot thickens, " Mercado said.

"Yeah, don't it though. So, Guzman says we can hop in our little car and drive on out of Telluride anytime we want to. We just have to leave the vault open and the, ahem, assets in it.

They say they'll send Paul along in a day or two, but no matter what else we decide, I am not going for that. They've got to deliver Paul back to us before I am stepping one foot out of this town."

"What have you guys talked about so far?"

"You know, I don't think any of us mind getting out of the business. We've had more fun and made more money than we had any reason to expect. And between the feds and competing cartels in Colombia, it probably isn't a bad time for us to fold our tent anyway. But leaving behind about forty millions of coke and cash is a jagged pill that we just can't swallow."

Mercado whistled through the phone, "Forty million. You've got to be shitting me!?"

"No, it's about half cash and half inventory that we have been building up here in case our supplies ever dried up for a while. We've been trying to get the cash to somewhere safe and were close to doing it, but they caught us at the worst goddamned time."

"So here's the bottom line. If they didn't have Paul, I think we would all just stand pat and wait this thing out. Even with their superior firepower, they aren't going to attack Fort Darren and get some of the good citizens of Telluride killed in the process. It probably would end up in a negotiated peace of some kind and we could live with that. But with them having Paul, there is no doubt in any part of my mind that they will torture the poor bastard and share their results with us. That sort of tips the scale more toward just taking our lumps and getting out of here with our lives."

"And how do Andy and Beto come down on this?"

"Well, I recognize they are in a little different boat than I— they weren't born with silver spoons in their mouths. Truthfully, my attitude toward Guzman getting our stuff has more to do with my balls than my net worth. But this is Andy's and Beto's "fuck you" money forever. You know Beto's favorite saying, 'Life's a shit sandwich. The more bread you have, the less shit you have to eat.' So, they have a little more motivation than I to hang on. I think that's how they're rationalizing that Paul's rolled over. It's easier to sacrifice him that way."

"Man, that's a little harsh. Do you really think that's what's going on?"

"I don't know, Billy. Between you and me, I don't really know what to think. What do you think?"

"Darren, I'm going to ask you a question to think about, okay?"
"Fire."

"Would Guzman be going to all this trouble if he didn't know-- for a fact--what you have hidden up there? It's not like this hasn't got risk to it for him. You guys have already flipped his bad asses once."

"That's been nagging at me more than a little."

༈

Lang and Jorge Guzman were closeted in the Winnebago recreational vehicle that had been modified to serve as a mobile command center. A full walkie-talkie panel and system was arrayed along one wall. All six deputy vehicles, Chevrolet Blazers and Jeeps, were equipped with walkie-talkies as well. Three telephone lines had been cut into a telephone system service box and were strung with temporary poles to the RV. Rumor in Southern Colorado had it that this expensively equipped deputy department was somehow funded by drug money and its real purpose was to protect certain citizens from a sneak attack by federal narcotic agents. Most scoffed at the rumor as preposterous, but recent events in Vail and Aspen had people thinking.

The Winnebago was parked about fifty yards off Airport Road. Three black and white Blazers straddled the highway, and an officer was stopping the few cars that were moving at this time of day and handing out coffee and doughnuts as part of a "citizen appreciation effort".

"So, when are you gonna give our buddy a call?" Joe Bob Lang, a transplanted Texan, drawled.

Lang looked over sixty but was only fifty-one. His sunburned red face, freckled and mapped with liver spots, sat atop a rounded mass of upper body that gravity projected over his belt in a muffin top. His eyes were just squints above jowls and what little hair he had left was widely spaced silver streaks combed from his forehead straight back. Blue jeans and boots were topped with a gray shirt with black piping and closed with lustrous snaps, except just above his belt where two had come undone. A three-inch shining five-point star announced him as "Sheriff". The back of his black belt further identified him as "Joe Bob" in white calligraphy.

"When I think it's time," was Guzman's curt reply, his opinion of the sheriff clear in the response.

"Well, la-de-dah," Lang sang back, irritating Guzman even further. "I'm going to check on my boys. Maybe grab a doughnut or two," he said as he opened the RV door and stepped down heavily, ponderously negotiating the ladder steps that swung down beneath the door, one rung at a time.

❦

After hanging up from talking to Billy, I showered and dressed. Normally, I would have gone for a five-mile run with Andy first thing, but that wasn't a choice today. I walked into the empty great room. I could hear Andy futzing around in the kitchen and the shower running upstairs where Beto was getting ready.

"What are you cooking, Andy?" I asked' strolling into the kitchen.

"*Huevos rancheros.* A g-g-good sweat breaking out on our, uh, foreheads will activate the creative lobes of our *cabesas.* Maybe we can figure a way out of th-th-this pickle."

"Great idea, partner. I'll heat the griddle for the *tortillas.*"

Andy had the green chile sauce warming in a saucepan, the pungent acidic aroma filling the kitchen. He stirred the sauce between flipping eggs on the adjacent griddle.

"Beto, get your ass d-down, down here," Andy yelled in the direction of the stairs. "Darren, I've got p-p-plates warming in the oven."

"Yep, perfect."

The assembly line was simple; the teamwork process, healing. Wearing a mitt, I pulled a plate out of the oven, slipped a tortilla off the griddle, laid it on the plate and held it outstretched to Andy. Andy flipped two eggs out of the frying pan and onto the tortilla, sunny side down and ladled a copious amount of the green chile sauce over the eggs and tortilla. I topped it off with a handful of shredded cheese just as Beto slipped into the room.

"Here, buddy, this'll put lead in your pencil."

I set the plate in front of Beto. "Watch out, that plate's sizzling."

Soon we were all huddled over our plates, stuffing forkfuls of tortillas, eggs, chile sauce and cheese into our mouths, each bite creating a blissfully painful explosion of heat that captured every taste bud in our mouths. I looked up and laughed. Beads of perspiration had sprung forth on all of our foreheads.

"I don't know how people live without green chile," Beto opined. "This stuff from Hatch is primo."

All three of us are members of an exclusive list of the in-crowd in Santa Fe who get the most select grade of green chiles from the Hatch Valley in Southern New Mexico every year. The farm does several custom picks as the chiles ripen, sorting the very best out for the elite customer group. The sort is based on three factors: the thickness of the walls of the chile; the outward appearance—regular shape and no pest damage, and heat level—the hotter the better. The chiles are hauled to a Silver City processor where they are perfectly roasted, veins and seeds removed, and quick frozen into two-pound packages. Club members all own old-style deep freezers mostly or totally filled with the chiles to be rationed out carefully to try to make them last for the full year.

The plates were all soon cleaned, the meal providing more than sustenance as we three old friends ate our "New Mexico soul food" together as we have done thousands of times before. Our appetites were sated and collective spirits somewhat renewed.

"So, so...where do we go from here, Dare?" Andy asked. "Did B-B-Billy have any great ideas?"

"Billy's noodling on it, but no, no real brainstorms yet. The more I think about it, the more I keep coming back to some sort of compromise end game. They can't afford to throw a full-on assault at us with Telluridians looking on...or worse, possibly being collateral damage, so it seems like we're stuck in a waiting game. Which one of us is going to blink first? Paul, however, is their wild card."

"Puts us in the old proverbial land between the rock and the fucking hard place," Beto added.

"You know, we have troops of our own that we could call in. Have you, ummm, thought about that, Darren?" Andy asked.

"No, I really haven't. What are you thinking?"

Beto jumped in. "Shit, Dare, most of the Poundmen are hitters. Truthfully, they are, like all of us, pretty much coin-operated. We're all in the game for the money. A few of them, half a dozen maybe, I think we could count on."

I had expected this. "Yeah, but even considering we might have six or seven soldiers with us, leadership is stuck up here in this fort. There's all sorts of logistical issues. And Guzman can probably put five times that many *pistoleros* in the field against us if he really needed to," I countered.

"I didn't say it was a fucking cake walk, Dare. I'm just raising possibilities," Beto answered.

"Sorry, you're right. We need to turn over every stone right now. By the way, and along the lines of our discussion last night, Billy raised this question—'would Guzman be coming at us this hard unless he is sure of what he is likely to get?'" I had already decided to share this. Truthfully, Billy's question rattled my absolute confidence in Paul and it was time to throw the boys a bone.

"If it's a lucky guess on his part, it's a damned sure good one. The timing couldn't be worse—for us that is," Beto responded.

"True. But they're going to--you know--put Paul in play no matter. We can bet on that," Andy added.

"Just in the spirit of full disclosure, Billy is more than a little concerned about Paul. You three have me thinking, anyway," I said. I appreciated that, knowing what a difficult admission this had been, Andy and Beto avoided looking at each other or at me. They just let the comment drop.

We discussed all the possibilities we could think of, outlining the pros and cons of each. We each took turns being Guzman and Lang in an effort to try to anticipate our adversaries' next moves. The conversation was mostly serious and productive, with occasional spurts of levity to break the tension. Beto did an impersonation of Joe Bob Lang that would have been good material for a *Saturday Night Live* "red neck revue".

＄

At just after ten, the phone rang. I let it ring five times before answering the great room line. Andy and Beto followed me in, to at least hear my side of the call in real time.

"This is Darren."

Surprisingly, it was Lang on the line. "Are you boys ready to come out of your cave? Darren, this game's been fun, but it's over. The quicker you fellers deal with that, the easier it's gonna be for all of us."

I substituted "You don't say" for my first impulse, which was "Go fuck yourself, you fat bastard".

"I do say. The only way you guys are getting out of my valley is on my terms. And my terms is that you plop yourselves in your car and drive on down here. We won't shake hands, but we can wave as you drive your sorry asses out of town."

"That just isn't going to happen, Joe Bob. I have a couple of partners up here who have a whole different perspective on whether you can enforce your rules or not."

"Well, that may be, but I can assure you that you ain't getting out of Telluride Valley unless you drive on out of here peacefully and quickly. These are some mean goddamned Mescans, Darren. They're about ready to carve your little buddy into pieces and start sending them up to you one at a time...just to encourage your speedy exit, you understand?"

"Paul's a big boy, Lang. He knew what he was getting into when he chose up with us. And when you've played that card, then, what next? Are you going to mount a full-scale raid on my house while the tourists and Telluridians dodge bullets? I don't think so. Even you aren't that stupid." I couldn't control my insult gland any longer.

"You know, Darren. You're right. You're a right smart, bright lawyer. But, me and the boys, we talked that little--how do you say it? see-nar-i-o? over. And what we come up with is a grave concern that the tailings dam above Telluride has developed a sudden lack of stability. We have such concerns that the recent rains and flooding have undercut the dam, well, that sucker might just bust sending a wall of toxic chemicals and water down over our good city. Our concern is rising to such a level that we might have to consider calling an emergency evacuation of Telluride's citizenry until we can get that damned dam stabilized. Now, what do you think of that, Darren?"

I didn't respond. This was a chess move that I—none of us— had thought of.

"We'll let you stew on that a bit. Talk ta ya later, podner." And with that, Lang hung up the phone on me.

Guzman said, sighing deeply, "Sheriff, hand me the phone. I'd better make a progress report to Cortez, though I'd rather have a root canal."

⌒

"Well, that was interesting," I said turning to Andy and Beto. "That fat redneck is a little smarter than I have given him credit for." "What'd he say?"

"What we expected—get out of town quietly, blah, blah, blah—and the "Mescans", as he called them, are going to start cutting Paul up any minute. But here's what we hadn't thought about--he's threatening to clear the whole valley due to impending doom from a leak in the tailings dams created by recent rains."

"Son of a bitch. Do you think he really would hustle everybody out of town just to come after us? That sounds pretty drastic," Beto said.

"I don't know if he'd actually do it or not, but it's a hell of a threat," I answered.

"You know, if you think about it," Andy paused. "It, it, it wouldn't take them more than an hour or so to get everybody out of Telluride this time of year. And, well, the greenies have made such a big deal out of the t-t-tailings dam, there's a built-in, how do you say it? plausibility factor, that would at least buy him a little time before the outside authorities and press could get in here. Umm, you're right, Darren, the old gent-gentleman is way smarter than we thought," Andy added.

"What do you read into Lang talking to you instead of Jorge?" Beto asked.

"Good question. Maybe the sheriff is asserting himself in this deal. You can bet he's planning on a nice payday out of this," I speculated, thinking it was very perceptive of Beto for picking up on this.

"So, so...what now, Darren?" Andy inquired.

"We wait for their next move. My gut says it won't be very long."

$\backsim$

Lang drove the sixty miles to Mancos and parked on the city square.

"Hey, Sheriff Lang, what's up?" Mickey Jenkins chirped in his always jovial manner. Mickey, a thirty-three-year-old drunk, was the county manager's nephew. He was on the county payroll with the title of maintenance worker, which meant he did a little of whatever needed doing to keep him busy. Today, he was acting morgue manager while he mopped the floors and cleaned the johns.

"Mickey, have they elected you mayor yet?"

"Oh, hell, Sheriff Lang, you're always pulling my leg. What are you doing over in these parts?"

"I heard a deputy picked up a John Doe down by the highway last night, and I'm sort of thinking he might be someone we got missing. Mind if I take a look?"

"No, nosirree. He's here in this drawer. Nope, must be this one. Yep, there ya go," Mickey said as he rolled out a cadaver drawer with a body bag resting on it.

"Dammit. Mickey, I think I left my camera on the front seat of the cruiser. Would you mind runnin' out there and getting' it for me? My old hip's been givin' me what-for lately."

"No, problem, Sheriff. Where'd you park?"

"On down by the park, Mickey." And with that, Mickey rushed off.

Lang pulled a plastic bag out of the left pocket of his jacket and a pair of wire snips out of the other. He quickly zipped open the bag halfway and pulled out the deceased's right arm. With a single snip, he cut off the pinkie finger just where it connected to the hand and let it drop into the bag, followed by the ring finger. Before he zipped the bag shut, he put the arm, minus two fingers, back inside the body bag.

After quickly stuffing the plastic bag and its gruesome contents into his pocket, Lang pushed the drawer closed and walked casually out of the morgue. He ran into Mickey on the front steps hustling back with the camera.

"Here you go, Sheriff. It took me a minute to find it."

"No, problem Mickey. Turns out not to be the fella anyway. Sorry to put you out. You tell your uncle hello for me; will you do that?"

"I shore will, Sheriff. Good to see you again."

$\backsim$

Hoping Billy had some inspiration, I rang him up. "Billy, Darren."

"How ya' holding up?"

"We're doing okay. Got a little call from our compadres this morning." "So, what did Senor Guzman have to say?" Billy asked.

"Actually, it was Lang that called," I said.

"Interesting."

"Mostly the call was what you would expect. Why don't you good ol' boys just get the hell out of my city? But there was a twister. Joe Bob is threatening to clear Telluride because of an imminent concern over the safety of the tailings dam."

"Hmmm, not a bad tactical move. It wouldn't hold water—no pun intended--for very long, but then, they wouldn't need much time."

"Exactly."

"As long as we're playing chess, did you hit Lang with the potential consequences to him if anything happens to you?" Billy asked.

"No, not yet, but it's probably time. He definitely put his nuclear option on the table this morning, and I have to say, I did not see that one coming. It sounds preposterous at first, but the truth is, it is a real enough possibility that we have to consider--they might go through with it."

"What about Paul?" Billy said.

"Oh, for sure, he laid that card on the table—how he wasn't going to be able to keep Guzman's *malo hombres* from torturing Paul. And, like the evacuating Telluride threat, they can make good on it. Any more thoughts on that score?" I needed Billy to tell it to me straight like he always has.

He paused. I understood his discomfort. This was a life and death discussion about someone he had worked closely with and come to respect and like. He was around to watch as Paul had first been brought into the group, and the challenge he had winning Andy and Beto over.

"The fact that Lang is threatening to clear Telluride and then wipe the three of you out and deal with the fallout from that—well, that doesn't mean much at this point. Until he actually acts, it could be just a bluff in a card game. But I am having a hard time getting around what has already occurred. They likely have hired serious professional help to blow you guys out of the sky. When Paul wasn't there, by the way. And they nearly pulled off an extremely well-planned sneak attack. It's just hard for me to imagine them going to all that effort if they weren't sure about the amount of the spoils."

"I hear you," I said grimly, silently thanking my lucky stars for Billy.

"Darren, have you thought about how Guzman would even know you guys were going to

Nassau and how you were going to get down there?" Billy asked.

"Yeah, Billy, I thought of that. I made the preliminary arrangements from my office in Santa Fe, but I scheduled the plane and confirmed the appointments from my home phone up here. Hell, I wasn't even thinking conspiracy at that point, so Lang likely was listening to every call going and coming."

"That makes sense. I don't envy your position, Darren. They're going to squeeze you with

Paul—and not too far in the future, I would reckon. You know that, don't you?"

"Yes, Billy, when I wasn't sleeping much last night, Paul was marching in the front of the parade of horribles."

"Darren, I just got an idea, but it may not amount to anything. Let me work on something from my end and if it has any legs, I'll call you back shortly."

"Sure thing, Billy. At this point, we'll take a National Guard air strike from the Santa Fe Armory if you can make that happen."

"You know, I just might could, but I'm not sure we would get away with that one. I'll call you as soon as I have traced down a couple of things."

"Call soon. We're sort of up against it, you know?"

 ~

I felt like a caged animal, even in the house I love. Twice I caught myself with my hand on the doorknob getting ready to go outside before my mind set off an alarm and brought me back to reality figuratively kicking and screaming.

"Andy, I've spotted two of the bastards in that stand of aspens just above the boulder, two more just the other side of the arroyo at two o'clock and then the Jeep down at the end of road," Beto said.

"Confirmed. Those guys have all been in place since last night," Andy said.

Beto was peering out the northwest-facing window of the loft bedroom with field binoculars. Andy had previously located and identified Guzman's and Lang's teams, watching their movements for several hours. Beto's reconnoitering confirmed Andy's.

"They have good visibility of the house on all sides except the south. You agree?" Andy asked, his voice calm and sure.

"I do," Beto said. "They must not be worried about that side since its right up against the bluff. They have all of the most likely access spots covered."

"So, bottom line, they've got us pretty well bottled up, then?" I asked.

Andy thought for a moment. "W-W-Well, I wouldn't go that far. After dark, we could all get out of the, um, house with a little effort, but we couldn't take much with us, and-and-and I don't know where we'd go. Unless we can...you know...figure out our next steps, just getting out of here, ummm, doesn't accomplish much more than if we just turned chicken, got in our c-c-cars and drove out of here empty handed. Does that sound right, D-D-Darren?"

"Yeah...yeah it does." Unfortunately, Andy was right on.

∽

The afternoon dragged on. To keep my mind occupied and avoid any unneeded questions, I conducted what law practice business couldn't wait, talking to several clients and lawyers in Santa Fe and Albuquerque. Andy and Beto took turns monitoring the bad guys' teams that were watching the house. They really didn't expect any activity, and none occurred. As is their way, they were just being extra careful.

Just before seven the house telephone rang. Darren let it ring awhile and then answered,

"This is Darren."

"I tried to call earlier, but your line was tied up," twanged Lang.

"How did you like all of the legal discussions, Joe Bob? Did you go to sleep listening in?" "Why, Darren, I'm offended. How could you even imagine that I would break federal law and have an unauthorized tap on your line? What do you think I am, a criminal?" He chuckled malevolently."Yeah, well, let's don't go there," I said. "So, are you fellers ready to scoot?"

"Put Guzman on, Lang." I wanted to push this issue and find out what was going on.

"We can talk, Darren. You and me...we've always been able to come to terms." "Put—Guz--man--on," I repeated, emphasizing each syllable and not hiding the undisguised hatred.

"Darren. How may I help you?" Jorge inquired in mock courtesy.

"Well, for one thing, Jorge, you can call off this charade before it turns into a debacle. You are fucking up a great business arrangement with your greed, and this can't turn out good for anybody, the way it's headed. You've lost two soldiers already.""Are they both, er, terminally lost?"

"Yes."

"That's not good. One of them is my sister's boy." "We can arrange for you to get the bodies, Jorge." "No, I'll let you deal with that issue for a while."

"Jorge, if this keeps going, you may need a lot of body bags. Why don't we call a truce, you go back to Mexico and we can meet in Las Vegas in a week or so to sort this out?"

"Yes, I can see how you would like that approach. That's not going to happen, Darren. You can easily solve the whole issue by climbing into your car with your two *associos* and quietly driving out of here. You have tons of money, leaving a little here is no big deal. You are the one being stubborn."

"Let's just say, for purposes of discussion, that I was willing to consider that. The only way, and I repeat, the only way, I would consider that is if you delivered Paul to us."

"Paul is our insurance policy that you won't try to turn around and do something stupid.

I don't see how we would be willing to give up our insurance."

"What if Paul and I traded places? I would be better insurance than Paul anyway." I had been thinking of this curve ball for a while. I need them a bit off balance.

"Now, that—that we might consider." I could hear Guzman's wheels turning. "Can I speak to Paul?" I asked.

"Hmm, yes, I think that would be okay."

I heard Guzman speaking in Spanish, the sound of a door opening and closing, and a minute or so of silence.

"Darren?" Paul's voice was raspy and cracked. "Hey, Paul, how are you holdin' up?"

"Reasonably well. They punched me around after the mess at your house but nothing since then. Guzman just told me there were two casualties, is that right?"

"Yes, it is."

"All these guys seem related, one way or the other, so that isn't going to help."

"Yeah, I know. I still don't think they're going to go loco. We'll get out of this mess, just hold on."

Through the receiver, I heard a gasp and what sounded like a struggle in the background.

Paul screamed, "No, no, God, no!" and the line went dead.

I slammed the receiver down, my heart pounding crazily. Trying to calm down, I recounted the telephone call to Andy and Beto, including how the call ended.

"Was it Paul--for sure--that screamed, Darren?" Beto asked.

I thought for a moment. "I think so, but I couldn't swear."

"I mean, this could all be for effect. I'm not saying Guzman won't hurt Paul, but..."

The sound of brakes squealing in front of the house stopped Beto in mid-sentence and he dove for his weapon. Andy had his drawn and moved in front of me so fast I didn't see him do it. Beto began to step toward the front door, when the doorbell rang. He swung to the side panel window on the right side of the double door and looked through the tempered glass. Then, we heard a car door slam and the vehicle peeled out and roared away.

"Bomb?" Beto mouthed.

"No," I replied quickly, "they aren't going to try something like that...not yet."

Beto carefully unlocked the front door and cracked it open. "It's an envelope," he said reaching around the door and pulling it inside.

It was a manila mailing folder. "It's got your name on it, Darren," he said handing it over to me.

I tore the flap open and looked inside, then dropped the bag in revulsion and jumped away from it. "Jesus Christ!" It was all I could do not to barf.

Andy picked up the envelope, reached in and pulled out a plastic baggie. Inside was a finger, bluish with bone and sinews exposed where it had been cut.

Andy, Beto and I had been sitting in silence in the great room for I don't know how long, when the house line rang. I let it ring seven or eight times and then calmly answered. "This is Darren."

"Darren, this here's Joe Bob. Did you fellers get yore special delivery package? And, what did you think about it? We hate to be rash, but you need to un'erstand—we's men of action."

I choked down my rage. *Geez, I'd love to strangle the fat fucker.* "We got it," is all I said.

"So, I wuz hopin' that'd bring a lick a sense to yore haid. Prope'ly sensin' yore desperate sitch-ashun, you'd drive on oud-a-yere."

"Thank you, Sheriff, for your kind offer. But we're not going anywhere."

"Sorry to hear that, Darren. You're a good ol' boy, but don't think I won't squish you like a bug if that's what's called for."

"Joe Bob, you need to think hard about this. You have been a co-conspirator with us. You have accepted bribes, bribes of significant amounts. You have lied to federal authorities, committed perjury, and facilitated interstate transportation of illegal substances in violation of federal and state law." I paused for effect.

"I assume you're getting to a summation some'eres in this mess."

"I have carefully documented all of your wrongdoing with evidence that a first-year prosecutor could use to convict you on all counts. I have records of cash transfers to you and a related list of assets you have acquired in Colorado and elsewhere. The documentation details you and your deputies' efforts to support our clandestine operations up here. And, you can bet one of those mealy-mouthed goons of yours will roll over for a plea." Again, I paused.

The line was quiet for a minute. The cracker was gone, replaced with a no-nonsense voice. "Now, let me guess. If something happens to you, this treasure trove of documentation, now being guarded in more than one safe location, will be released. Is that about right?"

"That's it, Lang. All of it is in place as we speak and will be unfolded unless I continue to walk and talk on this planet."

"I've thought about this a li'l, Counselor. And I think you're full of shit. You take me down with this crap; you take yourself down with me."

"I'll be dead. What the hell will I care?"

"You won't, but your snooty family will. Your daddy is as upstanding a citizen as New Mexico has. The family name smeared by a drug-smuggling son is not a pretty picture. You're a first-class bastard, Darren, but even you wouldn't do that to your family. Besides that, I'm not so sure any of that exists. I think we caught you pretty flat-footed."

For once, I was silenced. I knew what Lang said was true. But I didn't think Lang was smart enough to know it was true. Another lesson learned in underrating an adversary.

The hick returned. "And, one more thing, pod'ner, whilst we're talkin' on this. My share of the pie in your vault is sufficient that even if your little blackmail scheme were to be accidentally set into motion, I would be out of this country before the day was over and wake up on some sunny beach the next morning with a plump sixteen-year old beauty pourin' me a Bloody Mary and callin' me 'Hefe'. So, you can take that card off the table. It ain't worth shit."

"Looks like we got a Mexican standoff, Joe Bob."

"Yeah, right now it does. But, one way or the other, everything you have in your wine cellar, is going to be ours. I promise you that, Darren. Them's the spoils of war. You can only decide whether you want to stay alive or not. Don't fuckin' doubt my determination, pod'ner. That would be a mistake. In fact, Dare, here's my direct hot line number for when you come to your senses. " He rattled the number off and I jotted it down. Just in case.

I slammed the phone in the cradle. "Goddamned, if I could get my hands on that..."

Andy and Beto sat quietly. They are not accustomed to me losing it and get really nervous when I do.

Lake Vallecito

The girls had gone down to the lake to sunbathe and give the guys some needed time to get things ready for their wilderness trip. While they couldn't really understand the men's need to be completely out of civilization for a week, they did get that it was a serious endeavor that needed a lot of planning. Besides, they had things they needed to talk about without their men in earshot.

"How many nymph flies have we got?" Marc asked Ricky. "Five."

"What do ya think? Maybe another five or six?"

"Yeah, at least. Let's pick up ten to be safe. Bruce, you got that on the list?"

"Yep. Right after salmon eggs—whoops, no—I mean powdered eggs. But we need salmon eggs, too. Added. Rice, how much rice?"

As they readied for the second annual trip, Marc reflected on how much his life had changed in the past two years. When he started law school, he found himself transported from the stuffily conservative CPA culture to one of the most liberal environments in America. Daily dress changed from suits and ties to jeans and T-shirts. And daily human interaction could hardly have changed more; from an almost completely male society focused on a tiny sliver of highly technical information to an evenly gender-mixed population dealing with issues from every kind of human interaction.

He smiled. The change suited him well. He enjoyed the youthful brilliance of his classmates, the archaic background of English common law, and, for the first time in his life, had female friends that didn't include romantic entanglements. By studying hard and having a mind that easily grasped principles of law, he had placed himself near the top of the class. He wondered why he had ever had doubts about going to law school.

His attitude toward the wilderness adventure also changed drastically from last year to now. Never having been in the woods, last year he felt a lot more fear and apprehension than he tried to let on. Watching Ricky had quieted his concerns somewhat. For Ricky, getting ready for a wilderness trip was second nature, and his confident leadership was catching. But, in the final analysis, Marc thought, he was totally stoked about this year's trip; not fearful at all. And, he realized, it was his successful accomplishment of the trip the year before that filled him with confidence.

Even more amazing was how quickly the past year had just flown by. In a way it seemed like it was just weeks ago instead of last summer, when they hiked from just north of Vallecito Lake to Silverton and then on over Red Mountain Pass into Telluride. Round trip, they had covered nearly a hundred miles in their ten-day trip.

For this year's expedition, they had chosen Lake Como as a destination, about ten miles north of Silverton. On the way, they planned to fish half a dozen lakes and the creeks that connected them, some of the best trout fishing in the San Juan Mountains. While he was enjoying all of the partying, Marc was really looking forward to the isolation of the wilderness.

Donna had to be back in Durango Thursday night for a shift. Nancy and Barb planned to head back to Albuquerque on Friday morning when the guys took off for the woods. The Memorial Day holiday was ten days out. Nancy and Barb planned to drive back up on Saturday morning and Donna was going to join up on Saturday afternoon after her shift. They were all looking forward to the three-day weekend, which, they knew, would be crazy with the arrival of the summer crowd, much different from the deserted, solitary time they were enjoying.

"Do you think we're going to be ready to go into Durango shopping today?" Marc asked.

Ricky checked his watch and shook his head, "No, let's get our list finished and get up early in the morning and go over it one more time before we go get everything."

The phone rang and Ricky answered it.

"This is Billy Mercado. May I speak to Bruce, please?"

"Hello, Mr. Mercado, this is Ricky Gydeson. We met at the moot court competition at law school."

"Sure, hi, Ricky, how are you mountain men doing up there in the woods?" "Great. I think we're all starting to decompress from exams."

"Sounds just right. I need a word with Bruce. Is he around and sober enough to talk?"

Billy asked, trying to keep the conversation light.

"Yeah, sure, let me get him."

Ricky laid the receiver down and set out to find Bruce.

In a few minutes, Bruce got on the line. "Billy, hi, what's up?"

"Are you clear enough to think coherently?" Billy had to ask knowing Bruce's propensity to party to excess.

"Yeah, I'm fine. What can I help you with?" Bruce said.

"Bruce, listen, after your Vallecito trip last year, you came back all pumped up and were telling me about it...well, frankly, I was only listening with one ear. But did you say something about you guys hiking into Telluride?"

"Sure. We hiked from just north of here to Telluride and back."

"And didn't you say something about Ricky taking you guys on a trail, or something, that wasn't well known?"

"Er, yeah, sort of a, huh, secret, you know...but yes that's right. What's this about, Billy?" Bruce was more than a little perplexed as to why his boss would chase him down at Ricky's cabin to ask about a hiking trip.

"Was it something about a back way into Telluride that not many folks know about?"

"Yes, but I wish you'd keep that under your hat. It's Ricky's secret and I wasn't supposed to even say anything."

"Bruce, I'm getting in my car in ten minutes and coming up there. You guys wait at

Ricky's. DO NOT GO ANYWHERE. You hear me? This is important!"

"I'll call you when I get to the lake. Just sit tight for four hours."

Telluride

I was sipping Jack Daniels, neat, my nerves starting to calm when the phone in my bedroom rang.

"Darren," I answered in a shaky voice that seemed to come from someone else. It was Billy.

"You all right?" Billy asked.

"No, not really, man. We've not had a good day."

"Listen, Darren, I am working on a real long shot that may get you out of this mess. I repeat, it's a real long shot. I'm driving up to Colorado tonight and I'll give you a call once I've found something out."

"You don't want to say anymore?" I wanted more than anything (though part of me knew it wasn't that easy) that he was going to tell me that he had found the perfect solution. "No, not yet. Let me nail some things down first, then I'll call."

"Good luck, Billy. We could sure use some good news about now." *If I could pick anybody in the world to get us out of this mess, it would be Billy... or, strange thought, Dave Richardson.*

৵

"Thank God for Marta, "Beto chirped. "I'm going to give her a kiss and a hug she will never forget...when we see her."

Beto and Andy and I were huddled around the kitchen table hunched over large bowls of steaming green chile stew that Marta had left in the freezer. The only sounds were the clinking of spoons on pottery, the occasional slurp of the fiery broth, and various oaths that included the devil describing the heat of the green chile.

I looked up with a satisfied smile, wiped the perspiration from my forehead with my napkin and pushed back from the table.

"Billy is working on something, but he didn't want to say what until he nailed it down some more," I said. Andy and Beto both looked up inquisitively, Beto's smile widening.

"Ain't that like a frigging lawyer—promise but not deliver," Beto joked, until my feigned glare quieted him. "Oh, not you, boss, er...other lawyers."

"Well, he said he would call when he knew more, which I expect means tomorrow morning at the earliest. I am whipped. I think I'll turn in. Listen guys, I'm not sure how yet, but we'll get out of this. Get as much sleep as you can tonight—we're going to need to be at our best tomorrow."

"G'night, Dare."

∽

Applying blackface, Beto and Andy stood in front of the upstairs guest bathroom mirror. Each was dressed completely in black— black Levi's, lightweight black long-sleeve sweaters, black gym shoes and black woolen caps.

"If the bad guys don't get us, Darren will fucking kill us when he finds out about this," Beto grinned.

"Well, Beto, ummm...this is one of those times when it's better to ask for forgiveness than permission. S-S-Since we would never get it," Andy said.

They had brought their weapons cache up to the bedroom and were now making selections. Andy strapped on a hip holster. Picking up a Walther PPK, he inserted a clip and jammed it into the holster. He stuck two extra clips in each pocket and strapped a KA-BAR knife and holster to the side of each calf.

Beto chose two Browning High Power pistols and, like Andy, a knife for each leg. Andy and Beto had spent untold hours arguing the virtues of the Walther over the Browning and never agreeing. Both had been the weapons of choice in Viet Nam. As Beto put it, "it's a Ford-Chevy thing."

"It's been a while since we've done this, but it's sort of like riding a bicycle, I guess," Beto said.

"It is, but we don't need to-to-to kid ourselves. We can't pedal, ummm, as fast as we used to."

Andy stopped suddenly and turned to Beto. "The last time we suited up like this, you saved my b-b-bacon."

"Oh, bullshit, that's total bullshit."

In truth, both had been thinking about their last mission. Relying on bad intelligence, they had gone deep into Cambodia with a team of six operatives to rescue a pilot and walked into an ambush. A Khmer Rouge squad had deployed around the supposed location of the pilot and sprung the trap as the American team waded through a river. The jungle erupted in a cacophony of gunfire; bullets finding three of the Americans immediately. Andy, Beto and the remaining teammate were able to get to shore and return fire although pinned down behind a grove of trees. Beto broke free, dashing into the jungle just at the same moment that a bullet caught Andy in the leg and another hit the remaining soldier between the eyes. In what seemed like hours but was in fact less than two minutes, Beto shot, stabbed or slashed all eight of the remaining Khmer Rouge. Thinking back on it, all he remembered was throwing Andy over his shoulders and running back down the jungle trail that had led them into the ambush.

～

"You ready?"

"Let's roll," Beto said grimly.

They padded downstairs quietly. Darren had gone straight to his bedroom after dinner, but he wasn't asleep. They could hear him turning pages in bed. Normally, he would turn off his night light and go to sleep shortly.

Beto led the way to the window in the breakfast nook. He carefully and slowly turned the window locks, disengaging the locking lips protruding into the sash. Stopping periodically to listen for any response from Darren's room, he gently began lifting the sash a fraction of an inch at time. When the gap widened sufficiently, he turned to Andy, one last check. Andy nodded and

Beto rolled out of the window, making only a whisper of movement noise. Andy followed.

Once outside, they squatted perfectly still, leaning against the wall of the house to let their eyes adjust to the dark. After a couple of minutes, Andy slid in front of Beto and, stooped at the waist, began to creep softly forward, leading as he had always done in their missions. Beto followed a few paces behind.

Though it wasn't raining, heavy clouds hung over the valley, forming a roof over the valley floor. Reflected luminescence from the houses and streetlights down below lit open areas, but secluded stretches were dark as ink. Andy chose a path between a bluff of rocks and a stand of aspens that ran down to the streets below. They slipped into the darkness as if submerging into a pool of onyx water and soon exited a block away and out of sight of Guzman's sentries.

"Phase one," Andy whispered to Beto with a thumbs up.

Slipping into the middle of town, they made their way past houses with television screens casting dancing strobe-like shapes of light and dark around living rooms, laugh tracks and voices being broadcast into the night.   Exerting its domain over some nighttime rodent or other interloper, a dog barked a few houses away.

Beto followed Andy to a darkened street where they knew the homes were mostly owned by out-of-towners, not yet occupied for the summer season. Andy homed in on a black Bronco parked in the driveway of a house showing no signs of life, with a couple weeks of the local mailers strewn about the front porch and hanging off the doorknob.

"This one'll do," Andy proclaimed, signaling the execution of the next part of the game plan. They had previously decided to "borrow" a local vehicle to drive the two miles to Sheriff Lang's mobile command post and, assuming all went well, provide for a retreat. In seconds, Beto had the locked four-by-four door open and, a few seconds more under the dashboard and the starter motor began cranking.

Beto slid behind the wheel, pumped the gas pedal a few times. Andy assumed his position in the front passenger seat and, unable the resist the temptation of decades of habit, announced "shotgun". Beto backed the Bronco out of the drive and rolled slowly to the intersection before turning on the headlights.

"Phase two, check."

With great care, Beto maneuvered the car west through the back streets of Telluride following the path he and Andy had previously set. Soon, the pavement ended, and they drove on a continuation dirt road that twisted between rows of pine trees. Slowing, Beto turned off the headlights leaving the parking lights burning, providing enough light to make their way down the lane. An opening in the trees provided a space for Beto to back the car off the lane and park.

He cocked his head sideways, checking the gauge. "Plenty of gas. Let's leave it idling...just in case."

After softly shutting the doors, they jogged side by side down the pitch-black lane, aided occasionally by the quick beam of light shot out of a hand-held torch that Beto carried. In minutes, they came to the edge of the forest. Lang's outpost was clearly visible across the flat meadow about two hundred yards away. Lang's mobile unit and another RV were parked end- to-end. Several large tents were arrayed in a semi-circle around the RV's. All were lit by a large bonfire burning in the middle of the cluster, a gray stream of smoke rising upward into the darkness. They could hear voices, but not clearly enough to make out what was being said. The summer mountain air had gotten cold. Beto shivered involuntarily.

"You ready?" Andy asked.

Beto grinned. "I was born ready," he said. Despite their outward casualness, both were crazily energized, hearts pumping rapidly, breathing accelerated. It had been a long time since they had embarked on a mission of this sort, but their bodies reacted without conscious thought. The training never went away.

Andy led off toward the compound. Though he was only a few steps in front, Beto could barely see Andy's outline and could hear nothing as they covered the ground soundlessly.

In minutes, they were within twenty-five yards of the RVs. Three men sat around the bonfire talking, all with cups or glasses, sipping beverages. Paul sat easily on a camp stool listening as the man next to him talked. Still, Andy and Beto couldn't hear the words spoken, but as the man speaking emphasized whatever he was saying with wild arm movements, all three laughed loudly. Paul punched him playfully in the arm.

Beto whispered, "Well, there's our answer." "No doubt," Andy hissed back. "Let's do this."

With hand signals, Andy directed Beto to the front of the RV, while he moved into position at the rear. Andy gave the sign and, they sprinted across the remaining few yards of open ground and, just as the three men turned, Andy and Beto slashed the throats of Paul's two accomplices and, in the same motion, Andy hammered Paul on the side of the head with the butt of his knife. His knees buckled and he fell to the ground motionless. His two guards looked on in horror and disbelief, holding their necks in a hopeless effort to somehow keep the blood inside their bodies. One reached for Beto but crumpled to his knees and fell forward. Andy swung a backhand blow with the butt of his knife to the temple of the still standing guard, and he, too, fell face forward on the ground.

Andy re-sheathed his weapon and, wincing a bit from a still sore neck, threw Paul's motionless body over his left shoulder. He sprinted off across the meadow with Beto following. They were within fifty yards of the forest edge when, from the camp, came a loud cry, "What the hell," followed by loud shouts, curses and opening and slamming doors as the tents and RVs emptied to the call.

"Son of a bitch, I hoped we'd have more of a head start than this." With that Andy broke into a full sprint with Paul's body bouncing wildly on his shoulder. Beto ran ahead and opened the rear end of the Bronco. Andy unceremoniously dumped Paul's limp body into the back. Beto slapped handcuffs on him, although he didn't look as though he was going to join the conscious world anytime soon.

As they tore back up the dirt lane with headlights on--no need for clandestine efforts now—Beto yelled to Andy, "Here we are in the goddamned race we didn't want to have." When planning their mission, Andy had identified the greatest risk to be what would happen when their actions were discovered. Guzman's *pistoleros* and Lang's deputies would make a B-line for Darren's house.

The Bronco hit the bump where the dirt road ended and the pavement started and was airborne for a moment, slamming back to earth with a swerve that Beto expertly straightened. Screaming down the peaceful residential street at eighty, Beto threw a hard left turn, the backend of the Bronco sliding and then catching.

"Almost home, buddy," was quickly followed by "shit" as a black and white turned just in front of them by the old Sheridan Opera House, sliding around the corner and tearing straight up the hill toward Tomboy Road. Beto accelerated through the intersection.

"There's another one behind us," Andy informed Beto, looking out the back window as a Black Blazer spun around the corner.

Continuing to accelerate with his eyes riveted on the tail end of the cop car ahead, Beto caught the vehicle on the right quarter panel as it started to turn up Tomboy. The Bronco swerved across the road and off onto the dirt shoulder. Beto spun the wheel, and the Bronco shot back onto the road. Out of the corner of his eye, Andy could see the black-and-white hitting a dirt embankment and flipping, the bottom of the car rocketing skyward. The black Blazer was fifty yards behind and closing fast. Andy rolled down the passenger window, and leaning out, aimed his pistol at the windshield and fired three rounds, the muzzle flashes flared a white jet of light with only a "phhht" sound emerging from the silencer. The headlights of the Blazer nose- dived as the driver instinctively slammed on the brakes, the rear-end of the vehicle exchanging places with the front before skidding to a stop in a cloud of dust that totally obstructed all but the subdued hue of the headlights.

Beto slammed the Bronco through Darren's wrought iron security gate with a huge crashing sound followed by a screeching whine as the deeply-imbedded hinges were torn out of their stone mountings. Looking like a cowcatcher, the gate stuck to the front bumper. Andy and Beto leaped from the vehicle, Beto assuming a firing position as Andy dragged Paul, semiconscious out the tailgate and propelled him toward the front door. The Blazer appeared, squealing around the corner. Beto steadied, fired several rounds and ran to the front door.

༄

I was lying in bed staring at the ceiling. Twice I had turned the lamp off and, twice, turned it back on, exhausted but sleepless. Then, I heard tires squealing in the distance. Something didn't feel right. I got out of bed and padded down the steps, calling, "Andy—Beto—Guys?" The shrieking sounds of cars traveling at high speeds increased in pitch and volume getting closer. It didn't take much thought to put together that the absence of Andy and Beto and the commotion outside were related. As I looked out of the window next to the doors, a truck of some kind slid into the driveway and Andy jumped out pulling Paul with him. I threw the door open and standing just inside, rumpled from bed, asked "What in the Sam Hill is going on?"

Andy shoved a staggering Paul through the door and followed, with Beto bringing up the rear.

༄

Lake Vallecito

Bruce hung up the phone.

"Don't tell us. You've got to go back to Albuquerque because the Mercado law firm is falling apart in your absence," Marc teased.

The three couples had been enjoying the sunset on the deck when the telephone rang.

When Bruce returned, Marc was passing a number to Ricky. "No, something stranger. Billy's coming up here." "What? When?" Ricky asked.

"Tonight."

"Tonight? Hell, he can't get up here until almost midnight. And why in the hell would he be coming up here?"

"He wants to talk to us." All eyes were now on Bruce.

"To us? Bruce, what is going on?" Marc asked.

"He wouldn't say any more than that. He was adamant that we stay put until he shows up," saying no more, not wanting to say more, pondering how he could keep secret his indiscretion in mentioning the Telluride adventure the year before.

"Could this be about us?" Marc asked "A cheating scandal at law school, or dope or?"

"No, man, I don't think so. Let's don't freak. He'll be here in a little bit and we'll get the whole story."

Marc said "Thanks a lot, asshole. You have really bummed me out," which set them to snickering as they passed around the Oreos.

Despite the uneasiness caused by Mercado's pending arrival, the party continued, barbequing steaks and grilling potatoes on an outdoor fire pit. A couple joints of Acapulco Gold (probably acquired from some of Darren's folks) and a case of Coors beer worked to elevate the mood of the partiers.

ᔑ

Telluride

Andy and Beto took positions at windows facing the road, watching as two of the sheriff's vehicles cruised back and forth in front of the house. Paul was sprawled semiconscious on the floor, a gash above his eyebrow bleeding, his hands cuffed behind his back.

I asked, "How are we going to get their cuffs off of Paul? Beto, help me get him up on the couch."

"Leave him right there!" Andy snapped. "The fucker's dirty, Darren. Dirty as shit. And those are our cuffs, not theirs."

I plopped on the couch as my legs weakened under me. I was speechless—and stunned.

Yet, I knew it was true. I think I knew it the moment I saw Andy shove Paul through the door.

"I'm going to run upstairs and see where Guzman's assholes are. I'll be right back down," Andy said. Beto nodded consent as Andy's footfalls thundered upstairs taking two steps at the time.

He was back in moments. "Best I can tell--they are in the same places. No sign of movement, but it's really dark. I can't be sure."

Andy and Beto kept watch at the windows. After ten minutes of parading by the house, the police vehicles turned back down the street and headed back into Telluride.

"We need to keep an eye out, but I think this little episode is over. They went home to lick their wounds...again," Andy said grinning.

The phone next to me rang, its jangling causing me to jump. Frozen momentarily, I stared at it. "I'm not going to talk to them, yet. I need a little time to get my thoughts together, and you need to brief me on what happened." After ten rings or so, it stopped.

"I see Paul's got all his fingers," I said.

"Yeah, ain't that somethin'," Beto replied.

"I'll make coffee, while you guys keep an eye out," I offered.

Paul moaned and rolled his head but made no other sound. His eyes remained shut.

In a few minutes, I returned with a carafe of coffee, three mugs and a flask of brandy wedged under my arm. We all sat around the coffee table pouring java and Beto added a shot of brandy. I had thrown on some clothes, washed my face and combed my hair, and now felt wide awake. I also collected myself and resumed the demeanor of leader, though, for the first time in my life, I did not really want the job.

Paul was starting to regain consciousness, moaning and moving his legs. Andy picked him up by the seat of his pants and collar of his shirt, dragged him across the floor and heaved him into the love seat in the corner. Paul groaned, fluttering his eyes open briefly, and then passed back into unconsciousness.

I faced Andy and Beto. "Okay, so I get that you two didn't tell me about your little escapade. No need for further discussion there. It's done, let's move on. So, now, tell me what happened."

Over the next few minutes, Beto recounted the whole episode, Andy chiming in with added details.

"So, just for absolute clarity, when you saw Paul, he was sitting outdoors, talking with Guzman's guys, with no restraints?"

"No restraints...and he wasn't just talking. They were laughing and joking," Beto answered.

"Darren, there is no question. He knows these guys."

"The two guys you took out, they are for sure dead?" I asked.

The phone began ringing again. Again, I ignored it until it stopped, looking to Andy to answer my question. I had decided that I would initiate the next conversation.

"They weren't dead when we took off, but they couldn't have survived more than a minute or two. They're dead."

"Could they have been Lang's guys?" I asked.

"No, they were Guzman's. Hispanics, Mexican clothes. They both spoke pretty good English, but with heavy accents."

"So, now Guzman's got four casualties. The shit is going to hit the fan...somehow. They don't have any way of knowing for sure that we know Paul's flipped, do you agree?"

Andy and Beto both nodded.

"I don't know yet how it can work in our favor, but I don't see any reason to let on that we know. As far as they're concerned, we rescued our partner and got our necks out of that noose."

Again, Andy and Beto nodded assent, knowing the wheels were turning in my head.

♁

Paul started to come around, opening his eyes, shaking his head and testing his handcuffs in an effort to figure out what was wrong with his arms.

"Cuff his arms in front of him," I ordered. "It makes me uncomfortable looking at him wadded up that way."

Andy roughly rolled Paul onto the floor, not even attempting to protect his face as it slammed into the rug. Paul moaned. The cuffs removed, Andy roughly rolled Paul over on his back.

"Put your hands out," he ordered, but despite all efforts, Paul couldn't move either arm; a lack of circulation had rendered them useless. Disgust clear in every movement, Andy grabbed one wrist and then the other, pulling them together in front of Paul and snapped the cuffs back on. He reached down with both hands, grabbed the front of Paul's shirt, lifted his limp body from the floor, and tossed him back on the love seat. Paul sat upright slowly, opening his eyes and then closing them, shaking his head in an effort to clear the cobwebs.

Beto reached a glass of water toward him, but Paul couldn't raise his cuffed hands even off his lap. "Shit," Beto said and leaned in putting the lip of the glass to Paul's mouth, allowing him to drink.

"Thanks," Paul said hoarsely. He scanned around the familiar room, stopped, and looked searchingly at my face, and finding no answers, moved on. Beto put his arm around Andy and said softly, "I'll bet the last thing he remembers is talking to his new little friends."

Paul blinked, looked at me in recognition, and his eyes flew wide open before he buried his face in his hands and began to rock slowly backward and forward.

I assumed my level, lawyerly voice. "Paul, we now know which team you're playing on, so there's no need to have any discussion about that. I do, however, intend to find out how it happened."

Paul looked up, his face a grimacing mask of pain as he shifted his weight. "Darren, I swear, you guys have this wrong. I..."

"Stop, Paul, stop. Don't even start to insult me by some sort of bullshit denial. At the expense of repeating myself, we know you have turned on us. What we want to know is how it happened?"

"But, Darren..."

Before I could stop him, Andy smashed Paul just below the left eye socket with a quick jab that jerked his head back and split the skin under the socket, a line of blood starting to fill in the gash.

"The boss asked you a question, jerk. Just answer it."

Paul hung his head, not so much in defeat as in the knowledge that his life wasn't worth a nickel if he couldn't figure some way out of this mess. After a minute, he spoke.

"Guzman approached me a couple of weeks ago when he was in Albuquerque. He said he wanted to talk about some concerns openly, and he hoped I wouldn't mention our meeting. He said it would help if he could just talk to someone calmly about a few questions Cortez had without creating a big stir. He told me I was the calmest of the bunch and he felt we could easily resolve any problems. So, I said I would meet him."

"That was your first mistake." "Yeah, I know that now."

"So, what was Guzman's pitch?"

"Jorge said that Cortez was becoming increasingly concerned about management volatility with our group."

"Management volatility, is that what he actually said?" I asked him.

"Yes, he went on to explain that they were looking for a more low-profile posture, flying below the radar, particularly with some of the pressure that's starting to build on cocaine."

"I see," I answered. As Paul spoke, Andy's eyes focused into two black coals of hatred that seemed to bore through him. Paul glanced at Andy only once and then, jerking his head sideways, didn't dare to look in Andy's direction again.

"It wasn't supposed to be this way. More like a management transition in a large company," Paul fairly whined.

"And you were to lead the new regime?" I prodded.

"Yes. But nothing was supposed to happen to you guys. It was just going to be a palace coup, but I swear, there was never any talk of what has gone up here the last few days."

"And you didn't know that the Lear was sabotaged?" I asked.

I studied Paul's face as I had so many times in the years I had worked with him, recognizing genuine surprise. But surprise at what? The act? Or that the act had been discovered?

"That's enough for now. Andy, you and Beto lock him up in the guest bedroom." "Darren, listen, I, I..."

"I said 'THAT'S ENOUGH FOR NOW!'" I barked, thinking that if they didn't get him out of my sight, I might actually be tempted to kill him.

∽

When I rang Lang's number, I could hardly restrain my glee at making the call.

"Lang, here," he answered and didn't sound happy.

"Joe Bob, I just called to tell you that you picked the wrong team, you dumb red neck. Twice now my boys have got the best of your boys. And we are a long way from through. We have more tricks up our sleeves than you can imagine," I gloated. I really wanted to stick the knife in and twist it.

"I have to give your guys, credit, Darren, but nothing's changed. You won a battle, but the outcome of the war is irresistible. It'll end just like I said it would," spoken by the articulate Lang. I had to admit that his ability to change personas was a little unsettling.

"We'll see, Joe Bob. We'll see." And I hung up and scored myself a round. If nothing else, I felt like I could get some sleep.

CHAPTER 7

THURSDAY, MAY 25

Lake Vallecito

There was no way Billy could find Ricky's cabin at night without help, so Bruce had instructed Billy to call from a pay phone booth at the Shoreline and they would come pick him up. By midnight, the party had moved inside. The bunch were in the middle of a Truth or Dare game that included tequila shots and howls of laughter, when the phone rang. Bruce answered.

"Hey, guys, hold it down. It's Billy."

There was a pause and, then, Bruce said "Yeah, of course, the girls are here, too." Another pause and "We'll be right down."

When Bruce turned around, his party face was gone. "Billy wants to talk to the three of us for a little bit—in private."

He barely had the last word out of his mouth when Nancy jumped to her feet. "Who the hell does he think he is?! To come up here with all his secrecy—she grimaced and pulled a face— when we are vacationing? Tell him to go fuck himself." Classic Nancy.

Bruce fired back. "He's Billy Mercado, that's who he is! And I work for him. And something serious is going on. So just sit down and shut up for a minute!"

"Well, FUCK you too, Mr. Big Shot," Nancy shot back and stormed out of the room.

"Sorry guys," Bruce said apologetically. "Let's go see whatever the hell he has to say."

Telluride

"You don't believe his bullshit, for a moment, do you, Dare?" Beto queried. "No, hell, no. He's not the first general to try a coup and he won't be the last."

Paul was gagged, trussed, and tied to a bed in the first-floor guest room. Andy had made sure the ropes were a little tighter than they should be, giving each knot a little extra revenge yank. Turning off the lights in the room, Andy snarled "Sleep tight, prick" before slamming the door shut.

"What are we going to do with him?" Beto posed the question that had been on all of their minds.

Leaning back on the sofa, I pulled on my chin rough with a two-day beard. "I don't know, yet. Right now, he could possibly be an asset to us, but I haven't figured out how to play that card. Thanks to you rebellious teenagers, he's at least not a liability to us anymore. I grinned at Andy and Beto, one eyebrow raised, that said "Despite how much you two perplex me, all is forgiven." There was no need to say a word more.

"What other cards have we got to play, Dare? Seems like our options are getting a little skinny," Andy said.

"There's one. I have documents that will put him away forever and that will get released if anything happens to me. Guzman, and even Cortez, could care less. They have plenty of political cover in Mexico. But, Lang, he's another story."

"What are our other options?" Beto asked.

"Sittin' tight, I reckon. If I had to bet money, I'd say the bursting-dam scenario is one that Lang won't run...but I sure wouldn't give any odds. The longer we can stay in this standoff, the better for us. At some point, even the laid-back folks of Telluride are going to get suspicious. And the bunch Lang is truly fearful of is the Feds. He does not want them in his valley. That happens and his meal ticket is gone for sure."

Lake Vallecito

They found Billy parked by the phone booth where they all piled out of the van and shook hands, Bruce reintroducing Marc and Ricky. Bruce climbed in Billy's Jaguar XJS and they followed the Silver Goose back to Ricky's parent's unoccupied cabin, having to slow to a crawl in a couple of places where the road was so uneven that the low-slung undercarriage of the Jag would bottom out.

"Wow, this is off the beaten path," Billy said to no one in particular while climbing out of the driver's seat, stretching his arms and bending over touching his toes. The skies had cleared, revealing a black sky studded with stars so brilliant that, to people used to the city nights, the sight wouldn't seem real. The fragrance of wet pines and fireplace smoke from a neighboring cabin was pungently sweet, the mountain air, brisk and invigorating.

Ricky stepped on the porch, fiddled with keys a moment, and opened the front door.

"Come on in, Mr. Mercado, before you freeze." Ricky couldn't help but think of a mafia don when

he looked at the lawyer. His black hair was perfectly cut and swept back to a duck tail in back.

His coloring was dark matching the darkest brown eyes Ricky believed he had ever seen. At six- two or three, he was imposing. He always dressed to the nines—tonight black crisply-pressed slacks, a white shirt open at the neck, and a light-colored sport coat with a subtle blue and grey plaid pattern.

"Billy, just Billy, please. This is really nice, Ricky. What a great feel all the wood paneling gives. And it smells like heaven here."

"Thanks. You're welcome to stay here tonight. Wait till you see the views off the front porch in the morning. I can't do it justice describing it, so I'll just let you decide for yourself. Would you like something to drink? Coke? Coffee? A beer?"

"Beer, please, I need to wash the road dust down."

"I know you're damned curious about what I'm doing up here, so I'll get right to it. What I am going to tell you tonight is confidential—beyond confidential. Although you aren't covered by attorney/client privilege—all but Bruce—it will soon become evident as to why nothing we talk about can leave this cabin."

Billy stood up. "Are we clear on that? What you hear here, stays here."

Ricky spoke right up. "I've got a problem with that, Mr. Mercado, er Billy. I don't keep anything from Barb and I don't intend to start tonight."

Billy looked a bit shocked. He hadn't counted on this obstacle.

And, then, Marc chimed in. "Yeah, and the girls are back at Ricky's cabin waiting for us to show up and tell them what the hell is going on. Bruce and I aren't married, like Ricky, but I don't think I am comfortable telling you that I won't talk to Donna about whatever this is."

"Fair enough" Billy said, "but I don't think you are going to want to tell them about this conversation. It will be your call. Can we leave it at that for now?"

We all nodded.

"I think you all know that Darren Jacobs is a client of my firm. He's in really serious trouble, and you may be able to help. I am not overstating the case when I say you may be able to save his— and others'—lives. "

"Geez, Billy, of course we'll help if we can," Ricky said, before a troubled look crossed his face as he realized what a dumb carte blanche statement he had made.

"Not so quick. I'm going to tell you everything about this deal. I will answer every question you ask me. If—and it is a big if—you decide to try to do this thing, you are going to have as complete a picture as I can paint.

First, Darren is in the cocaine business in a big way. He and his organization control coke distribution over a vast area."

Billy stopped to let it sink in, looking carefully from face to face. His audience didn't look shocked as he had expected.

"You don't seem surprised?"

Bruce spoke up. "Rumor on the street has it that Darren and his guys are involved in some way. We've talked about those rumors, before. But that he's the guy—that is news."

"Well, he unquestionably is. Or has been. That's the issue. The Mexican cartel that supplies him has decided to oust him and take over his organization. That in itself is not problematic. Darren is probably ready to quit. However, in his house in Telluride is a vault and security system most banks would kill for. And inside that vault is twenty million in cash and twenty million more in uncut coke."

Bruce whistled. "That's a lot of dough."

"Yes, yes, it is, and the cartel has an army in Telluride and has told Darren to get out of town and leave it all behind. Darren's holed up in his house now with a couple of his generals." "Andy, Paul and Beto?" Marc asked.

Billy looked shocked, again. "Yeah, how did you know that?"

"We ran into them at City Market a couple of days ago. They were headed to Telluride from Denver," Marc said.

"Surely, they can't imagine that they could get away with storming an American's home in an American city, even a small one like Telluride, and making it back to Mexico without getting caught?" Marc asked.

"It's complicated. The sheriff, a guy named Joe Bob Lang, and his deputies have been on

Darren's payroll for years. Darren picked Telluride because of its remoteness and access. Despite

suspicions that smugglers were up there, the federal drug enforcement agencies know they can't spring a raid on Telluride because the local cops provide protection and an early warning system. The runners and their evidence would be long gone before they got close.

But the sheriff has turned on Darren and sided with the cartel. Right now, the whole canyon is boxed up. Between the deputies and the cartel's henchmen—we don't know how many, but 'more than a few'—every road and Jeep trail is covered.

And...they've already made two attempts on Darren. They sabotaged his plane." "We saw that on TV news. It sounded like an accident," Marc said.

"Yeah, that's still the official story. But the cartel's people tampered with the plane in Nassau. Tuesday night when Darren showed up in Telluride, they tried to ambush him and very nearly got away with it. Guys, this is seriously dangerous. Darren's guys have now killed some of the bad guys."

That got their attention. A conflict between a drug dealer and his supplier is one thing. Dead guys are something else. Looking rattled, Ricky stood, walked over to the sink and filled a glass with water from the tap and drank deeply. Billy's tale had shaken all of them and wasn't over yet.

"Billy, why are you telling us all this?" Bruce asked. Working with Billy as closely as he had, he was the only one of the three comfortable enough to blatantly ask the question.

"I'll get to that, here shortly. But I want you all to have the whole background story first.

Marc, you are right that these guys aren't going to just raid Darren's house with the good citizens of Telluride watching on. So, to get around that problem, Lang has concocted a game plan to evacuate the town on the premise that the tailings dam above town is near failure. He says if Darren hasn't cleared out, that he and his deputies will evacuate Telluride. With the full run of the place, they would overrun Darren, even with Andy and Beto as good as they are, pretty quickly."

"Shit, Billy, this just doesn't seem real," Bruce said, "More like a movie." "Well, it's real. A couple of dead guys can certify to that."

"So, where do we come in?" Bruce asked, though at this point, he was starting to get the picture.

"I remember you telling me that on your wilderness trip last year, you hiked into Telluride some way that no one knows about."

"Bruce, goddammit," Ricky stood and glared at him, "That..." His voice trailed off in frustration.

"There'll be time for that later. Right now, you fellows have a decision to make. What I'm proposing is that if you guys can do that again, maybe you could get Darren and his boys out of there."

"Billy, why don't they just take the peace offer and drive out of there?" Marc asked. It's just money.

Billy put his hand on the young man's shoulder. "Marc, that's a reasonable way to look at it. I believe that if Darren thought the offer was genuine, he would take them up on it. But he doesn't believe that. He thinks that, now that these guys have shown their real spots, there is no reason to believe they would leave Darren—or his guys—upright on the planet."

Locking eyes with jury members when delivering the clincher was a skill Billy had developed over decades of practice and scores of summations. Tonight, he applied the same skill to the three young men, in essence pleading for the life of his friend and client. And then, the closing argument.

"And one final thing—there is a million dollars cash for each of you if you can get Darren and his guys out."

The three living-on-shoestrings law students looked at each other in astonishment.

∽

Culiacan

"Hold all my calls," Esco Cortez instructed his secretary as he walked briskly by her desk on the way to his office. He had been in a meeting down the hall when Guzman's call came in. *"Hola. Digga mi?"*

"Esco, this is Jorge. We've had something of a setback. We.."

"Fuck! Don't 'setback' me. What the fuck happened?"

"Jacob's henchmen attacked us. They killed Mario and Ernesto." "You've got to be kidding me! How many were there?"

"Two, but, Esco, these guys are—"

"Yeah, I know who those guys are. I wish they were working for me instead of you, you incompetent son of a bitch."

"There's more. They got Paul."

Esco Cortez screamed in rage and threw the telephone across his office. It smashed into the closed double doors and shattered it into pieces. All Guzman heard was the beginning of a high-pitched whine before the phone went dead.

A moment later, the phone in Lang's command unit rang. Guzman stared at it, screwing up the courage for what he expected was coming. "*Hola, hefe.*"

"No, Senior Guzman, this is Estella. Senior Cortez asked me call to tell you that Carlos was on his way."

Guzman hung up the receiver without bothering with a goodbye. Heavily, he dropped into a desk chair and stared at nothing, wishing only that he had never heard of cocaine. Carlos Durant held the distinctive position of being Cortez's go-to enforcer.

～

Lake Vallecito

"We need some time to talk this through, Billy," Bruce explained after Mercado finished laying out his case. While all four of them were exhausted from the discussion, and Billy additionally so from road wear and the effects of the past days, no one was the least bit sleepy, although it was after two in the morning.

"Yeah, kid, I know you do. This is a bolt from the sky."

"Before we go any further, you guys need to understand," Ricky said, "that I don't know exactly how I feel about this deal. I feel the responsibility is squarely on me, since I am the only one that can get us in—and hopefully out—of Telluride. I won't say the money doesn't matter. A million dollars is a huge number. But what I really can't get out of my mind is that I may have the key to save these guys lives. That's heavy. "

Billy started to speak, but Ricky held up his hand.

"But no matter, I have to include Barb in this decision. Of that I am sure." Silence ensued as Ricky's words sunk in.

"That means Nancy and Donna will be part of the equation as well," Bruce said.

"I agree. We can't go back to Ricky's and make a decision without all of us being in on it.

I don't even know if Donna will want to weigh in, but she's just sort of sucked up into the mess with the rest of us," Marc explained.

Billy stood up. "I don't have a wife, or even a serious girlfriend, I guess just because of these situations. So, it's hard for me to understand. But, Ricky, I do feel for you. You're in the

toughest spot of all of us. And I respect your decision about your wife. All I can say is that we haven't got much time. If you are going to do this, you need to be in Telluride tomorrow night— ugh, I mean tonight—around dark."

Ricky stayed back talking to Billy a bit, while Bruce and Marc climbed into the van. Bruce smiled at Marc. "May you live in interesting times, grasshopper."

Marc just slowly shook his head. "This is unreal. I keep pinching myself hoping I'll wake up any minute."

"Yes, but the real question is—do you want it to be a dream?"

"Shit, man, you are loco."

Ricky came out and started the van for the short ride to his cabin. All three were silent, contemplating the upcoming discussion.

"I wonder if the girls will still be up," Bruce asked.

"Of course, they will," Ricky said with disgust. "Geez, Bruce, sometime your denseness amazes me." This wasn't like Ricky. The pressure was showing.

"Sorry, man, you're right. Besides, they're women. Curiosity will keep them up if nothing else. So, I wonder if Nancy will still be pissed?"

Ricky just looked at Marc and shook his head.

Before getting to the cabin, the three had a discussion and decided Ricky was the right spokesperson to break the news to the girls. Not only did he have the biggest dog in the fight, he was the most undecided and, therefore, likely to portray the situation most fairly. Bruce was staunchly in favor of jumping in; Marc, equally opposed.

The three women were sitting around the fire in the little living room when the men returned. Nancy had, in fact, cooled down and was about to say something smart, when the stricken faces looking back caused her to bite her tongue. Barb rose and hugged Ricky, instinctively picking up his heavy mood.

"What's up, darlin'", she asked, searching his face.

"Long story, honey. Long—and almost unbelievable. In fact, I wish more than anything that it weren't true. But, it is," Ricky said. "Let's all sit down and talk it through."

Ricky spoke uninterrupted, Barb sitting next to him holding his hand, his comments directed to her—and to Donna, cuddled next to Marc on the couch, and Nancy, now snugly under Bruce's arm. The women exchanged frightened looks of disbelief and shock but did not interrupt.

"So, that's about it. We have a few hours to decide if we are going to try to get these guys out of their mess, or let them fend for themselves," Ricky summed up.

"And don't forget, make a million dollars apiece in the bargain," Bruce chimed in.

Barb spoke first. "You mean, YOU have to decide. You are the critical component, no offense Marc or Bruce." The computer wizard hit the nail on the head.

Ricky turned, his face a few inches from Barb's, and said, barely audibly, "I knew you would get it."

"And, let me guess, Bruce—you have already decided. You're in?" Barb asked.

Bruce nodded.

"And Marc, you are out. Am I also correct?" she asked, turning to him.

"Yes, absolutely. I think the whole idea is preposterous, crazy and dangerous. I can't believe we are even talking about it," Marc said.

Donna, ever the optimist, said, "There has to be some other way to save those men's lives. There just has to be. Even if it means calling in the federal legal authorities. So they go to jail for a while? It beats dead."

Ricky answered. "What you say makes sense, Donna, but Darren and Billy have talked this one through. They are sure the feds won't act, even if Darren were to call. They would just wait for the outcome and then ride in as though they were the saviors. Both Darren and Billy agree on this."

"Oh, my god, this is insane," Donna said. "There has to be a better answer than Ricky and Bruce putting themselves in danger. There just has to be."

"There may be," Bruce allowed, "but we only have a couple of hours to find it."

"Barb, how do you feel?" Nancy asked. "My 'man' (spoken with distaste) has made his mind up without consulting me. But I really want to know. What are you thinking?"

Until that moment, Bruce had not understood the damage he had done, though everyone else in the room had. He sputtered and tried to explain, but Nancy wouldn't even look at him.

"Barb?" Nancy said.

"Of course, I don't want him to go, but then, I'm not in his shoes." She stroked his face with her hand and the tears flowed from Ricky's eyes. Barb wrapped him in her arms as he dissolved into sobs. Marc and Donna went outside to the front deck, Nancy; to the guest bedroom; and Bruce, the back porch; giving Barb and Ricky the privacy they needed to talk.

The mountain air was cold, so Marc and Donna threw logs on the hot coals in the fire pit which burst into a roaring fire in seconds. They stood with their arms around one another, facing the fire.

"I still can't believe this, Marc. It just doesn't seem real—more like we got caught in an episode of 'The Twilight Zone'. What do you think Ricky will do?"

Marc was silent for a moment. "He's going to go. He's a lot like you. He can't let someone die if he has a chance to save them."

Donna pulled Marc close and began to cry. "Oh, Marc, I am so afraid for them. What would Barb do if she lost him?"

They held each other, standing in front of the warm blaze with the first light of day just starting to peep over the mountains, when Ricky opened the door.

"You guys want some coffee?"

∽

Bruce had come back in at some point and was, head down, drinking a cup of coffee at the little kitchen table. Nancy joined the group in the kitchen, all fixing cups of coffee and finding seats in by the fire.

Ricky's voice was hoarse. Barb's eyes were red from crying and brimmed over again when he spoke. "I've decided that I have to try. These are human beings. We saw them just

Tuesday. They aren't some anonymous drug gang." His voice cracking, he went on. "They are

Darren...and Andy...and Paul...and Beto."

At this point, Barb clung to his shoulder sobbing and there wasn't a dry eye in the room. "Marc, I hope you can understand," he said looking directly at him.

"It's not for me to judge, man. I don't think I could find Telluride driving on the highways. I sure couldn't find how we got in there last year. You're the one on the hot seat."

With that, Marc hugged him and, now his voice cracking, said, "I just don't know what

I'll do if you don't come back." And, turning to Bruce, "either of you."

Bruce stood up and walked over to Marc. "Are you sure you won't come with us? We'll be back here in less than twenty-four hours. Rich heroes, at that." "Right, if you come back," Marc snorted.

Bruce put his hand on Marc's arm. "Man, you're so worried about getting killed. But for student deferments and lucky lottery numbers, we could have got our asses shot off in 'Nam while doing sinister shit...and got paid next to nothing. Think of it this way—we take a risk, possibly save a few guys' lives, and walk away millionaires. We could have gotten drafted, killed in 'Nam and not have a damned thing to show for it. How can we not take a little risk?"

As Marc watched Bruce speak, he understood why he had a reputation as one of the best extemporaneous debaters and moot court student lawyers in the country. Simply by rephrasing the risk in terms of a bullet they had all dodged, Bruce had them looking at the whole question

differently. Plus, Bruce called into play Viet Nam, which, because of Marc's long-standing hatred and bitterness about the war, caused him to be off-balanced.

"So, I take it you've made your mind up, Bruce?" Marc said.

"Fuckin' A. A shot at a million bucks and an adventure we'll never forget. That's a no- brainer."

"Some of us don't look at the world like you, Bruce." Marc said. "In other words, you won't take a chance? You're too afraid."

"Hell, yes, I'm afraid. What's not to be afraid of? Law students getting in the middle of two groups of brutal killers? Sure, that picture scares me to death. By the way, as I understand it, Billy hasn't even talked to Darren about this yet. Is that right?"

Ricky nodded.

"Sounds like you guys are jumping the gun a little bit. You don't even know if Darren is going to go for this half-baked scheme. My guess is that he won't," Marc said. "Have you really even thought this through?"

"Marc, you raise good points. I think I have thought it through, go over it with me," Ricky said.

"For starters, we have all the gear and supplies we could possibly need. We're prepared to leave for a seven-day trip, so we're certainly more than prepared for a trek into Telluride."

Ricky stepped over to a small desk in the living room and, after sorting through a stack of maps, pulled one out of the bunch and spread it out on the kitchen table. All had gathered around the table now watching.

"We would go back through Durango and drive almost to Silverton," he said, tracing his finger along the route. "But we'd get off right here at the forest service road and drive through this meadow and camping area and find us a place to park the Goose. Look, here's where we walked from Silverton last year. Do you remember walking through this camping area?"

"I do. I remember being surprised that so few people were there," Bruce said.

"From there, it's a six-to-seven-hour hike down under Ophir Pass and over through the spot we weren't ever supposed to talk about," he said looking disgustedly at Bruce.

Bruce flashed his most charming smile and put his arm around Ricky.

"We'll come out there by Bridal Falls and walk into Telluride just like we did last year," Ricky continued.

"So, what if the sheriff is watching that whole area? What if you get stopped by one of Lang's fuzz?" Marc asked.

"We say we've been camping up there. We've got our gear and I'm sure there are other hikers and campers coming down into Telluride," Bruce proposed.

"Yeah, I think that's right. But Jacobs' house is being watched, so clearly, we can't just march up to his front door and ring the bell," Ricky countered. "We don't know how we'll get into his place."

"So, let's leave that problem alone for now. Once we get there, we can go to the French Bakery and call from the pay phone, so they'll know we're there. Then, they've got to figure out how to get us into the house," Bruce said.

"And if they can't do that?" Ricky asked.

"Then, we hike out of town and nobody's the worse," Bruce answered.

"So, let's say they figure out a way to smuggle us into the house. Then what?" Ricky asked, challenging Bruce.

"They have to get us all out of the house—with the goods—without the bad guys knowing.

That's all there is to it."

Marc's patience was gone. "Don't be so fucking glib. That's where the risk comes in, you asshole. That's the risk we're supposedly trying to define by this little exercise." Donna reached out and held Marc's hand soothingly.

"So, it boils down to whether Darren's team can get us in and out of the house safely.

And we can't know that until we talk to Billy and he talks to them. Bruce, you agree?" Ricky said.

"I do. Might as well start the ball rolling," Bruce said, picking up the phone and handing it to Ricky. "I hope Billy will answer the phone in your folks' house."

Billy did answer...on the second ring.

"Billy, Bruce and I are in..." Ricky said. "GREAT, oh, man, Ricky, that is great!"

"Wait, Billy. You didn't let me finish. We know we can get into Telluride. What we want is for Darren to tell you that they have a plan to get us into his house and back out of town that he believes has a high likelihood of success. We are willing to go on those terms. But not if this is just a 'Hail, Mary'. That's our deal," Ricky said.

Ricky, surrounded by his friends watching intently, his wife's arms wrapped around his chest—her head on his back, listened for a minute and hung up the receiver.

"Billy said he would call after he talked to Darren."

လ

Telluride

I was twelve again, standing on the bank of the Rio Grande wearing nothing but cowboy boots and a red baseball cap. A duck floated by quacking. It's quacking was really irritating and wouldn't stop...

And then I started edging back into consciousness and grabbed the phone. "Lo". "Darren, did I wake you?"

I nestled the receiver to the private phone to my ear. "Umm, yeah, hold on, Billy."

A trip to the bathroom for a pee and cold water on my face brought me to full awareness.

I padded back to the bedroom. "Okay, shoot."

"I may have something, Darren. I don't know. It's a long shot for sure." "A long shot is better odds than we have right now," I said.

"Yeah, well, hear it out first. I'm up here with Bruce—law student, clerking for me—you ran into Bruce and two of his buddies, they said. "

"Sure, when we stopped in Bayfield."

"Well, I am at one of their cabins over here at Vallecito Lake." "That's over the other side of Durango, right?"

"Yes, that's right. Darren, Ricky grew up in these mountains. He's like fourth generation Southern Coloradan. At any rate, his granddad showed him a back way into Telluride that he says nobody else knows about. It was covered up by mine works decades ago. Bruce hiked it with Ricky last year, and he says it's completely hidden."

"Interesting. Where does it come out?" "Up by Bridal Falls."

"Okay. I'm with you so far."

Billy continued. "We have been discussing the possibility of them hiking the back way into Telluride later today and leading you guys out of there tonight. They have little doubt that they can get into Telluride without a hitch. So, here's their question for you: once they are there, how can you guys get them into your house? And then how can the whole bunch of you get back out of the house with the goodies without getting killed? They're waiting for the answers to those questions before they decide to take a swing at it. Oh, by the way, I told them you'd pay each of them a million bucks each if they pulled it off."

"I like how you spend my money, *consigliore*. I'm going to have to think on this some, Billy, and talk to Andy and Beto. I really don't like the idea of getting those kids mixed up in this mess—what are they twenty-three, twenty-four?"

"No, Darren, these guys are in their late twenties. I mean, they're still damned young, but they all three were out in the world a while before going back to law school."

"Any military or law enforcement experience?"

"No, hell, no, I think they were all draft dodgers. Not really, but they are definitely not the military type. However, they are all three horses. They go on extended hikes into the back country, so they are definitely competent mountain guys. But as for experience under fire, I'm sure not."

"Let me think on it. The money's fine. Spending three to save forty is a pretty easy call. But I just don't know if I want to bring them into this. Have you been straight up about how bad this has gotten?" I asked.

"You are only spending two million. One of the guys, Marc, is not in," Billy said.

"Sounds like he's the only one with good sense. So, Billy, I'll ask again. Did you level with these guys completely?" I wanted Billy to answer this question—for my own conscience, I suppose.

"Sure, I told them there were two casualties already. I haven't held back anything. You know what I think of Bruce, and these other two guys are good young men, too."

"Correction, Billy. The total body count has risen to four of Guzman's hombres. I haven't had a chance to bring you up to speed on recent happenings. Andy and Beto launched a sneak attack last night and got Paul back."

"Hell, Darren, that's incredible news!" "Not so quick—Paul is definitely dirty." "Darren, I'm really sorry..."

"Thanks" I said, "it was a hell of a shock but at least we are clear on who's on which sides.

Let me talk this over with Andy and Beto. I'll call you back in a bit."

"Don't take too long, Darren. If they're going to do this, they've got to get going." "Believe me, Billy, no one is more aware of the ticking clock than I am." I wrote down the number Billy gave me and sat with my legs hung over the bed in the dark of my room. *Do I really want to drag innocents into this mess?*

❧

I dressed quickly and dragged myself downstairs into the great room just as the first sunlight seeped in. It was a scene of contradictions. Andy was rolled into a fetal position, his back jammed against the seat of the couch. Asleep, he looked like a ten-year-old cherub, his arms clutched to his chest. On the floor lying on its side just under the sleeping Andy, was his M-16. Similarly, Beto was asleep in the lounger, his cheek pressed into the leather, his right arm flopped over the chair arm, his fingers resting lightly on the muzzle of his M-16 which leaned against the chair.

Sensing some activity outside, I approached the window by the front doors carefully, tentatively pulling the blinds aside and aligning my left eye, my right closed, to peak through the crack. Two patrol vehicles were in the street outside, both idling with their drivers' doors open. Their drivers were working as a team, stretching "CRIME SCENE" tape, fluorescent yellow with bright red letters, from pillar to pillar across the drive, sealing the Black Bronco inside, with the gate still wedded to its grill.

"What's up, Dare?" Beto mumbled softly, not waking Andy. "I'll swear I don't know."

Beto and I moved into the kitchen to get some food ready. We tried to be quiet, but Andy was, evidently, awakened when sounds of food preparation clattered out of the kitchen.

"Good mornin', gents," Andy greeted Beto and I as we prepared coffee and microwaved frozen pastries.

"Hey, Andy. Take a look outside and see if you can figure that little scene out?" I asked.

Andy, yawning, slowly dragged himself across the great room floor and returned to the kitchen. "Man, that's weird. Why would they do that?"

No sooner was the question asked than the ringer in the kitchen wall phone rang. I looked from Andy to Beto, set my jaw, and picked up the receiver. "This is Darren."

"Hey, buddy, this is Earl. The spit-and-whittle club heard you got caught up in the excitement in Telluride last night."

Darren turned to Beto and shrugged before saying, "Yeah, I guess I did."

"Sheriff said they chased the car thief all over town before he crashed into your drive and took off into the woods. Frankly, sounds like Keystone Kops to me, but don't tell Joe Bob I said that. He'll figure out some way to write me a ticket." Earl laughed and I laughed along with him. Earl Straighter sits on the Telluride City Council and is one of my favorite neighbors.

"You gonna come down and have coffee this morning?" Earl asked.

"No, Earl, I've got some business associates in town, and we're trying to get some work done. Tell the boys 'howdy' for me."

We said goodbyes and I hung up the phone.

I couldn't hide my smile. Turning to Andy and Beto, a grin breaking through on my face, I said, "Seems like a car thief stole that Bronco crashed out in my driveway, and the cops nearly caught him before he jumped ship and got away."

Andy poked Beto in the arm. "Y-Y-You have to give it to our notorious sheriff—he can, uh, you know, sure spin a tale when he needs to."

"Sit down, guys, let's talk. Billy called this morning". I recounted my conversation with the lawyer. "So, the ball's in our court. They want to know if we can get them in and out of here in one piece. What do you think? Do we want to take that on?"

Beto reacted in a blink. "Wow. It's great to have an alternative to think about—like fresh air. I know we can get them in here okay. That's no sweat. All of us getting out of here? A bit trickier, but we can do it? Hell, yeah, what do you think, André?"

"Well, I don't know. Darren, do you think they, uh, you know, have been told the who- who-whole st-st-story?" Andy asked.

"I do, Andy. I trust Billy has leveled with them."

"Then, I am for giving it a, umm, go. There's-s-s-some risk. B-B-Beto and I will manage that, th-th-though. But, er, I think we should pay them well. You know, we h-h-have Paul's, er, share, n-now." Andy said.

I liked what I was hearing from Andy. "It's a go and we pay them three million each. You guys okay with that?" Beto and Andy looked at each other and then nodded affirmation to me.

"So, I need to call Billy. When they get here, they are going to call our 'secure' line from the French Bakery. Then what?" I asked.

"They should time it to arrive at dark. Tell them to order a pizza and hang out on the front porch. Beto will pick them up and bring them back over here," Andy said in the concise and clear manner that coincided with his taking charge. The makings of a tactical plan were already forming in his head.

ᔐ

Vallecito

Once Ricky had spoken to Billy, there was nothing to do but wait. Despite the tension, fatigue had set in and all three couples drifted to their quarters and some badly needed sleep. Billy's knock on the door woke the sleeping cabin. Marc let Billy in and started coffee as the group drifted slowly into the kitchen, yawning and finding chairs. Ricky was the last to arrive and Billy addressed him before he could sit down.

"Darren says they are confident they can get you guys into and out of the house safely.

In fact, there is an update you should know about. Last night, Andy and Beto snuck out and retrieved Paul," Billy said.

Barb's eyes flew open. "Billy, doesn't that change the balance of things. I mean, now they don't have a hostage."

"Quick analysis, Barb. If you ever want to get into law... But, no, unfortunately Paul has been working with the bad guys all along. And another thing you should know—in the process of retrieving Paul, Andy and Beto killed two more of the cartel's men. There is absolutely no peaceful way out of this now," Billy said.

This news chilled the room. Barb looked at Ricky and shook her head softly.

"Listen, I know that's frightening news. But the other side of the coin is that Andy and Beto got out of the house without the cartel figuring out how they did it. The bad guys changed out the guards around the house, so Andy believes that the assumption they are operating under is that the guards went to sleep and let Andy and Beto sneak out. The fact is there is a way in and out that is not covered. So, to answer your specific question, they are now very confident they can get you in and back out of the house safely. They have tested it," Billy said making every effort to keep his persuasive skills in check and just relate the facts.

"And a small detail—Darren said I was being too stingy. Pull this off and you each get three million."

"Holy shit!" Bruce jumped out of his chair. "Holy fucking shit. That is a lot of dinero." "Decision time, men. What's it going to be?" Billy asked.

"Hell, yes, Billy we're in—for three mil—you bet'cha," Bruce piped up.

"I'm not in," Marc said staring right into Bruce's eyes. "I don't care if it's thirty million. I don't want to get killed in the middle of a drug deal gone bad."

Bruce turned to Ricky. "You in?"

"Yeah, I'm in," Ricky said and turned to Marc. "Marc, think about this. Man, I respect your decision, but you're only looking at this from one view—failure. Step back from the edge for a minute and think about the view of success. Not only do we get these guys' necks out of nooses, we walk away incredibly rich. I know money is not a big deal for you, but this kind of money means you can live your life any way you want. You can travel anywhere, anytime you want. Have a yacht in the Caribbean. Any damned thing you want. Just think about it. That's what success looks like."

Marc shook his head. "No, you two idiots go get yourselves killed. I know I can't stop you, but I'm not going to follow you over the cliff."

Billy was headed for the door. "Ricky, may I use your phone? Darren's waiting for my call."

∽

Telluride

Andy and I were so focused on our conversation that the ring from the upstairs phone startled us. "You girls a little goosey?" Beto teased.

I just grumbled and headed upstairs to my room, taking the steps two at the time. I was reeling a bit from an epiphany that truly surprised me—how much I love my Telluride home and how personal this had become for me. While my logical, business mind argued *it's just real estate*, another part of me felt deeply the connection with my castle brought to life by my own creativity. This wasn't a Jacobs Family asset passed along to the heir; this was something I dreamed up, planned and built with my own money—ill-gotten as it may be. The thought of Lang and Guzman pushing me out of it makes me nearly physically ill.

"Hello, Billy. What's the news?"

"Reinforcements are on the way—Ricky and Bruce. Marc opted out. They say they will be in Telluride just before dark. They are going to go to the French Bakery, where they feel they will blend right in with the college kids and hippies. Bruce will call you from the pay phone. You take it from there."

"Good. We're ready. Billy, these guys know what they're signing up for, right?" I really want these guys to come to our rescue, but I want my conscious clear as well.

"Darren, I promise you—I laid it on thick—held nothing back. Ricky's doing this because he can't sit by and let you get killed.

Bruce, some that, some the adventure and some—maybe more than some—the money. They'll be fine."

"Anything else?" Darren asked.

"Nope, just take care and I'll have you martinis ready tomorrow afternoon."

"I hope like hell that's exactly what we're doing this time tomorrow. But, Billy, if this doesn't end well, know that you have been a great lawyer and a better friend. No matter what happens, you've gone above and beyond."

"I appreciate the kind words, Darren, but I have no interest in handling your estate. Just get your sorry self over here tomorrow."

Andy and Beto watched me like a pair of hawks as I came back into the great room. If the situation weren't so serious, I would play them a bit. But I just don't feel like it.

"Game's on. Bruce and Ricky are headed this way—should be here about sunset. They're going to the French Bakery and wait for us to come pick them up."

Beto jumped up ready to respond when the house line rang. I paused a moment, took a breath, got into character. Then, I answered in my most officious tone. "This is Darren".

"Darren, ol' buddy, this here's Joe Bob. Time to decide, Dare, are you gonna fish or cut bait?'

Billy's call was a game-changer. Now, I needed to buy time. "We're reasonable men, Joe Bob. We have a proposal," I said. "And that would be?"

As a good negotiator would do, I paused a moment before speaking. "I suspect you have a pretty good idea of what's in the vault. We'll drive out of here with the cash and leave the inventory in the vault." Andy and Beto both looked at me like I had lost my mind.

"Darren, you know that isn't going to fly," he replied.

"Wait, Joe Bob, there's more. We have some conditions about exactly how we leave

Telluride, you know, so that we do, in fact, get to leave Telluride," I further relayed. "And, Lang, you don't have the horsepower to make this call by yourself, so talk to your cutthroat partners—they think like businessmen—and let me know.

"I will, but I can tell you right now, what you're suggesting just isn't going to work," he said.

"And one more thing, Joe Bob, don't do anything stupid while we're trying to work something out here. If certain parties don't hear from me by eight o'clock tomorrow morning, my dossier on you will be released to the DEA."

I clicked the receiver down. Both of us were lying—me saying we were considering leaving, and Joe Bob pretending he was going to let us go. But that doesn't matter. I started a conversation that could buy us the time we need.

∽

Lake Vallecito

Billy stepped into the cabin where Ricky and Bruce were creating a beehive of activity. He had waved at Marc who stood dejectedly at the far end of the porch, staring off at the lake. Marc didn't respond. Barb and Donna were seated at the kitchen table, both looking like hell warmed over.

"How's it going?" he asked.

Ricky was totally focused but looked up absently. "Fine. We're nearly ready."

"I'm thinking all we need to take is enough water and energy bars for a day and camping gear to support our story, if we have to tell it," Ricky said as he pulled clothes, dry rations, and fishing gear out of his backpack.

"Yeah, and we can dump the camping gear once we get there. We sure won't need it on the return trip," Bruce said.

"We still need to stop in Durango and pick up enough backpacks to bring back what you're going for," Billy reminded them.

"Yeah, La Plata County Sporting Goods will have them," Ricky said.

Billy pulled his Jaguar by the back porch and opened the trunk. Ricky and Bruce tossed their backpacks in.

"You guys are welcome to take the Goose," Marc said. "We've got Donna's car. She's going to work a shift tomorrow...and, uh, then come back here."

"No, you guys may need it," Ricky said. A chill went down Marc's spine thinking why that might matter...and that Ricky had the presence of mind to think about it.

Barb clung to Ricky sobbing, her strength finally giving way to her fear. He held her away, his hands on her face, his eyes locked on hers and said softly, "I promise you that I am going to be right back here with you tomorrow afternoon, and I have never broken a promise in my life. Do you believe me?"

Marc remained on the porch, the distance between the friends felt like an ocean. Nancy hugged Bruce before he waved at Marc and jumped in Billy's car. Grinning, he stuck his head out the window. "See you tomorrow. As they say, keep the porch light on for us."

Ricky bolted up the steps and grabbed Marc in a bear hug, not willing to leave the young man who had become almost like a brother on such awful terms. "See you tomorrow, man."

"Keep your head down," Marc said, his voice husky with emotion.

Marc and the women watched them drive off. Bruce had, as usual, claimed the shotgun seat, with Ricky in the back. Billy eased the Jag forward, weaving to avoid chug holes and protruding rocks. The car windows were down, letting in the sounds of chirping birds and quarrelsome squirrels and the heavy, rich aroma of the forest floor spiced with the pungent scent of pine. Splashes of brilliant morning light successfully dodged the thick boughs overhead, illuminating the interior of the car in fits and starts. Ricky turned and looked out of the back window and, just before the car disappeared into the trees, flashed a smile and the peace sign. Tears welled in Marc's eyes. *What if that was the last time he saw Ricky alive?* But he didn't have long to dwell on that—Barb collapsed in a sobbing, heaving heap and he and Donna rushed to her. Her face twisted in anguished pain, Barb fought to get the words out... and finally, "He may never know his child, or even of its existence."

᧠

Winding their way along the twisting Florida Creek, the Jaguar purred down the mountain lane, ultimately arriving in downtown Durango. Billy angle-parked in front of the sporting goods store on Main. All three poured out of the car, intent on buying the extra backpacks, a final mundane task marking the end of normalcy before embarking on an undertaking that was to be anything but mundane.

In ten minutes, the three walked out of the store, Ricky carrying a large paper shopping bag containing the four backpacks.

Bruce laughed. "Son of a bitch, Billy. Look at that piece of shit smudging your car."

Marc was leaning against the Jag, his eyes peering sheepishly out from under a blue cap with an orange Bronco's logo. The Silver Goose was parked a few spaces down.

"Hey, asshole, did you finally come to join the party?" Bruce asked, putting Marc in a headlock before he could answer.

"Are you sure, Marc? You had good reasons for not coming in the first place?" Billy questioned.

"Well, it finally dawned on me. If I'm dead, I'm dead. I can accept that. But the thought of living the rest of my life as a working stiff with these two knuckleheads becoming millionaires and holding it over me...man, that was just more than I could stand."

"If you're sure?" Billy asked.

"Yeah, Billy, I'm sure. Actually, it was Donna that made the difference. She said I would always have second thoughts about myself, and she was right."

Ricky said, "Billy, you know you're welcome to go back to the cabin and wait if you wish."

"Thanks. I'm going to go up to Darren's condo at Tamarron and see if I can get some work done. Fat chance, but I'll try. Those three guys stuck in Telluride are as close to me as my real brothers. I can't tell you..." and his voice broke. He turned his back quickly. "See you guys tomorrow."

$\backsim$

After Marc left to join up with his friends, Barb and Donna sat around the kitchen table sipping tea.

"I just found out and was going to tell Ricky last night. But, then, all hell broke loose," Barb said and started sobbing softly again.

Nancy emerged from the back room and joined them at the table, where Barb shared more of the news.

"Oh, my god, a baby. You're already off on your dream come true," Nancy said, jumping up and throwing her arms around Barb's neck, practically smothering her.

"Yes, except for this nightmare," Barb said, bringing the celebration to a quick stop.

An uncomfortable quiet filled the room.

Nancy spoke softly. "Ricky will get them back fine. You know that. Now, don't get yourself worked up. Tomorrow night, you're going to be wrapped up in that man's arms in that bedroom in there. Just keep that picture in your mind."

Barb took her hand. "Sweet words, friend. And just the ones I need. Thanks."

The day drug on for the women, each, despite their efforts, checking the wall clock every few minutes. They had talked about walking by the lake but rejected the idea, not wanting to get away from the phone. Nancy withdrew to her room, so, Barb and Donna sat and talked and waited.

"If something happens to Marc, I don't know how I will come to live with myself," Donna said. "I feel like I practically shoved him out the door."

"No, you were right. He wanted to go. He made the call. It was what he wanted," Barb said.

"Yes, but if I had said 'don't go', he wouldn't have gone. True?"

"You don't know that. I think it's more likely that he would have sat here another thirty minutes, and then, gotten up and ran after them, anyway." Barb went on, "This may sound selfish, but I'm glad that he is going to be with Ricky. I know Ricky relies on Marc's good judgment—he's always asking his opinion. And, who knows, Marc's being there may make the difference between...well, you know, success or failure."

The word "failure" was still lingering in the quiet room when Nancy came out of the guest room carrying her bag. Barb and Nancy both looked up with surprise.

"Nancy, what's going on?" Barb said, rising and tucking Nancy under her arm. Nancy put her head on Barb's chest and, letting it all out, shook with sobs, wetting Barb's sweater with tears.

Nancy pulled away; turned her back to the other women; blew her nose; rubbed her face, and, summoning her courage, gradually controlled her weeping. "I'm going back to Albuquerque. I'm throwing the towel in with Bruce." Getting the words out was the limit of her composure—she broke down, wracked with crying again.

Barb and Donna gently escorted her to the couch and sat down next to her, while she again tried to calm herself.

"Bruce is never going to be what I want in a partner. It became crystal clear to me when he made the decision to go to Telluride without giving one thought about me. You heard his decision at the same time I did. I mean, I'm not the easiest person in the world to live with—I'll give you that. But most of our fights are caused by him forgetting something he committed to do, or making decisions that affect both of us without a thought of talking to me about it, or just flat forgetting I'm around sometimes."

"Nancy, don't you think Bruce loves you, though? I mean, he followed you out here, and you've been together so long, now?" Barb asked.

"You know, he does in his own way. It's just that he's so wrapped up in himself. I have pretended that I am happy as an independent businesswoman with a 'modern' relationship. And I do want a career. But I also want a real husband…and a home…and a family. Bruce isn't ever going to make that dream come true—not the way I dream it, anyway."

Donna and Barb exchanged a look that said neither of them knew what else to say. Because they both felt Nancy was right. They just wrapped her up in a group hug and Barb said, "We're always going to be here for you. Don't think for a minute that you and Bruce splitting up is going to change that."

"Well," Nancy said. "The first thing I need is a ride to the airport so I can catch a flight home. Donna, do you mind taking me on your way into town?"

Nancy's broken heart took Barb's and Donna's minds off their own problems for a few minutes, but only for a few minutes; soon, the three resumed the vigil of worrying about their men. And, despite Nancy's revelation, it was clear to Barb and Donna that she could not be more concerned about Bruce. Clearly, she was still in love.

Donna and Nancy left late afternoon, allowing plenty of time for the trip to the airport and then, for Donna to get to the hospital on time. Before leaving, Nancy extracted a promise from Barb that she would call as soon as she got any news from Ricky.

Left alone, Barb pulled down a box from the closet that contained photographs taken at Vallecito. One by one, she relived every memory of the times recorded by the visual records; all their friends and family; lingering any time Ricky's face was in the photo and taking comfort from the reality of the visage and the certainty that it could not disappear from her life.

Ricky drove, Bruce rode shotgun, and Marc perched on the backseat alternately sitting back to look out the windows or leaning forward to talk although the conversation was sparse. Heading north toward the Silverton "Million Dollar" Highway, they were soon past the Durango motels and burger joints gearing up for the upcoming season, and out into the countryside. Steep red cliffs rose claustrophobically on the left side of the road. On the passenger side, the valley broadened into a flat green expanse dotted with cattle and cut by the snaking Animas River, its path marked by newly greened willows and bushes, the whole scene backed by pine- and fir- forested bluffs and copse of white and shimmering lime green aspens. Still snow-covered Engineer Peak popped in and out of view as the highway twisted and climbed northward and upward.

Thick black smoke and the nausea-inducing heated smells of coal and tar trailed through the valley.

"There she goes!" Bruce hollered, rolling down the window.

Just ahead the Durango & Silverton train appeared, rolling northward on ancient tracks at the bottom of the canyon floor. The black, puffing engine pulled a load of four bright yellow passenger cars and a brown caboose, taking it easy before the onrush of tourist dollars would add another dozen cars and make the steep climbs almost unbearably difficult. A few passengers waved out open windows. Bruce rolled down the side glass and waved back. Ricky honked and the engineer responded with two loud blasts of the whistle with matching puffs of steam.

"Damned that was fun last year," Marc said. "We need to do that again. The girls loved it."

Marc thought back to the previous October. The three couples had ridden the D & S to Silverton during the height of aspen season. The ride was spectacular at any time, but especially so in the fall when the aspens turned ridiculously luminous shades of yellow, orange, and red, dramatically contrasting with the surrounding hues of evergreen forest and red rocks.

"I've even hung that stupid picture over the fireplace back in Albuquerque. Everybody loves it," Ricky added.

After shots at a couple of Silverton saloons, the six-some had stumbled into a photography studio that specialized in old-timer photos, where they had several made with the guys decked out as gun-toting cowboys and the girls as saloon floozies complete with wigs, garters, fishnet hose and heavily rouged faces. The sepia-toned photos perfectly captured the wild-west frontier spirit fully felt by the tequila-fueled subjects.

Though unspoken, all three veered into similar private thoughts about whether they would be around in October. The rest of the ride was broodingly silent.

Diving down into a dirt road that stretched out across the meadow to the other side of valley where the signage for the campground could be seen in the distance, Ricky turned the van left across the Million Dollar Highway. Slowly, they wound their way down the dirt lane flanked on both sides by reeds and spring mountain flowers. The van splashed through a creek just before climbing slightly into the campground area and passing the U. S. Forest Service sign advising that "overnight camping is limited to two nights". A few tents were set up, but no campers appeared. Ricky drove the van to the end of the lane and pulled left into the last camping spot.

The three stepped out into the mountain sunshine, feeling the seemingly illogical simultaneous skin sensations of cool breeze and intensely burning sun. Ricky opened the back van doors and handed out packs to Bruce and Marc, who stuffed the new backpacks into each before they strapped them onto their backs.

"Daylight's burning" was all Ricky said as he strode up a path with Marc and Bruce hurrying to catch up. Soon, they were in the familiar groove of almost meditative silence as their legs reached out and their heartbeats became stronger and faster. Red-winged blackbirds called to one another as a mockingbird screeched and clacked. Ricky pointed and Bruce and Marc followed the direction to a red-tail hawk high over the valley circling on a thermal.

The trail soon rose into dense evergreen forest, predominantly pine and fir with the occasional blue spruce. Rainwater stood in low-lying puddles that the three dodged around. As the hikers moved through cool, dark forest shadows interspersed with blindingly bright openings pierced by rays of sunlight unimpeded by the thin, mountain air, the aroma of wet pine needles and pollen from flowering plants filled the air.

They climbed steeply for over an hour before Ricky stopped and turned. "Let's take a break."

"Shit, yes, about time," Bruce said spinning out of his backpack and bolting to a tree, the sound of forceful piss following shortly. "Oh, my god, that feels good."

Marc smiled at Ricky and took a swig from a canteen, savoring the sweet coldness of the Vallecito water. Ricky followed suit as Bruce tore open a protein bar, gobbled it in three bites and then crammed the wrapper into his pack. Ricky had been fanatical about teaching Bruce and Marc to always "pack out what you pack in", so that it had become instinctive, even to Bruce.

"Whadayathink? Five more hours like this?" Marc asked Ricky.

"Yeah, that's about right. We'll hook up with the trail we took from Silverton last year in about a half hour."

"Lots of water, guys. It may not feel like it, but we need to keep rehydrating."

For a moment, Ricky's familiar coaching made it seem to Marc that the three friends were just out on another hike. After one last drink, they threw their packs on and Ricky headed up the trail with Bruce and Marc in tow. True to his prediction, the trail ran out into a small meadow in about thirty minutes where it intersected with the main track from Silverton.

"Okay, guys, here's where we see what you're made of—two thousand feet of grade change between here and the pass, remember?"

"Oh, fuck yes I remember. I thought I was gonna die," Bruce said, grinning. "I also remember that you're a mean bastard as a platoon leader, Ricky."

"It wouldn't have anything to do with those cancer sticks you keep putting in your mouth, would it?"

"Fuuuuck you. You know that is not a topic for conversation. Period."

Amid forest sounds and occasionally the crunching of gravel underfoot, they climbed for another half hour before coming to a plateau that opened to a sweeping Rockies panorama.

"Oh, yes, brothers! I remember this!" Marc said. "How could anyone ever forget this view?"

Their eyes scanned the horizon, scored by a dark violet jagged line created by a collection of snow-covered mountains bare from tree line to their peaks, and below, bright red slashes of decomposed granite cut under the peaks, leaning right and left at angles that marked the dizzyingly steep elevations. At the tree line, dense old forest of the deepest green was interspersed on either side of rocky slide areas with the fresh lime green of aspen leaves and occasional sparkles of white trunks.

∾

Ricky, Bruce, and Marc had been steadily at it for three hours. If they continued on their current path, a dirt forest service road, they would eventually top out at Ophir Pass, the second highest pass in the country negotiable by a vehicle. Initially, the lane was built as a toll road back in the late nineteenth century as a shortcut from Telluride to Silverton, but it fell into disuse with the silver bust and was now a forest-service-maintained wilderness road.

"This way," Ricky motioned to Bruce and Marc, walking to the right off the path and into a boulder field that was left from a slide that began several hundred yards up the mountain and continued several hundred more yards below the old road.

The three hikers picked their way carefully through the giant rocks and slippery shale for over fifteen minutes, Ricky leading the way all the while picturing his grandfather walking in front of him as he had so many times. This was their special secret. The field ended abruptly, and they found themselves standing on the remnants of the old mining road.

"Déjà vu, dudes," Bruce announced, "just like last year. Ricky, I don't know how you do it. It's like you have a homing signal in your head."

"Let's take a break," Ricky said, putting his backpack down.

They all three set their packs on the abandoned mining road and gave tired legs a rest leaning against the rock wall. Canteens and snacks were pulled from backpacks. The road could only be discerned from their vantage point, and even then, it just looked a little unusual, like an unnatural ledge on the side of the mountain. Brush and scrub pine grew in the roadway, blending imperceptibly into the surrounding forest.

"Look at that." Marc pointed to the west. The beginnings of giant cumulus clouds— thunder boomers—were starting to mount in the west, rocketing skyward in lumpy white columns out of heavy gray foundations. While the sun had moved into the western sky, the earth would need to spin a while longer before it would be blocked by the clouds.

"Yep, we may get wet before we get to Telluride," Ricky opined. "Guess we better get rolling."

Bruce stood with a groan and Marc followed, both slinging their packs over their backs and then hurrying to catch Ricky as he weaved and bobbed between the tree trunks. The shade created by the green canopy was welcome as the afternoon mountain sun was taking its toll on the travelers. All found walking through the cooler pine-scented air a welcome relief.

The men continued in this way, silently striding one behind the other, weaving between trees while pushing limbs aside from time to time, until they suddenly broke out of the trees into a bright, sunny patch. A clearly delineated roadway spread straight out in front of them bare of any vegetation as none could grow on the steep rock wall to the right of the path, and to the left, the edge of the road fell off into nothingness. The three walked out on the patch of road and looked over the side, the scene both frightening yet breathtaking. The canyon wall plunged straight down almost a thousand feet, tapering only at the bottom where the residue of sheets of rock had been falling off the cliff and piling up for eons.

The view, like something drawn in a Roadrunner cartoon, was mesmerizing. Marc stepped back giving way to his fear of heights. "Let's keep moving. Nothing to see here, people." He took the lead wanting to get off the ledge before dizziness set in.

Disappearing into a dense tangle of undergrowth and vines, the roadway ended abruptly in about fifty yards. Marc waited as Ricky passed him and, approaching the wall of vegetation, chose a spot. He put his arms in front of him, his palms together, wedging them through hanging vines and parting an opening wide enough to walk through. Marc and Bruce followed Ricky through the green curtain. Inside, Ricky had turned on the flashlight, revealing the beginning of the tunnel. The rock walls were about eight feet apart and showed vertical drill marks where the original cuts had been made. Ricky flashed the light on the roof of the tunnel about ten feet overhead. Water dripped continuously from tiny cracks. Remnants of abandoned rails and rail ties were strewn across the floor of the shaft.

"God, I don't like this. I had forgotten how bad it stinks," Bruce whined. "It smells like giant dead rats."

"Yeah, well, let's just keep trucking and we'll be out of here in a few minutes. Marc, do you want to turn on the other flashlight?" Ricky asked.

Marc did. The three marched forward, being careful not to trip over steel rails or waste rock that had broken loose from the ceiling. The shaft curved to the right in a gentle arc and descended slightly. The would-be spelunkers followed the two shafts of light, walking steadily for almost half an hour until the rays rested on a solid blockage at the other end of the shaft. Just like they entered the tunnel, Ricky stepped forward through the vegetation wall spreading the growth and letting a burst of light into the darkened cave. Marc and Bruce followed through the opening and burst into the bright sunlight. Squinting all the while, the three blinked their eyes repeatedly until they became accustomed to the sun.

Unlike the entrance to the tunnel on the other side, here, Marc could barely make out the roadway as it was mostly covered with overgrowth.

"Quick break, mates?" Bruce asked. Without reply, they all sat, glad to rest a bit and really glad to be out of the tomblike mineshaft. Sprawled on the mountain grass, they drank the last of the water and finished off the granola bars. The sound of rushing water from deeper in the valley floated up.

"Is that the San Miguel we're hearing?" Marc asked Ricky

"It is. Let's just bushwhack down there rather than staying on the old road. Just to be safe. We'll run into that path that runs along the river and we can follow it down right into town."

They had just set out through the heavy brush when the sky blackened as the huge thunder clouds covered the sun. The air cooled markedly, and a rumble of thunder announced itself from miles away, reverberating up the valley. Ricky scrambled down the hillside with Marc and Bruce following. The threesome headed deeper into the woods, constantly moving toward the river sound as it became louder. They emerged into a clearing next to the river with a path meandering through the middle of it.

As they walked on the path out of the canyon, they could see Telluride houses and buildings occasionally through breaks in the trees. The nearness of the danger loomed as they followed the path until coming to a paved road.

"Showtime," Bruce said in a weak attempt to defuse the building tension.

A few blocks on, they walked into the center of Telluride just as the sun began to set and lights peep out of the buildings around town. Monstrous thunderheads loomed over the tiny city, jagged tributaries of lightening sizzling on their faces as explosions of strobe lights framed the three young men's bodies. Sonorous rumblings bubbled out of the sky and poured down the canyons, ricocheting from wall to wall. Marc wondered, *Was the charge in the air was from the storm—or a warning of what was to come?*

Telluride

I don't ever remember time passing so slowly. Andy, Beto and I enjoyed a few minutes of celebration after Billy's news that redemption might be coming, but then we faced the reality that we were stuck in the house for a long day of waiting. I could deal with the waiting much better if I could sit out on the deck. But sitting outside might be pushing our luck; the *pistoleros* might be crazy enough to take it if they got a clear shot at me. So, Andy, Beto and I played poker and drank sodas all afternoon.

Lang and I had several conversations. As I expected, they rejected my initial settlement offer, but, after much wrangling, we mutually agreed that we could take five million in cash. We also agreed on protocols on how we departed Telluride. One unarmed man was to inspect the car at my house to see that we only took the five million. At which time, Lang's troops would open up the road out of town and keep all of their people out of the way. Lang tried to negotiate that we were to have no weapons in the car, but I didn't let that go anywhere. "If you're going to stay out of our way, why do you care if we are armed to the teeth?" This whole "let's pretend" discussion was sort of fun for me. Me, pretending we were actually going to be around tomorrow morning. And, Joe Bob, pretending that he was going to let us go.

Black, heavy thunderclouds rolled over the valley as the sky grew dark and thunder roared in the distance. Under normal circumstances, nothing would have delighted me more than a summer mountain storm setting in, but today it just magnified the already tense atmosphere. It didn't help matters that about every fifteen minutes Beto said, "I wonder where the guys are now? What if it rains so hard, they can't get through?"

Beto and Andy periodically checked on Paul, took him to the restroom and gave him something to eat or drink. After one such round, Andy sat down in front me.

"Okay, D-D-Darren, so what's the game p-p-plan with, uh, Paul?" It pained me to see Andy so tormented over confronting me.

"To tell you the truth, I don't know."

"There's room in the meat locker, Dare. Andy and I can make that happen," Beto piped in.

I shot a perturbed look at Beto, "thanks for the offer. I'll keep it in mind. Actually, I have a hunch that we don't want to let Lang and Guzman know that we have the goods on Paul. Somehow, I think we can use it to our favor."

"Or is that just a stall to avoid making a hard call?" Beto asked.

"We're taking him with us, and then I'll decide what happens to him." I looked from Beto to Andy and back. "Any questions?" There was more edge in my voice than I intended, most likely because Beto was closer to the truth than I wanted to admit. Despite Paul's treachery, I just couldn't bring myself to allow his execution.

Both shook their heads in submission to the alpha dog, and we returned to our poker game. Beto looked at his watch for the hundredth time. "It's seven-fifteen, Darren; you reckon we should go look for them yet?"

I opened my mouth to answer and the phone rang. I sprinted upstairs. "Hello, Bruce?"

"Yes, Mr. Jacobs. We made it fine. We're at the French Bakery. Sorry it took so long, there was a line at the pay phone—kids calling home to get money wired from what I could hear."

"No problem. We actually needed to wait for the dark anyway. Sit tight and Beto will be over to get you as soon as it gets a little darker," I said.

"We're starving—will we have time to eat some pizza?"

"Of course. You'll need your energy so load up." Something about the normalcy of a hungry young man wanting pizza made me smile. "See you in a little bit, Bruce."

I looked around to find Beto and Andy standing in the doorway.

"They're here. Everything went fine.

Beto snuck out the side of the house just after it got dark, a repeat performance except solo—Andy stayed back with me, just in case. The best they could determine, Guzman's guards were all in the same places, and a black and white sat at the end of the street maintaining surveillance. We took comfort that, at least by outward appearances, they weren't escalating, so maybe believed we were going to leave in the morning.

Beto was to head over to Bill Thompson's house, a friend of mine and part-time resident of Telluride. I kept sets of keys to his house when he was out of town and, since Bill was traveling to the East Coast, we agreed Beto would "borrow" a van that Bill kept in the driveway.

〜

Ricky, Bruce, and Marc sat on the front porch of the French Bakery, virtually inhaling their food. Though wrestling nerves, the long day's march had stirred up the young men's appetites and they quickly put away two large pizzas.

A black and white blazer with Telluride Sheriff's Department markings pulled up to the curb in front of the busy restaurant. The driver eyed the crowd like a wolf looking over a herd of sheep. Ricky said, "Shit, the timing couldn't be worse."

With that, Bruce stood up and marched over to the police vehicle. Marc and Ricky looked at each other with "what-now" expressions.

"Good evening, officers. I am a law student and soon to be an officer of the court. I take this responsibility seriously. I understand that if I know of a crime being committed, it is my duty to report it to the appropriate authorities." Bruce spoke with the perfect tattle-tale indignation in his voice, not unlike Eddie Haskell from "Leave it to Beaver."

"And what crime do you think is being committed, Mr. Law Student?"

"A group of hippie-looking kids just left here. They were talking about breaking into the city pool and robbing the vending machines. And that's not all. I think they had marijuana with them, and they even were talking about...skinny-dipping."

The two officers smiled at each other. "How long have they been gone?"

"No more than ten minutes. There were maybe ten of them, boys and girls, although it's hard to tell the difference with that type, you know."

With a "thanks" the driver shifted the vehicle into gear and drove off.

"Jesus Chris, Bruce, you've got the balls of god," Marc said. "What were you thinking?" "I was thinking that I'd better get rid of those keystone cops before our ride shows up.

Raising the possibility of them catching naked hippy girls was just an inspiration. Speaking of which, there's Beto now. Casual boys, very casual."

With that word of caution, each picked up his backpack and sauntered to the blue and white van. Bruce climbed into the front passenger seat while Marc and Ricky slid the side door open and climbed into captain's chairs arrayed around a Formica-topped table.

Beto smiled at Bruce. "I never thought I would say seeing a hatchling lawyer would be a sight for sore eyes, but I am sure glad to see you."

"Beto, you remember Marc and Ricky," Bruce said, nodding toward each.

"Are we glad to see you guys! Marc, we didn't expect you?"

"Yeah, I reverse chickened-out at the last minute," Marc said sheepishly. "Is it okay that I'm here?"

"Hell, yes. One more strong back to carry out the loot. You bet. We are truly and sincerely glad you are here. Let's roll. We'll have plenty of time to catch up at Darren's before we slip out of here tonight."

I couldn't imagine how the tension level could ratchet higher, but when Andy closed the window that Beto had just rolled through, the pressure in the house was almost paralyzing for me.

"Gin game—b-b-buck a point?" Andy asked.

"No, thanks, Andy. I don't think I could focus enough to play 'Go Fish'."

This was something of an admission for me, as I have never before let pressure bother me. One thing my fiercest adversaries would admit of me is that I am always cool under fire— in the critical moments of a trial or in the climax of difficult negotiations. But this was different; I have never had my life on the line before. And my closest friends and now three young men.

"Dare, do you mind if I ask you a really personal question?"

"Geez, Andy, you know everything about me. What could you not already know." I chuckled. "Of course, ask away."

"Wh-wh-why do you d-d-d-do these crazy things?" I didn't expect this. "What do you mean, Andy?"

"Well, umm, you've always sort of lived two l-l-lives. Even when we, uh, met as kids, you, you know, were sneaking out— hiding things fr-fr-from your folks." This was the worst I had heard Andy stutter in a very long time. "I-I-I mean, you were born into r-r-r-royalty. Why would you r-r-r-risk so much?"

I was stunned into momentary speechlessness. Believe it or not, this question had never occurred to me. The first thing that flashed into my mind was my father saying to me, many times in my life, "you're one of those people who do what's and how's with little interest in the why's". Maybe the past few days opened the door for Andy, probably the only person on earth who could do so, to ask the question.

I don't know how much time passed in silence. I was truly dazed.

"G-g-gosh, Dare, I-I-I didn't mean to up-up-upset you." Andy's face showed nothing more than his deep concern for me.

"Andy, I'm not upset. I just don't know what to say. You asked me too good a question, my friend." He smiled a bit with relief.

"You know I don't like to shoot from the hip, Andy, and you've caught me totally flat- footed. I suspect I'm going to be doing a lot of thinking about your question over the next little while, but I will tell you the first thing that came to my mind.

"I have never liked rules, for as far back as I can remember. I can't tell you how many conversations I had with my parents about following rules. 'You have to do this because blah, blah, blah'. And I would drive them to distraction with 'questioning the purpose of the rule' until I would get the ultimate show-stopper—'because that's the way it is, young man'.

"But— having said that out loud— it's more than that. Part of me has always dreaded the boredom of my parents' life. Don't get me wrong, they are such good people and I respect them tremendously. You know that, right?" "I do, Dare, for sure."

"...and, yet, the thought of settling down, getting married and having another brood of Jacobs kids grates on my mind like fingernails on a chalk board. I feel like I'm different than other people—separate. I truly don't understand what makes the average Joe tick. Does that make me a weirdo, Andy?"

"No, it's just who you are. Not b-b-bad or g-g-good. Just Darren."

I laughed. "You're a hell of a lot better at figuring life out than I am. There's one more thing, Andy, and this one won't surprise you—I get a huge rush from taking chances. HUGE RUSH! From driving crazy fast to...to dealing with Mexican drug lords...to doing lines of coke in the bathroom of the Roundhouse in Santa Fe during legislative session. I love the danger while it's going on, and the euphoric feeling of getting away with it. It just makes me feel incredibly alive, like all my senses are working overtime. I don't know how else to put it."

A "bump" startled both of us. Andy grinned. "Just P-P-Paul rolling off the bed, I sus-suspect."

With that, Andy took off down the hall and I headed to the kitchen for water. The thought of a shot of tequila was really tempting, especially after that conversation, but I knew that all my faculties needed to be sharp. I sat down at the kitchen table, trying to clear my mind of the flood of thoughts opened by the discussion with Andy. After ten minutes, I was becoming concerned that Andy hadn't returned, but then the commode flushed and, a minute or so later, I heard his steps on the stairs.

And then, a "tap" at the window made me jump nearly out of my skin.

‿ჿ

Beto drove the van cautiously back to Bill's. On the way, he explained to his charges that they were going to take the back way into Darren's house and that he wanted them to follow close to him and watch his every move. He would have preferred to have had time to train these new recruits in hand communications and stealth movements, but, of course, that was not possible.

They returned Bill's van and, following Beto's lead, tried to appear to be out on casual stroll as they headed to Darren's. When Marc thought about what they were doing—sneaking into a house being watched by an army of criminals—his first impulse was to turn around and run. But he had come this far.

An uneventful stroll and a few minutes later, they were in the dark outside Darren's house looking through a lighted window. Beto tapped on the glass and it slid open immediately. Beto motioned his three charges through the window ahead of him before sliding smoothly through himself.

Breaking into a jail is one thing; breaking out, quite another.

Carlos Durant and Joe Bob Lang sat in facing bucket chairs in the communications vehicle, Guzman in the corner, now clearly demoted. As Durant spoke no English, Guzman was permitted in the command post only because he was needed for translation.

Durant asked Lang if he really thought Darren would just drive away peacefully in the morning.

"There's a part of me that can't see it, frankly. But maybe Jacobs doesn't see any other way out. The big sticking point is that his partners don't want to give up their wealth. If they do leave in the morning, my guess is that Darren has made a deal with them. He could make them very wealthy and barely miss it."

Guzman translated and the new jefe nodded.

"Just in case, however, we have every available man, yours and ours, on the roads tonight. If they are going to try something, we had better be ready because Darren's two soldiers are as salty as they come."

Again, Durant nodded and said something to Guzman in Spanish.

"Carlos said, no matter what, they aren't leaving town alive," Guzman relayed.

The sheriff was examining his hands and, not looking up, said, "Yeah, I know that. I know."

❧

"Bruce, welcome to my home. Sorry you couldn't come through the front door. It normally is a very dramatic entrance, but I'd say your entrance was dramatic enough, considering the times," I said.

"That's okay, Darren. From what I've heard, we'll take a pass on the front door tonight. You remember Ricky...and Marc."

"I guess I'm a little confused," I said. "Marc, I understood you weren't coming." "Last minute change of plans, Mr. Jacobs. Hope that's okay?" Marc said.

I was really pleased that he had changed his mind, for a lot of reasons, not the least of which is that we need all the able-bodied hands we can get to take our property with us. I put my hand on his shoulder. "Yes, for sure we are glad to have you."

Bruce's demeanor surprised me. Ricky and Marc looked like they could bolt and run given half a chance, but Bruce seemed to actually be enjoying the adventure.

"There just are no words to express our gratitude to the three of you," I said in all earnestness.

I herded Andy, Beto and our three new co-conspirators into the great room where a coffee carafe and tub of soft drinks on ice were waiting on the coffee table. Taking extra caution, I dimmed the lights. The darkened room and thunder rumbling outside didn't help the overall tension levels.

"You guys help yourself to Cokes or coffee and have a seat, make yourself comfortable."

I looked at Beto, "everything go?"

"For sure, boss man. No hitches."

I got a kick watching our three new colleagues checking things out. Ricky and Marc at least tried to be circumspect and steal glances here and there, occasionally letting their eyes rest a bit on the huge glass wall with the lightening sizzling under the retreating clouds while outlining the mountain peaks. Bruce, on the other hand, made no bones of it—he just openly gawked and finally got up and walked around the room inspecting the art appreciatively. "Great house, Darren. This is just beautiful."

Thinking this is a guy who wants it all made me smile.

"Thanks. Let's not push our luck walking around in front of windows. Come on over around the dining room table, shall we," I tried to say calmly, not wanting to freak out our new guests any more than they already were.

I sat at the head of the table. "I know Billy has done a good job of explaining our predicament to you and I couldn't be more impressed and grateful that you have taken on the role of heroes, because for us, that's exactly what you are. But bear with me; I want to be sure that we are all absolutely clear with one another. We only have a few hours before we take off, so it's now or never. Does that make sense, fellows?" I addressed the question to the three newcomers, who nodded silently back at me.

I pressed on. "Andy, Beto and I are in the cocaine distribution business. In a big way. We run New Mexico and Arizona exclusively. Though the source of the coke is Colombia, it comes to us through a Mexican cartel that we have worked well with for years. Until this week. They are now putting a power play on us, both to take us out of the business and to grab about forty million of coke and cash that's here in my house. This much, I believe, you already know."

Again, nods from the couch.

"What you may not be aware of yet is that we have had a traitor in our organization who has given the Mexicans the chink in the armor that they needed to try to pull this stunt."

Bruce said, "Yeah. Billy told us. You must be pretty sure?"

"There is no doubt. He has confessed. The point I want to make with you guys is that we are dealing with some really dangerous characters. Surrounding this town right now is a mix of Mexican cartel pistoleros as well as the corrupt sheriff and his deputies, all of which are now working for the cartel. They used to be ours," I said with a wry smile.

"You guys have given us the trump card, or, otherwise, we would be toast. The only thing we have going for us is that they feel confident that this thing can only end one of three ways." Counting on his fingers: "One, we make a charge for one of the passes. Two, they clear the town in the morning and come straight at us here. Or three, we drive out of town in the morning like we have said we are going to do. And, speaking frankly, I am not sure that we would ever get out of town alive, even if we took Door Number Three. We feel pretty sure, though, that they don't have escape by other means as part of their defense strategy, so we do have surprise in our favor.

That said, there is still plenty of risk in what we are proposing to do. I want you three to be one hundred percent sure before we start this gig. It's not too late to go back out the window you came in and head over to the hostel, no one the wiser."

"We've already been through this, Darren, and we're in," Bruce answered.

I looked at Ricky and then Marc. "I would still like to hear it from you guys." Ricky and

Marc looked each other a moment followed by nods.

"I'm in," Marc said.

"Me, too," Ricky followed.

Beto clapped his hands. "Hot damned!"

"Again, I want to say how grateful we are." I wanted to confirm the compensation arrangement before going further. "Three million dollars sounds like a lot of money to a young guy, I know, but it takes a potful of courage to step up like you have, money or no. Any questions?"

"Well, as long as we have time to kill, I'd really like to hear the story of how you got into the toot business," Bruce said.

I saw Marc's jaw drop in surprise. "Good God, Bruce."

"It's okay, Marc," I said, "What the hell. I guess we don't have many secrets at this point."

Actually, keeping these amateurs' minds occupied struck me as a good idea. I poured a cup of coffee and took a sip, holding the cup in silent thought for a moment before beginning.

"Where to begin? Andy and Beto and I have been getting in trouble together since we were just kids. El Tres Musketeers we named ourselves early on."

Despite being nearly paralyzed by fear, the young men were fascinated about what was unfolding. One of New Mexico's wealthiest and most powerful men was disclosing the secret side of his life story. After recounting several tales of his, Beto's, and Andy's encounters, he moved on to more current history.

"Long story short, Beto, Andy, and I bought the El Patio while I was still in law school back east," I continued.

"Let's be accurate, Darren," Beto interrupted. "You bought the El Patio and let Andy and me in as sweat partners. Hell, we couldn't pay our bar tabs there some nights, much less buy the place."

"Okay, that's true. But Andy and Beto worked their butts off and ran the place like a business...no, more like a military operation.

We put the business in a corporation, El Tres Musketeers, Inc. and reported a strong profit the first year we filed a tax return. And then,

Beto got us in a new line of business—a cash business that didn't go through the bar's books.

Beto, this part of the story is yours."

Beto grinned. "Well, I spent some time south of the border. I had family in Acapulco who I went down to visit regularly. One trip, my cousin, Ruben, quietly put me in his truck one day and drove me up in the hills...to his marijuana plot. He asked me if I thought I could sell some of his crop out the back door of El Patio. 'Hell, yes' sez I, and we were in business."

Ricky smiled. "That adds up. When I was in school, everyone knew you could get weed at El Patio. Good shit, too."

"Yep, Ruben delivered genuine Acapulco Gold. The business grew leaps and bounds. Andy and I could pretty much run El Patio in our sleep, so we started building a network. We were careful who we picked for dealers and my job was to, so to speak, keep the wolves away from the door. Between my friends and family, we could share a little mordito—that's a taste of the honey—around with cops and even the judiciary. They became silent partners in the business and never gave us any trouble. You know New Mexico. We have our own way of looking at sin and grass was definitely venial in the Catholic lingo. Looking the other way was both spiritually satisfying and profitable."

I butted in, "I found out how profitable when I came home for Easter of my last year at Harvard. After closing up El Patio the first night I came back, Andy and Beto took me into the office, opened the safe and handed me my share of the take, $20,000."

"Yeah," Andy said. "D-D-Darren even tried not to t-take it. Said he hadn't done, umm, anything to earn it, but we con-con-convinced him that was not cor-cor, uh, right. Without El

Patio, we wouldn't have had a place to st-st-start."

I went on. "El Patio rocked along, pouring out money like a slot machine. We would get together quarterly and split up the dividends from the real business with a check and the distributions from the dope business in cash.

"Then—I'd been practicing law about three years in Santa Fe—Andy called me for a special partners' meeting. Giving me a bit of a preview, he told me Beto had been approached by a Mexican cartel to handle cocaine distribution on this side of the border. I will never forget that night, a real life-changer. I got us a private dining room at the Palace Restaurant off the plaza."

Beto took over. "I had gotten a call from a guy that my cousin Ruben knew in Culiacan. He said that his group could get Colombian cocaine and were looking for partners. Did I want to come down to talk about it? I didn't know shit about cocaine at this point, but I figured what the hell, so I drove down to Juarez and caught a plane to Culiacan.

"These guys were real businessmen. They had already put together truck routes and warehouses. They showed me some of the product, as they termed it. I felt like a bit of a hick. I had heard of it but never seen any. They laid out a few lines and showed me how to roll a bill and snort it. It nearly took my head off. The buzz was something else. But what really got my attention was when they told me it was selling in Los Angeles for over a hundred bucks a gram.

Another group was handling that distribution."

"So," I cut back in, "we meet at the Palace and Beto brings us up to speed on all of this.

We can have New Mexico if we want it, but the kicker was that a "good faith deposit" of a hundred grand was required to seal the deal.

"We didn't even have a drink, as I recall. This was a serious proposition. We talked back and forth for hours. Weighed the pros and cons. Andy had reached out to some of his buddies in L.A. for intelligence. They confirmed everything the cartel said about the demand and profitability. We learned that a couple of the key guys had bought mansions in Beverly Hills and Ferraris.

"At the same time, stories about the ruthlessness of these guys were getting around.

Evidently one of their partners got sideways with them and turned up in a gully, and...well, let's just say he didn't die an easy death. That bothered me because Andy and Beto were going to be on the front line, not me, so I wanted them to be damned sure."

I poured myself another coffee and paused for a minute, thinking back to that conversation. "We had been at it for hours when Beto turned to me and spoke softly. I will never forget Beto's face and the words he said, quote:

'Darren, you have no idea what Andy and I have done and are capable of doing. We don't talk about 'Nam because it's just shit we don't want to remember. But, also, because we were in situations where it was kill or be killed and you or nobody else needs to know about those times except Andy and me. But believe me when I say we can take care of ourselves.'" I was watching Beto, and he seemed okay, so I kept going.

"Beto had never spoken to me this way. When I had asked about their time in Southeast Asia, they told me that it was a long vacation with the best dope and sex in the world. Andy even allowed as how he felt bad taking the government's money. But now, all the joking was over. Let me just say that they convinced me that they could take care of themselves in any situation. And, you have to admit, the last few days have borne that judgment out. Our Mexican brethren have had more than their hands full with Andy and Beto." I beamed at them—Beto smiled back broadly, and Andy just looked down, checking out his shoes.

"My other concern was the law. Grass was kind of innocuous in New Mexico, but I wasn't sure that cocaine was going to get the same hall pass. Long story short, we voted like we always did, thumbs up or down. And with three thumbs up, we were in the cocaine business. I already had a name picked out—Cerberus, the three-headed dog from hell."

Beto interrupted, "You know, Dare, I'll bet, tonight, Guzman thinks our business name is a pretty goddamned good fit. What do you think?" Beto got the laugh from the group that he was after and, in the break, Andy stood to speak.

"Here's, uh, here's where our m-m-mentor, Darren, started teaching Beto and me some lessons. He said the hundred grand was okay but we couldn't go back without, ummm, negotiating, so we had Beto tell them that we were in if we got New Mexico and Arizona. They, uh, said 'si'."

"So," Marc asked "these are the same guys that are screwing you over now?"

"Aa-ah—aaah," I said, raising my right pointer finger in correction, "trying to screw us over.

Thanks to the three of you, well, we'll see how it comes out,."

Andy took over, telling how the business was built. I was extremely proud of him. It was not his way to speak much, but I believe he could tell his audience was intrigued and knew from years of leading innocents into battle that it was good to keep their minds off of what was coming.

He explained how he had worked with the cartel convincing them to bind the packages in one-pound blocks, shrink-wrapped in plastic. Transportation of choice was almost always by small, over-wing aircraft that could fly below radar and land and takeoff from short dirt fields. Pilots were recruited from the ranks of Viet Nam vets looking to make a good chunk of change in a short period of time and then get out (though most of them didn't until they crashed at least one plane). Flights were generally planned in two legs: the first a hop from Colombia to Central Mexico and the next from there to some remote area just north of the U.S. border in New Mexico or Arizona. Landing fields were bulldozed into the desert, abandoned and new fields created regularly. All landings were at night, the makeshift strips lit by bonfires and the headlights of waiting cartel employees, heavily armed men there to make sure things went off without a hitch. A high percentage ended in crashes, which was thought of by the cartel as just another cost of doing business.

I enjoyed watching our three newcomers intensely listening to Andy. But then, how many people get the building of a cocaine empire explained to them by one of the architects. He went on. The coke was moved from the transport plane into a waiting Cerberus van, the money counted by the cartel agent and, then, given to the pilot. In the first years, the pilot returned the

U.S. dollars to Colombia, but with sophistication, the cartels bought banks in Miami and established routes to get the money to El Paso and then on to Miami. The little planes took off into the night, the vans roared off with the blocks of coke to processing centers located outside Tucson and Las Cruces, and the bonfires eventually burned out.

Andy went on. Processing stateside consisted of preparing the coke for street delivery and repackaging for shipment. The one-pound blocks of pure cocaine, solid bricks from the Colombian labs, were first ground into fine powder in an industrial grinder, configured with dust retention vacuums to prevent the escape of any of the precious material. The coke was then cut, in Cerberus case, and mixed with an equal amount of powder. The result, street coke, and the Cerberus coke at 50% pure, had the reputation of the best on the street anywhere. The mix was readied using sophisticated packaging equipment; the end result, one-pound rectangular blocks that were then hermetically sealed in plastic wrappers and ready for the next step in the distribution chain.

"But Darren's business genius was—you know—what really made us run like a Swiss watch," Andy interjected. "He created a simple but effective p-p-pyramid system. At the, um, highest level we have, er, "P-P-Poundmen". Um, there are four, one in each terri-territory: Albuquer-quer-que, Santa Fe, Phoenix, and Tucson, all hand-picked by, uh, me. We, kind of, established delivery schedules for each area based on how much blow is moved. The Poundmen s-s-send the cash back to 'Home Office'—exchanged for each pound, uh, received."

I would have bet a lot of money that Andy would never do a lecture like this, but he continued. "Sixteen Ouncemen report to each Poundman. Ummm, and so the Ouncemen are recruited by the Poundmen, but vetted carefully by us. Poundmen divide the pounds, uh, into sixteen one-ounce bags. Like the level above them, the Ouncemen, ummm, deliver cash to the Poundmen with each cycle."

Beto jumped in. "Ouncemen maintain their own dealer networks. This is where the rubber meets the road—the product gets into the hands...and ultimately noses...of the consumer. Again, as with the Poundmen, the Ouncemen measure out nineteen individual grams from each ounce of coke, bagging the 'individual servings' in paper envelopes, universally recognized packaging by all blow users. Heck, you may have seen some of our product?" he asked with a wry smile looking at the young men quizzically.

Well, you know, while delivering the blow to the dealers and collecting cash is their first job, er, Ouncemen also are responsible to make sure their dealers understand that should they decide to cut the product, they would be caught and, shall we say, enforcement action invoked. We had one unfortunate episode, but the punishment example has stuck," Beto clammed up realizing this last explanation was probably not the best timing.

I stood. "Do you guys need a facility? Just down the hall there."

After the break, everyone returned to the table. They noticed that Beto had gone upstairs for a while and couldn't help but wonder what he had done—yet, not really wanting to know.

"So, Ricky, I understand your family was sort of pioneers around this area?" I asked.

"Yeah, I guess we sort of are pioneers. My great-grandfather came to Telluride in 1878 for the silver mining, and we've been around ever since."

I immediately liked Ricky's style. He spoke softly and slowly. He recounted the family lore that he had heard his whole life. "The first of the story that we know for sure is that his daddy, Nathaniel, was one of the original Forty-Niners. Supposedly, he had been a teenager working on the family farm in Pennsylvania and struck out to California with his best friend. Since there aren't any California banks with my family name, he obviously didn't hit the lode."

"So then, after that what do you know?" I asked. Keeping these guys talking has got to be a good thing, I figured.

"We don't have good family genealogy. We keep talking about having one done, but you know how those things are. The family story is that Nathaniel married and had six or seven kids but only two lived, one of which was my great-grandfather, Leo. Moving back eastward, evidently, they worked mining claims in Nevada and Northern Colorado and finally settled up around Grand Junction. From what we know, the family had had enough of moving around, but Leo was drawn to the silver in Telluride."

"The rest of the story, we have pretty good records. Leo married an Ouray girl and they had six kids, one of them my grandpa, Matthew Gydeson.

With the local knowledge of his father's forty years traipsing the Umpanaghre and San Juan wilderness areas, Grandpa became a highly reputed hunting and fishing guide. When he was really young, he built a client base of wealthy Easterners. Then, when he started slowing down physically, set up Jeep rental and tour companies in Durango and Silverton."

"Your dad didn't take to the business? By the way, I have had cases with him and hold him in high regard."

Ricky didn't miss the fact that there was some high irony in this drug lord complimenting

Ricky's father on his ethics.

"Thanks. No, Dad was not taken by the outdoors. As a kid, he loved reading and things orderly, so law school was a logical choice for him after college. He got his law degree from the University of Colorado and set up his law practice in northwestern New Mexico."

"So, how did you get so into the outdoors?" I asked, exercising my genuine interest in people. Downright nosey some people say.

"I spent every possible minute with Grandpa Matt. We were inseparable in the summers. By the time I was sixteen, I was supposedly working for Grandpa at the Jeep rental business. But most of the time I was off in the mountains on three- and four-day hiking trips around Ouray, Silverton, and Telluride by myself. Grandpa and I had a deal that we didn't talk about my summer adventures so as not to worry Mom and Dad."

"So that's how you learned about the secret way into Telluride?" Beto asked.

"Earlier. I must have been about ten when Grandpa took me through the old shaft.

Seeing him pack a flashlight for a day hike, I was curious and asked him why. He told me to hang on to my hat; that I was in for an adventure. And he wasn't exaggerating. To this day, I remember how my skin crawled walking through the shaft listening to creatures scratching around us, the air smelling yucky, and water dripping constantly on us from the ceiling. The only thing that got me through was holding on to my grandpa's hand, and even so, I was really glad when we came out the other side into the sun. After that, it was our special secret and we hiked it every year until Grandpa couldn't...and then I just did it on my own."

"Well, I'm tickled as shit that your grandpa knew about it and showed you," Beto said.

Ricky glared at Bruce. "And that one of us has a big mouth," he said and punched Bruce in the arm.

That brought a badly needed laugh from the group. I said, "Yes, and thank goodness for that, too. And, Marc, are you a mountain man as well?"

"Not hardly. The only night I ever spent in the mountains before meeting Ricky was at a golf resort in Vail. Definitely not an Eagle Scout. But first year of law school, Ricky talked about his beloved mountains and Lake Vallecito so much that Bruce got hooked. The two of them started planning the First Annual Monster Mountain Trek. The thought of living in the woods for over a week scared hell out of me, but I didn't want to be left out, so I finally jumped on the train."

Marc told how they had alternated weekends; one weekend dedicated to shopping trips led by Ricky to get Bruce and Marc properly equipped, and the alternating weekend for training hikes up the face of the Sandia Mountains to the Crest. Though both Bruce and Marc were former athletes in reasonably good condition, the first few hikes nearly killed them. The vertical elevation change of over three thousand feet over the sixteen-mile hike carrying a fifty-pound pack wore out their legs and, totally winded, required numerous resting breaks. Marc smiled telling how Ricky never slowed once, striding at the same steady pace from the bottom to the Crest while he was sweating profusely and his heart pounding. By the fourth hike, however, Bruce and Marc were getting conditioned, and all three marched to the Crest together.

"And now I love it. This year, I couldn't wait to get back up here."

Smiling with understanding, I asked, "These mountains have a way of getting to you, eh?' "So it doesn't sound like any of you guys wasted your life getting your ass kicked by a jackass sergeant and sleeping in a pup tent?" Beto asked.

All three shook their heads.

Ricky spoke. "All three of us had student deferments and then drew lucky lottery numbers. Bruce told us coming over that you two spent a lot of time in 'Nam."

Marc kept quiet. He had drawn a low number, 110, but his grandfather was a doctor and friends with cronies on the draft board. He carried a 4F classification somehow.

"Yeah, in Viet Nam and some other places we officially never saw," Beto said, smiling broadly.

Ricky said, "It always makes me feel like a shit when I meet a vet, like you guys carried the load for me."

Andy stood up and, putting his hand on Ricky's shoulder, said, "You-you-you shouldn't ever feel that way. I don't. It was just a, um, mess and, for me, I'm glad every —uh, uh, one of you guys didn't have to be there. Beto and-and I got out okay... and that's saying a lot more than a lot of p-people we knew."

"I have never understood this Viet Nam guilt you guys that didn't go seem to come down with?" Beto asked.

"I have thought about this for years and even talked to a couple of my buddies who went and got home, mostly in one piece," Ricky said. "It's not that I've changed my mind about the war. I protested against it then and still think our politicians made horrible decisions. What bothers me the most is how you guys have been treated since you came home. I never even considered participating in some of the antics the hard-core resisters set up to shame vets when they came home. I thought they were wrong. But I also never did anything in support of the vets. It's complicated."

"Do you guys feel that way?" Beto asked Marc and Bruce.

"I couldn't have said it better," Bruce replied.

"For me, it wasn't just that I hated the war. Frankly, I was scared shitless," Marc answered. "I didn't worry about getting killed so much as turning chicken when things got bad. I'm not proud of it, but that's how I felt."

"Hell, Marc, that's called good sense, not cowardice," Beto said. "Those of us, like Andy and me, probably should have been in institutions but they needed us to do the crazy shit. I have zero resentment for the guys that didn't go. Hell, I'd go so far as to say that if Darren had tried to sign up, Andy and I would have come home, kidnapped him and locked him up somewhere."

"I'm glad we had this talk," I said, glad that the conversation had happened but also wanting to move away from the topic on a high note. "I can tell you that Andy and Beto have told me how they feel over and over, but I still am troubled by the 'Viet Nam Guilts'. From what I can tell, the guys that have grudges are the guys that are still back in 'Nam in their heads and just can't let go."

"You hit the nail on the head, partner," Beto said.

I gauged the comfort level in the room to be as good as I could have hoped for. Andy and Beto radiate confidence, which I think our young associates pick up on. So, I moved the conversation to small talk and the time passed easily as we exchanged stories.

Ricky described to Andy and Beto the route, and answered their questions about terrain, visibility and other tactical issues as best he could for an amateur. We decided that we were going to "begin the operation", as Andy put it, at midnight. I checked my watch absently, the hands seeming to be frozen. But eventually, the big hand and the little hand lined up on the twelve.

CHAPTER 8

FRIDAY, MAY 26

"It's time. Okay, men, let's get this thing done," I said standing briskly and leading the group downstairs to the vault.

Andy swung the vault door open and our three law students peered inside. I almost laughed out loud at the look on their faces. Their jaws dropped and they could not take their eyes off the stacks of money and white blocks of cocaine. Marc spoke first. "Is all of that going to fit into seven backpacks?"

"It will, with a little room to spare," I answered. "But they're going to be heavy—eighty pounds or so. Marc, if you hadn't come, we would have had to leave some of the coke behind."

Andy lined the seven backpacks up against the wall next to the vault door, and he and Beto began sorting the blocks of coke and cash into them. Within minutes, the vault contents were transferred to the waiting backpacks. My calculations had, thank goodness, been right: all of it fit snugly into the backpacks.

I addressed an envelope "To Lang" and taped it to the doorjamb of the vault; turned and spoke to Andy and Beto. "You guys get Paul. Stretch his legs and get him ready to roll."

And then to Bruce. "How are you three doing? You ready?"

"No doubt," Bruce answered without pause. I glanced at Ricky and Marc and wasn't so sure. We each grabbed a loaded backpack—Andy grabbed two—and proceeded upstairs.

"Everybody hit the head for a protective piss before we roll," I cautioned and then disappeared into Marta's room. Andy and Beto followed me in, closing the door.

Beto said, "The son of a bitch is no fucking use to us and may be trouble. I say we leave him here...dead."

"I told you already that I am not ready to make that call, yet, and that's the end of the discussion," I said. "Besides we need him as a pack mule."

Beto was getting worked up and opened his mouth to speak again, but was cut off by Andy. "D-Darren, you need to know that I'm with Beto on this one. He's done us enough d-d- damage, and I don't want to give him a, ummmm, chance to do more."

"Fine. I hear both of you, but I am pulling rank. Bundle him up. He's coming with us and that's the end of it. Or would you rather leave six mil in coke behind?"

I swung the door open and burst out. Despite my every effort at control, I could feel my face white with anger. I had never been so totally pissed off in my life. Was it because Andy and Beto defied me? Or because I was so wrong about Paul? Or—this possibility bothered me the most—I knew Beto and Andy were right but just couldn't take the needed step?

Marc and Bruce were standing in the hall waiting for the restroom. The look on their faces told me instantly that they had overheard every word of the argument. *Well, welcome to the family, kids, and all its dirty linen.*

I pushed by Marc and Bruce, glaring wordlessly, but stopped at the end of the hall when I heard the bedroom door open. Beto shoved Paul through the doorway, stumbling, and Marc gasped involuntarily. Paul's left eye was swollen shut and a cut over his right eye was covered with dark brown clotted blood. His clothes were splattered with blood, wrinkled and torn; his shoulders slumped in defeat. Marc and Bruce backed up against the wall as Beto shoved Paul by them.

"Listen, you sorry asshole, if it were up to me, you'd be in the meat locker with your comrades. But Darren has other ideas and he's the boss. We're taking you with us. One fuck up, though, and..." With that, Beto pulled his KA-BAR knife out of its sheath and held it to Paul's throat.

"Have you got that?"

Paul nodded slightly just as Ricky stepped out of the restroom and recoiled from the sight of a horribly bloodied man with Beto holding a knife to his throat. I saw the look on Marc's face and realized that, for him at least, all of our *cumbaya* goodwill had quickly disappeared. I suspected that the deal was over. Andy stood in the doorway at the end of the hall and our eyes met, judgment in his.

"We'll leave the three of you to talk," I said. "I'll restate my offer; I'll have Beto escort you out so you can go to the hostel—no hard feelings. But once we leave here, there is no turning back. Is that understood?"

$\backsim$

Minutes passed, some of the longest minutes of my life. Andy, Beto and I sat on the couches, in the dark, in the great room speculating on our next move, assuming, as we all surmised, we were going to be on our own. We couldn't hear the words coming from the hall, but it was a spirited discussion. And then silence and Marc rounded the corner with Bruce and

Ricky in tow. Marc looked at me and said, "Darren, we're in. All three of us—unanimous." Ricky and Bruce nodded their agreement. Silence reigned as we all now shared a common fate. Andy spoke up, "We will get you home safely." I sensed that the simple words from the big man had a powerful effect on us all.

As for me, I just watched and smiled to myself thinking it was probably fortuitous for The Three Musketeers that our three rescuers had seen all that money in the vault. Maybe a bit cynical, but then, we are all coin-operated. I made one final call to let Billy know that all had gone as planned to this point and that we were getting ready to exit.

"Billy sends his best. Says he will see us in a few hours."

$\backsim$

We circled up around Andy in the kitchen while he did a quick final run through. I watched Marc, Ricky and Bruce trying to listen, but they kept stealing glances at Paul who was starting to look stronger but still covered with blood. "All eyes on me after we leave here. I will take the lead and give you clear commands. You follow them. We've got a critical half hour or so and then we're cool. Beto is going to bring up the rear."

Beto had told me many times that when Andy was in command and needed to communicate clearly, his speech issues disappeared. As Beto predicted, there was no evidence of his halting speech. He was in charge. He began to quietly open the window...

I heard SPLAT. SPLAT. SPLAT from the great room, and then cracking glass!

"Get down," Andy ordered, somewhat unnecessarily as everyone but he and Beto had already dived for the floor. When I looked up in no more than a second or two, Beto was crouched on one side of the kitchen door with his weapon aimed into the great room; Andy, standing on the other side of the door, his arm swinging, sweeping the pistol from one side of the room to the other and back.

Minutes, each seeming to be an hour, passed in silence.

"Paul, if you move a muscle, I will put a bullet between your eyes," Andy warned. "Darren, they've shot the glass out of the front doo..."

And the telephone rang, causing even Beto and Andy to react. After a half-dozen rings, I rose carefully and answered it. "Darren, here."

"Hey, old buddy, are ya' need'in to change your drawers?" Lang said, genuinely laughing.

"What the fuck, Lang. We have a deal," I said indignantly.

"Yeah, yeah, yeah. We'll see you in the morning. I di'n't like how dark an' quiet it was up yore way. We just wanted to leave you a li'l reminder 'at we're still around." Then, he laughed and hung up.

Feeling a room full of eyes on me, I put the phone back in the cradle. "That was the good sheriff. He said he just wanted to give us a wake-up call a little early." "What do you guys think?" I asked.

"I don't know for sure, but I'd say that if they were really coming after us, they wouldn't have stopped with three bullets," Andy replied.

Beto chimed in, "I agree with Andy. He's just fuckin' with us...I think." "So," I asked, "just lucky timing when we were heading out?"

"Only one way to find out. You guys keep your heads down until I get back." Andy rolled through the breakfast nook window into the darkness. Beto pointed his weapon at Paul menacingly, then, turned and assumed a firing position through the open sash. My new young friends and I could do nothing but lay on the floor and exchange worried looks and wait.

Beto slipped out of the way, and Andy rolled back inside. Speaking softly, "The coast is clear, guys. Never a better time than right now," then giving us no time to think, went back out through the opening, pulling Paul through with him. I followed Andy's lead, with Bruce, Marc and Ricky close behind. Beto handed the packs out to each of us and then, silently slid through the window himself.

Andy paused holding up his hand, I figured to allow our eyes to adjust to the darkness and our ears to the quiet. Though it wasn't that cold, I couldn't stop shivering. After a bit, Andy raised his hand higher and, palm flat, axed the air and led the group back on the course they had just followed hours before. We swiftly climbed the steep rock outcropping behind the house to be swallowed up by a stand of welcoming pines. The relief I felt at getting out of the house passed quickly as I became certain that gunmen were behind every tree.

And then, my fears were confirmed. The sound of limbs crashing to our right was followed immediately by a dark shape leaping from behind a tree. As I dove to the ground, I saw the flash of a gun behind me and heard the muffled "phttt" from a silencer; then the whiz of the bullet followed by contact and a strangled gurgle. When I summoned the courage to look up, I saw the dark shape fall to the ground.

Beto, in a forced whisper, said, "Sorry, guys. Everybody stay cool. It was just a deer."

The animal struggled on the ground, twitching, until Beto took two quick strides and, holding the young buck by an antler, slit its throat and ended its misery.

With his foot on Paul's back holding him down, I could barely see Andy as he held his pointer finger over his lips signaling silence as we all pulled ourselves up off the ground, brushing pine needles and dirt away. We stood motionless; all ears trained to see if we could catch any sign that we had been discovered.

Andy put his arm around my head, pulling my ear to his mouth. "How are you, Dare? You okay?" he whispered softly. He held me there for seconds, somehow transferring his solid calmness to me.

"Yeah, I'm fine, Andy," I whispered back. "You ready to roll?"

"You bet," I said softly. "Let's get this thing done."

Andy moved on to Marc and Ricky and then Bruce, in the same quietly confident way, whispering and encouraging, before taking his lead position. He looked back to see that we were all lined-up and Beto in place bringing up the rear. Then, he held his hand up and motioned us forward again.

The calm Andy had engendered in me quickly passed, to be replaced by a royal bout of nerves. I thought back to my conversation with him not much over an hour ago, talking about how I loved risk. *I am not loving this. I have had enough risk to last me a lifetime.* And we are a long way from safety. Once we leave the cover of the little wood patch, the only way to get to our escape vehicle is to walk down a series of residential streets where we will be totally exposed. While Andy assured us that there was no reason for Lang's men to be looking for us, I just kept thinking *sometimes bad luck just happens.*

As we passed the first houses, two dogs began to bark. To me, it sounded like *HERE— THEY—ARE, COME—AND—GET THEM.* But we continued down the street and the dogs quieted. Thankfully, all of the houses were darkened, either not yet occupied for summer, or the occupants long asleep, the only lighted area being one streetlight on Bill's corner.

The rest of the walk to Bill's house went without incident. Had one of Lang's patrols run into us during this phase, we would have been ruined. I noticed Andy keeping a close eye on Marc. Even though the night was chilly, Marc was clearly terrified. His shirt was soaked with sweat, and he periodically spit dryly. I wondered if being positioned in the middle of the line of marchers was the only thing that kept him from running away into the safeness of the dark woods. *And who could blame him?*

Andy quietly slid the side door of the van open, shoved Paul roughly into the back of the vehicle, and climbed in. As always, Beto climbed in behind the steering wheel to drive, while I took the front passenger seat. Bruce and Ricky took chairs next to Andy, while Marc crawled all the way to the back where Paul was laying, now hand cuffed. Backpacks holding the net worth of some countries lay on the floor.

Beto cranked the engine. "Shit" I swore softly; it sounded like a jet taking off in the quiet of the mountain town night. He backed the van out and headed west through the deserted Telluride streets, winding around to the left and then right onto Tomboy Pass Road. I thought if our good luck holds, we will be at the jumping off point in a matter of minutes.

It did not. After traveling a mile up Tomboy Road, we came around a corner only to meet a pair of headlights coming in our direction. "Fuck, gum ball machines," Beto swore as the lights on top of the vehicle stood out. As the vehicle, a Blazer, came alongside, it was easy to see the distinctive black and white markings of the sheriff's department. The two vehicles passed each other, each going about twenty-five miles an hour. Beto watched in the side rear-view mirror as the cruiser pulled by. I sneaked a peek out the van's rear window. For a moment the thought that we might be in the clear filled the van with euphoric hope, but then the Blazer's flashing lights sprang on as the driver threw a hard U-turn and accelerated rapidly toward us.

"Flashing lights, what the fuck?" Beto said loudly. "At least we got a rookie behind us."

Beto tromped on the accelerator pedal and the van sprang forward. I looked through the back window to see the blinding cloud of dust we were throwing behind us. Andy signaled Bruce and Ricky to get down. Paul was already handcuffed on the floor in the back, Marc next to him.

Andy opened the side door window while pulling his Walther out of its holster. He had just extended the gun through the window frame when the rear window exploded raining glass shards inside the van. Marc let out a yelp and Ricky shouted to the back, "Marc, you okay?"

"Yeah, yeah...the glass just stung. I'm fine," Marc yelled over the screaming engine and gravel cracking the bottom of the van.

When I turned my attention back in front of us, my heart nearly stopped. We were screaming toward blackness, when Beto put the van in a power slide at sixty miles negotiating the hairpin corner perfectly. I turned back again just in time to see the Blazer, framed through the shattered glass of the back window, as it failed to make the corner. It crashed through an embankment which launched it skyward before it slammed into the ground nose-first, sending it tumbling end over end, the emergency lights creating an eerie scene of flashing red strobes spinning wildly through the dust storm it had created.

Beto slowed the van when he spotted the police cruiser crashing through the brush in the rear-view mirror, clearly no longer a threat. I turned around, "everybody okay back there?" I asked. The tangle of arms and legs unwound and slowly returned upright to the van's seats. "Bruce?"

"Yeah, I'm fine. Marc, you and Ricky okay?" "I'm good."

"Me, too," Marc was able to utter, though none too convincingly.

"I'm not. I am bleeding all over the place," Paul whined, curled up in a ball on the floor, his hands cuffed behind his back.

"Yeah, well, we weren't asking about you, asshole," Beto responded. "What do you think,

Dare? Was the dumb shit smart enough to get off a call before he came after us?"

I shook my head. "We'll know pretty soon, won't we, buddy."

Now more than ever the mission had become a race against time. We had to assume that the deputy had gotten out an alert and that other cruisers were headed our way. I figured that we only had to cover three miles on Tomboy Road in the van before we'd be at the spot where we could abandon the vehicle and begin the trek cross-country. Once into the woods on the other side of the San Miguel River, we would be hard to catch.

Beto covered the distance in less than five minutes, driving on the very edge of out-of- control. I watched Beto hit brake, clutch and accelerator pedals at a furious pace, while sometimes turning the steering wheel fractions and, at other times, whipping it wildly, a magician hurdling the van up the twisting dirt lane.

I yelled into the back of the van, "Ricky, you'd better get up here. I think we're close to the spot you pointed out on the map."

I saw that he was looking out into the darkness, finding milestones along the way. "Now, Beto, now!"

With that, Beto slammed on the brakes and the van nosed down and slid sideways across the road in a beautifully executed telemark turn, the van stopping perpendicular to the roadway with the rear doors facing the river. Though I was forcefully slammed into the side of the van, it didn't hurt—*interesting stuff, this adrenaline.*

"Let's go, let's go, we've got to get out of here," Andy yelled. Doors sprang open and I raced around the back of the van to claim a pack. Beto yanked Paul out of the van. He winced and let out a cry of pain. "Not one peep, mother fucker. And you better move your ass or I swear to God, I will take immense pleasure in cutting your throat." With that, he spun Paul around and hung the straps of the backpack over his shoulders.

Beto froze. "Listen!" In the momentary silence, the sound of car tires sliding on gravel rang out and seconds later headlight beams appeared careening around the corner. The car, another deputy department Blazer, slid to a stop in a thick cloud of dust, the rear end slinging around so the car ended up pointed across the road fifty yards from the van. As the dust cleared, the passenger and driver, visible momentarily, had disappeared.

"Stay behind the van!" Andy ordered as all of us but he and Beto had already scrambled for the cover. Beto positioned himself behind the front of the van, Andy at the back, both with their weapons drawn. Shots came from the direction of our attackers and the van's windshield shattered. I pressed myself as close to the van as another coat of paint, my legs shaking uncontrollably, my heart reverberating off the sheet metal. Strangely, I heard Andy in my head from just a few hours ago saying, "Darren, why do you do this?"

"Fuck, Andy, these guys know what they're doing." Beto said, ducking behind the van. At that moment, bullets struck the ground under the van and ricocheted into the undercarriage.

Out of the corner of my eye, I saw Andy give Beto hand signals. He pulled his other Walther out of its holster and stepped out from behind the van. He walked steadily—I heard the slow rhythmic crunching of gravel—with both pistols returning fire toward the enemy. At that same moment, Beto stepped out from behind the van and unloaded a clip from his Walther. I could hear Andy's rounds crashing glass, pinging off metal, and finally an agonizing scream from the direction of our attackers. Beto continued to exchange fire with the remaining attacker. Then, Andy reappeared, crawling behind the van holding his stomach while forcing a clip into his pistol.

Bruce and I pulled him over to us, when, Marc rose, took Andy's pistol out of his hand and, in a flash, ran around the van. With a blood-curdling scream, he ran toward the enemy firing round after round. Marc's attack was too much, and the remaining attacker turned to run, only to be cut down by Beto's fire.

Beto signaled for Marc to get down, but he stood frozen in the road. Beto crept behind the police car, his pistol drawn at ready. "They're both down!" he yelled and, running back toward the van, grabbed the gun out of Marc's hand and pulled him along.

Marc shuffled with him and in a trancelike voice said, "Thank you, Beto."

∽

"Let's go troops--let's go! We've got to get the fuck out of here. NOW." Beto shouted, and then he saw Andy propped up on the van holding his guts, blood on his hands. "Beto, get me bandaged and on my feet."

"Get your packs on, all of you. Darren, here's a gun. You're in charge of Paul," Beto ordered handing me the weapon.

Beto found a T-shirt in the van and began ripping it into pieces, which he laid in a pile. One by one, he wrapped them around Andy's wound. Andy winced only once when Beto wrapped the bandaged area with his belt and pulled it in tightly. Field dressings applied, Beto helped Andy to his feet.

"Hand me that pack," Andy ordered.

"No way, you stubborn asshole, we'll carry the pack," Beto said in Andy's face.

Andy gritted his teeth. "Beto, put the goddamned pack on my back and let's get going."

Andy turned his back to Beto, who then grabbed a pack and slipped the shoulder straps over Andy's shoulders. "Ricky, you're our guy. Lead on and we'll follow," Andy said through gritted teeth.

Ricky didn't hesitate, wanting more than anything to get off the road and up into the mountains. He took off down the embankment by the road with all of us following behind. Bruce dropped into the back slot. As he passed Paul, he smacked him in the back of the head. "Give me a reason, you sorry sack of shit, and I will take you down before you know what hit you."

Now, that was interesting, I thought. *Bruce seems to take to this a little too easily.*

Beto came alongside. "I'm going to get rid of the van, and then I'll catch up. I don't want Lang's boys to find it." Minutes later, I heard the engine roar to life and , a short while later, heard the van crashing down the valley wall, finally settling far below us. Ricky stopped, so I explained, "no worries, just Beto taking care of business," and we continued walking. A few minutes more and Beto returned breathing heavily. "I rubbed out the tracks on the side of the road where the van went over. They won't find it—at least for a while." Smart boy, my Beto. He relieved me of the weapon I was holding and resumed guard duties on Paul, as we trudged on following Ricky up the dark trail.

We had been steady at it for about an hour when Beto called a halt. "Let's take a break," Beto said, though Andy grumbled through gritted teeth that we needed to keep going.

If Beto hadn't called for the break, I was going to. I'm in reasonably good shape, but I'm not accustomed to hiking with eighty pounds on my back. My legs were getting damned wobbly, and, for the life of me, I don't know where Andy gets his strength.

I had just wrestled the pack off my back and sat on the ground next to Andy when Beto said, "Hush," and signaled all of us to be quiet. As I listened, I became aware that the thunder and lightning had stopped, but the wind was whistling noisily through the tops of the pines.

From far off, I heard something, but I couldn't name it. Beto did. "Fuck me, Lang's goddamned dogs from hell." It didn't take but a minute for the barking and howling, though still far off, to become clear enough to confirm Beto's alarm.

"On your feet, men! We're in a race now. Ricky, how much longer to the tunnel?" Beto asked.

"An hour...maybe a little less," Ricky responded.

We all quickly replaced our backpacks, Beto helping Andy get into his, and resumed the climb with heightened urgency. Nothing like a shot of adrenaline to make the tiredness disappear. But how long can we hold out with just adrenaline? Especially Andy? The sky was clear, now, and the moonlight provided just enough light to make out our shifting outlines.

We had been hard at it for maybe fifteen minutes. The sound of the pack of dogs, at first sporadic, was now constant...and louder. Not thinking particularly well, it took me a while to figure out that they were gaining on us because the dogs' handlers weren't carrying heavy backpacks. I could visualize the dogs pulling along their trainers, lurching along much faster than we could walk, even with the dogs having to stop occasionally and test the scent. The image of Lang wheezing along, stumbling in his cowboy boots almost made me laugh, but that fantasy soon passed, replaced by a truer vision of the fat fuck sitting in his RV up on the road waiting for them to bring us in. That thought got me so revved up, I inadvertently almost ran over Marc before I got myself back under control.

"Ricky, hold on a minute," Beto snapped. We all stopped and Beto herded us into a small huddle.

"I'm going to go back and slow these pendejos down a bit. You guys keep going. I'll find you," Beto said.

"Beto, how in the hell are you going to find us? You stay with us," I said, trying to hide my panic.

"Don't worry, Dare, I'll find you. If I don't do this, Darren, these guys are going to be on us in ten minutes or so. Believe me, I know what I say...and I know what I'm doing. Now, we're fucking wasting time, so you guys get going. I'll be along soon." And with that, Beto leaned his backpack against a boulder, and ran off into the darkness.

"Let's go, men. You heard Beto. We need to keep cranking," Andy spoke in clear words, though through gritted teeth obviously in pain.

Paul started to say something, but Bruce smacked him in the forehead ending that, and we fell in behind Ricky's lead. As we trudged on, my thoughts went to the three young men that had joined us in the middle of this debacle: Ricky's quietly assured leadership; Marc's totally unexpected heroism; and Bruce's toughness. Who would have guessed? I was thinking, when gunshots rang out somewhere below us. The dogs let off loud howls coupled with men yelling. We instinctively stopped, but Andy ordered, "Keep moving. Just Beto doing what Beto does best." We continued on and in silence for a few minutes, when the sound of the howling pack of dogs pursuing us resumed. My heartbeat raced, fearing for Beto.

We had covered maybe another half mile when gunshots erupted again. And, shortly thereafter, the loud howling from the pack (wishful thinking...or are there fewer?), men shouting, and then minutes of silence, before the insistent bay of the hounds resumed, but this time not nearly so close. *Ah, Beto, what have ye wrought? And, then, oh, Darren, what have ye wrought? Andy shot and Beto deep in danger—all because of me.*

～

We waded across a shallow spot in the San Miguel and, Ricky leading, climbed up a steep stretch on the side of the mountain. Though the going was difficult for all of us, Andy kept up, though his breathing was labored. We could still hear the dogs baying, but far below us now. Now, every minute of Beto's absence seemed to reinforce in my mind the truth that he would not return.

"This is it," Ricky announced.

I moved up next to Ricky and asked, "This is what?"

"The old mining roadway. Ricky flashed the light he was carrying down the slope and back up. "The trees and shrubs have grown over it, Darren, but see how flat it is? There's a spot right there"--he flashed the light onto the side of the hill—"where they cut-- and you can see the spoil off the other side"--pointing the light at a pile of rocks that formed the downhill side of the road.

"I'll be damned." I turned to look at Ricky, "If you didn't know what you were looking out, there's no way you would even notice it."

"Yes sir, I guess that's why it's still such a secret." Ricky pulled back a thick tangle of brush and vine and shone the light on the walls of the tunnel inside.

"I'll be damned. You'd have to literally fall into it before you would know it was there," I said. "Let's have a quick rest here before we go in—enjoy the fresh air." And, though I didn't say it, give Beto one more chance to find us. Now that I had seen it, I knew even Beto couldn't find us once we went through nature's drapery.

Gratefully, we all found places to sit and rest and unburden ourselves of the backpacks that we had lugging for over two hours. Andy was off to the side with Paul. I sat down next to him and handed him the only canteen of water that we had been able to bring. He drank deeply. I put the light on his wound where large spots of red showed through the makeshift bandages.

Andy had read my thoughts. "He'll be here. Don't worry, Darren. You know how the little dude likes drama."

And, before I could reply, we all spun toward a voice coming out of the dark on the path behind us. "What? Are you girls tired?"

I shined the light at the voice and was never so happy in my life to see, shining back in its beam, Beto's gleaming teeth. Andy jumped to his feet, along with the rest of us, and swarmed Beto. "You, okay, man? You okay?"

"Hell, yeah. I'm fine. I had me some fun down there, did you hear?" Beto said laughing.

"God, Beto, we sure heard. No doubt, you saved our bacon—again," I said, tucking him under my arm. "I am never--never, letting you out of my sight again, though."

The dogs bayed again, but somewhere far below us.

"I felt bad about shooting a couple of the dogs; the penche cabrones—not so much. So, why are you resting? How far to go?"

"We're here, Beto," and shined the light on the over-brush covering the portal. "That's our escape, right there. We were just waiting for you to show up, late as usual."

"Son of a bitch. We made it," was all he said.

We decided to stay outside in the fresh mountain air a few more minutes. The clouds had cleared, the moon now providing enough light to clearly see each other. However, with the sound of the pack getting closer, we rose to enter the tunnel.

I had been watching Marc lying on his back staring at the sky. He hadn't said a word since the shootout. Bruce was standing over with his arm extended. "Give you a lift?" And he pulled Marc up. "That was an impressive piece of work you did tonight. What in hell were you thinking?"

"You know, Bruce, truthfully I wasn't thinking. I don't know how else to explain it. I just remember seeing what needed to be done and knowing I had to do it. If I'd thought for a second, I probably would have frozen. I just acted."

"Well, I'm sure glad you did, man. You know why?" "Why?"

"We...are...rich mothers, man. Rich, rich, rich!"

"My mom used to warn me about counting chickens, Bruce. We aren't out of this yet."

"Sure we are, little big man, the rest of this is a cake walk."

We all passed through the leafy curtain and into the chamber lighted only by our flashlights. Ricky shined his light down the tunnel, revealing the sundry broken parts of the old narrow-gauge rails between the shaft walls. I whistled. "Thank our lucky stars for this old shaft. We'd be toast without it. That, and you guys," I said to our three rescuers.

The feeling of relief was palpable. We helped one another remove our backpacks. A celebration broke out, hand shaking, back-slapping, and even hugging. All participated but Paul, who sat quietly against the wall of the tunnel.

"Can you believe it, man, we pulled if off!" Beto said slapping my back.

"I just wish I could see Jorge's face when he opens that note," I said.

"We did it. We fucking did it. Yahooo!" Beto's joy could not be contained.

The celebration was short-lived though as Andy's knees buckled and he fell heavily to the ground. As Beto rolled him over on his back and helped him stretch out, I put a pack under his head.

Weakly, Andy said, "I'll be fine in a bit. Just let me rest and then I'll be ready to go," before drifting into unconsciousness.

Beto and I took all the cocaine blocks out of the packs. I located a recessed area in the mine wall and we stacked the cocaine deep in the hole. Once it was all stashed away, I stood and, wiping my hands together, said to Beto, "it's going to feel weird leaving it here, but if you really think about it, there can hardly be a safer place on the planet."

"I've been thinking, Beto, worse case, we can leave Andy here and go into Durango and get a litter to carry him out." I spoke softly, not wanting the others to hear my thoughts.

"I can almost guarantee you that when the sun comes up, Andy's going to stand up and walk down this mountain. But, in case

I'm wrong, it's cool that you are thinking of alternatives— as usual," Beto answered.

I turned facing the group. "Let's rest in here until sunrise. It doesn't make sense to risk walking down the mountain in the dark. It would be a hell of a note if, after all of this, one of us went over a cliff. Beto, cuff Paul up and let's all get some rest. If we can't sleep, at least we can recharge our batteries."

Beto was snoring within minutes. I walked over and sat next to Marc.

"How are you doing, buddy?" I asked. "I'm....um...okay."

I wanted him to understand my gratitude. "You know that what you did tonight likely saved all our lives?"

He was quiet. "I don't know about that...but I know that it saved my life. It's hard to explain. I mean, you don't know me." He paused again. "I didn't realize it until now, but I've lived fearfully my whole life. Worried more about mitigating damage than drinking life up. Carpe diem was meaningless to me."

"And now?" I asked.

"One thing I am sure of is that my life will never be the same. I don't understand it yet, but it just feels like there's a different guy living in my skin."

"Maybe something good has come out of all this mess, then," was all I could muster. "Get some sleep."

Despite the excitement of the day and the uncomfortable, freakish location, the physical requirements of the men's bodies soon took charge, and all drifted into deep sleep—including Marc. As tired as I was, I suppose I wanted to make sure all my charges were okay before resting myself. As a good leader would do. Eventually, I drifted off as well.

～

I had not been asleep long when I jerked to wakefulness and jumped up. Barking dogs and men's voices were nearby. It was completely dark in the cavern, so I took a chance and switched on the flashlight. Beto was already in firing position, with guns in both hands.

Everyone but Andy and Paul were on their feet when Bruce slugged Paul and he fell in a heap on the tunnel floor.

It sounded as though the dog pack was just outside the tunnel, baying constantly.

We waited and listened. Then, I heard a man's voice drawl, "Goddamned dogs, led us up here on a wild goose chase. There ain't nothin' up here "

And, then some cursing in Spanish.

"It isn't the dogs fault. They are just spooked," another voice answered, while the dogs continued to growl and bark.

"Yeah, well, their getting' spooked lead us way off the path. Them fuckers doubled back and are back in town, now, I betcha. You get to tell Lang yore theories about the dogs. I ain't gonna. Let's go."

We listened as the dogs' barking started to move away. Suddenly, Paul yelled "Hel...", not finishing the word before Bruce knocked him to the ground and kicked him in the ribs.

From outside. "Did you hear that?"

Beto stepped silently to the tunnel mouth, both guns drawn.

"Hear whut? Nothin' but them worthless dawgs howlin," "I'll swear I thought I heard a voice, or something."

"Now, you're as 'spooked' as your stupid dawgs. Let's go."

I took a deep breath, realizing that I hadn't for a while. The sounds of the dogs and the men subsided, and then, were gone.

"I know it's a cliché, but-- 'that was too close for comfort'," I said. "I really think we're okay now, don't you, Beto?"

Beto confirmed my opinion and we quieted down again for the night.

CHAPTER 9

SATURDAY, MAY 27

"Up and at 'em, guys," Beto chirped. "Daylight's burning." I could see a soft glow of light barely visible far into the darkness, *an exit sign of sorts* I thought. We were all slow standing, even Ricky, but eventually, we all roused ourselves stiffly to our feet. Ricky and I turned on the flashlights. Feeling as stiff as a tin man, I leaned against the mine wall stretching first my left hamstring and then my right. I was tired, sore and...momentarily euphoric!

And then I saw that Andy had not moved, even with all of the commotion. Beto couldn't get him up, so he poured water from the canteen over Andy's face. Sputtering, he took a swing at Beto before blinking his eyes and shaking his head several times, restoring consciousness in the process. Pulling his legs under him and grabbing the rough wall, Andy managed to get upright. I slung on my much lighter pack with only the cash inside and handed packs to Ricky, Bruce and Marc which they slung over their shoulders. Beto removed Paul's handcuffs and shoved him in front of them, all falling into a single line in a slow march following the beams of light. Close behind, Beto supported Andy's unsteady first steps. I could hear Andy's ragged breathing and grunts of pain as he walked. But with every step we made, the blackness of the tunnel diminished until we finally broke through the wall of vines and hanging limbs and into the morning sunlight.

Blinking and rubbing my eyes, I finally got where I could keep them open and focus in the glaring sunlight. We were standing on the narrow rock shelf just outside the tunnel entrance. Looking over the valley as the sun's rays fanned across the sky in spears that sprang from the outline of the distant peaks, I thought I had never seen a more beautiful morning.

Ricky turned to Marc and smiled. "Great to be alive, eh, buddy?"

I was about to burst. "I've got to pee like a racehorse," and, with that preface, began urinating over the side of the cliff, my stream disappearing into the canyon below. The best piss of my life, no doubt. Soon, all my comrades joined in, puffing their cheeks and blowing air in satisfaction and relief and Beto farting loudly causing us all to laugh. Paul looked longingly at me and I nodded back, so Paul joined the phalanx. My grin expanded until it felt my face might crack just thinking how good it felt to be standing in the sun peeing.

I stared, disconnected from the moment, down the side of the cliff intuitively searching for the bottom of the canyon when a flash of motion to my right jerked me back to the present. I turned instinctively toward the motion and to the sight of Paul being violently propelled out into space, arms windmilling and legs churning in midair while accelerating into an arched downward trajectory. I watched mesmerized in disbelief, as Paul's body tumbled noiselessly through space until colliding with a rock outcropping hundreds of feet below with a cracking thud and clipped cry, crazily bouncing once before disappearing from sight.

I snapped. There is no other way to put it. My legendary, tightly controlled mind, already reeling from the events of recent days, seemed to explode as if one electrode too many had fired. A moan escaped from somewhere deep inside me as I frantically tried to connect the dots. Seconds before, my former right-hand man was standing next to me—alive. In an instant he was somewhere down there—certainly dead. How could this be? Slowly, the realization formed in my barely functioning brain—*Bruce pushed Paul over the side!*

As if seeking confirmation of the unthinkable, I turned and looked from face to face. A whimper escaping from deep in his throat, Marc's legs buckled and he dropped to the ground like a rock. Ricky looked dazedly from where Paul had been just seconds before to where his body had flown through the air and then back to the spot on the ledge. His lips moved, but no sound came out. Even Beto and Andy were looking at each other in disbelief.

Then next thing I knew, I spun on Bruce, grabbed him by the front of his shirt with both hands and drove him back against the rock wall on the far side of the path. "What did you do? What in the hell DID YOU DO?"

Bruce looked me in the eyes calmly and, speaking softly said, "Darren, it needed to be done and I just did it." Beto grabbed me by the arm and pulled me down the trail away from Bruce and the narrow ledge. Andy suddenly sprang to life and leaped to Beto's side, grabbing ahold of my other arm as I screamed in rage and tried to shake the men off. But, even with the adrenalin of my rage, I was no match for the strength of Andy and Beto as they pulled me down the trail and talked me down from the temporary insanity that consumed me.

"I'm okay now, guys. Let me go. Beto, bring me my pack and let me walk ahead for a little while. Round the boys up and let's get the fuck out of here."

Beto helped Ricky and Marc with their packs and pulled them to their feet, giving them pushes down the road toward Darren. "Bruce, stay back here and help me with Andy." Andy was tottering, the exertion sapping his last strength so that he didn't resist when Beto and Bruce each slid one of his arms over their shoulders and the three men trudged after their group.

～

After two hours of steady walking ending in the difficult negotiation of the boulder field, my heart jumped when I saw the Forest Service road ahead. Luckily, the late spring aquifer pressure forced water out of fissures along the roadway so that we had plenty of water to drink. The sun was already intense. Andy, though, was weakening, his face covered with perspiration, and he was having difficulty focusing his eyes. Beto was watching his every move and sending me worried looks. Not a word had been spoken since we left the tunnel. Marc seemed particularly lost in thought.

᠙

Step by step, Marc's head cleared. At one point, I saw him look at Bruce and literally shudder in revulsion. I wondered what Marc and Ricky were thinking. When they set out on this adventure, they each knew their lives would never be the same. But they could not have anticipated the events that unfolded. Before their very eyes, had Bruce become someone totally foreign? Their friend gone?

᠙

Andy stumbled, though Beto kept him from falling. "All right, guys. Let's rest a bit," I announced breaking the uncomfortable silence.

The men found places in the grass alongside the road to rest. Marc sat next to Ricky and they talked quietly. Andy lay on his back while Beto rewound the bandages, now soaked with blood. Bruce sat away by himself.

When I walked toward him, he stood and watched me warily as I approached. I stood close to him. I wanted our conversation to be private, so I spoke softly. "So, now, Bruce, I am asking you in earnest to tell me what you were thinking."

"That Paul was a problem that had to be resolved and there would never be a better opportunity. He has disappeared. No one will ever find his body in the bottom of that canyon," came Bruce's calm, almost cold reply. "And that it was a problem between you and Andy and Beto, which I could resolve. So, resolve it I did."

I stared into his face for a long time. He held my look, not flinching or looking away.

"So, what do you want to happen, now?" I asked.

"Well, after all this, I can't see myself opening a law practice to handle DUIs."

"I'll think on where we go from here. I want a little time and to talk to Andy and Beto, of course. But let me say this, as we have walked down the mountain, and Andy has gotten worse, the only thing I regret is that I didn't push him over the cliff myself." *As I said it, I wondered if it were really true.*

Bruce smiled. I put my hand on his shoulder, showing forgiveness in an alpha dog way.

When I turned around, all eyes were on us. Even Andy had risen up on an elbow.

"Home stretch, guys. Let's finish this off."

꩜

Downhill most of the way, the final leg was fairly easy. A cool breeze was blowing, and clouds floated over, occasionally blocking the sun. Yellow butterflies fluttered just over the tall meadow grass and, twice, we startled mule deer that ran off into the woods. Even so, Andy's stride weakened until he was barely putting one foot in front of another, leaning more heavily on Beto and Bruce. His breathing had become even raspier, and he asked for water every few minutes. Finally, he lost consciousness, his legs collapsing. I sprang to his side, replacing Bruce. "Hang on, man, you're going to be fine." In this manner, Beto under one shoulder and me the other, we carried Andy the last hundred yards to the campground.

Ricky's Gray Goose was the only vehicle in the deserted lot. Beto and I carefully laid Andy on the carpeted floor, while the others stuffed the backpacks full of $20 million cash into the overhead cabinets next to life preservers and towels.

"Ricky, let's have Beto drive, don't you think?" I asked. Ricky gladly relinquished the keys to Beto, and we all piled in for another driving exhibition. Expertly guided by Beto's driving skills fueled by the desire to save his oldest friend's life, the Gray Goose screamed down the Million Dollar Highway with all of us rocking and swaying inside.

I gathered my thoughts, finally thinking straight.

"Listen, guys, we've got to take Andy to the hospital in Durango. But I can't be with you. The press is going to have a field day as it is, so I need to distance myself as far away as possible. So, drop me off at the Ore House and I will go inside and call Billy to come get me. Ricky, write your phone number down for me. When you get to the hospital, here's the story—you were all at Lake Electra for lunch. Andy's pistol fell out of his holster getting out of the van and fired when it struck the ground. Andy has a permit to carry, so that's no problem. He'll just be mortified about his professional reputation when the story gets out. Everybody got it?"

I got nods from everyone. We screamed down the mountain for another forty-five minutes until Beto skidded to a slow roll by the side of the road across the street from the restaurant. I jumped out while the car was still moving, slapped the door and gave Beto the thumbs up to go. Which he did.

There was a pay phone outside the restaurant. I called the operator and placed a collect call to my condo at Tamarron.

The phone rang only once before Billy grabbed it up, "Hello."

"Will you accept charges for a call from Darren Jacobs in Durango?" the operator asked. "You bet," came Billy's immediate response.

"Billy. Darren. Can you come pick me up? I'm at the Ore House on the north side of Durango"

"Shit yes, I can come pick you up. You're okay?"

"Yeah, I'm fine...Andy, not so good. Come get me. I'll tell you everything then." "So, did you get everything out?"

"Yes, yes we did. Come get me, Billy, we've got things to do."

I knew it would take Billy a half an hour to show up, so I went into the cool darkness of the lounge and sat at the bar, its sole occupant.

"What can I get you sir?" the bartender asked. I wondered if he thought I was out all night on a bender.

"Black Jack, rocks, please," which he delivered quickly. I rattled the ice around in the glass and took a sip. Never, ever in my life had a drink tasted so delicious. The bourbon moved through my system quickly, warming as it went. Part of me felt like letting out a war whoop and running through the Ore House naked. And, part of me wanted to cry.

Soon, the bartender was back. "Another, sir?" I nodded and he brought the second round. I sipped this one a little more slowly and just let my mind wander. Suddenly, a calm came over me, and the thought raced into my mind, *Andy's going to be fine.*

～

Honking the horn, Beto skidded the van to a stop immediately below the Emergency Room sign at the Durango Regional Hospital. The van ride had been an experience. And they were lucky on two counts: traffic was light and they encountered no police cars. Using every inch of the serpentine road for sliding turns, Beto pushed the van to the limit.

Two men in light blue scrubs ran out of the building and to the rear of the van where Ricky and Marc had thrown the doors open. Andy lay unmoving in the back of the van, blood from his bandages covering most of his upper body. The older of the two men plugged the stethoscope draped around his neck into his ears and placed the diaphragm on Andy's chest in several places. An orderly had brought a wheeled gurney alongside the van and together, the three got Andy moved from the van to the gurney and rolled him briskly inside the building, Beto at his side. Marc overheard the medic who had checked Andy whisper, "I couldn't find a pulse".

～

The three young men stood outside, alone together for the first time since, it seemed like a lifetime ago, they were eating pizza in Telluride. Their comfortable camaraderie had disappeared, replaced by tense silence. Finally, Bruce said, "Well, did I tell you guys or what? We're rich and we have a story we can tell our grandkids."

Ricky looked at Bruce, shook his head and said, "I'm going to move the van", and walked off.

"What did I say to him?"

"I don't even know who you are any more, man. I'm not sure I ever did," and having said that Marc walked through the Emergency Room doors and found Beto sitting on a bench in the hall, his face in his hands.

"Any news?" Marc asked.

"No," Beto looked up and replied, "I stuck my head in there a moment ago and got shooed out. I can't even count how many people are working on him."

Marc sat down next to Beto to wait. When he let his imagination run and ponder all that Beto did in his "line of work", the images horrified and repulsed him. Yet, he was also drawn to him, now feeling a perverted form of kinship. Something about his love for his friend and his loyalty to Darren was noble. *Honor among thieves.*

The swinging doors to the emergency room opened and the medical staffer who had first examined Andy walked through pulling down his protective mask. Donna, head down, walked behind him. She was reading a clipboard when she looked up and saw Marc. Her professionalism shattered instantly—she dropped the chart and ran into Marc's arms, leaving her associate staring gob-smacked.

Marc stood to speak, but seeing Donna, he felt a lump rise in his throat and tears filled his eyes. She pulled him to her. "Honey, what's going on?"

Time passed. Marc just held on to her while he steadied his emotions. He knew she might be on duty but had not prepared himself to see her sucked into the middle of the drama. "How's he doing?"

"Who?"

"The patient. Andy. We brought him in."

"Oh, he's stabilized and we have called in the duty surgeon. He's in really bad shape, but he seems strong as a horse. That bullet needs to come out of him quickly. What do you mean, '—brought him in?—'" Donna asked.

"He and Beto—pointing to the man sitting on the bench— work for Bruce's boss. We met them up at Lake Electra for lunch."

"Oh?" Now, putting the pieces together, "And so what happened?" Donna asked.

"Andy is a professional bodyguard. He dropped his gun getting back into his car and it went off."

Donna pulled him close again, whispering in his ear, "Thank god it wasn't you. Thank god it wasn't you." And, pushing back to look in Marc's face, "Ricky and Bruce?"

"They're fine. They're out in the parking lot."

◡

Telluride

"They are still somewhere in Telluride, I will guarantee you that," Sheriff Lang said emphatically to Guzman who translated Lang's words to Durant. They were sitting in the great room of Darren's house. They had been there since shortly after the reports about the troubles up on Tomboy Road started coming in late the previous night from Lang's troopers. Lang immediately alerted all the squads guarding the passes to be prepared for Jacobs and his two henchmen to try to crash the barricades and redeployed a contingency of his troops to seal up and search the village.

Lang, broke through the front doors of Darren's home, Guzman and Durant followed him in and went straight to the basement. The vault door was open, an envelope taped to the doorjamb. Durant ripped it off the door and tore into it. It contained one sheet of paper on which Darren had written:

"Sr. Cortez—You lose".

He folded it carefully and put it into his billfold and, glaring at Guzman, said something in Spanish. Guzman turned to Lang. "He said to tell you that you had better be right—that these *pendejos* are still in town." Lang blanched as the blood drained from his face. Durant spat on the carpet, put on his sunglasses, and growled, "*listo*".

While moving the Grey Goose out of the emergency lane and parking it in the lot, Ricky saw a pay phone booth outside the front entrance of the hospital. He sprinted around the building and, digging in his pocket, was relieved to find a dime, which he inserted into appropriate slot, pulling the booth door closed behind him.

"Ricky! Ricky, is that you!" was how Barb answered the phone. "Yeah, sweetie, I'm in Durango and fine."

Barb's sobs over the phone broke Ricky's heart and he found himself trying to sooth her while crying himself.

"I love you, baby. Please come home—as fast as you can—but safely," Barb said. "I will, sweetie. I'll be right there."

"Oh!" Barb said in surprise, "what about Marc and Bruce?"

"They're fine, too. Marc and Donna are inside talking now. I'm sure they'll want to come out as well. Maybe Donna can get someone to cover for her?" Rick guessed. "And Bruce is around here somewhere."

"Nancy went home."

"What? Why, must be some emergency?"

"No, she says she's done with Bruce. Come home and we can talk about it. I promised to call her to let her know you guys were okay, which I will do as soon as we hang up," Barb said.

"What do I tell Bruce?" He's going to be crushed.

"I'd recommend just tell him to call Nancy in Albuquerque," Barb said. "Just come home, honey, please come home."

CHAPTER 10

SUNDAY, MAY 28

Vallecito

I t was a spectacular sunrise. Thunderstorms had shaken the rafters until three in the morning, followed by a soft summer rain that whispered against the tin roof for several hours. Ricky had driven back to his beloved cabin, to find Barb waiting outside for him. The tearful reunion quickly turned into a riotous celebration when Barb whispered, "Welcome home, Daddy- to-be." Donna and Marc showed up a while later. They had stopped at the store and picked up T-bone steaks, baking potatoes, salad fixings and a couple bottles of red wine to help celebrate the many joyous events in their lives, including being alive.

Ricky and Marc sat on the porch drinking coffee, their hands wrapped round their mugs for warmth. Neither felt much like talking. Sitting quietly together was enough. Barb and Donna were still asleep inside, worn out from the activity of the past days. Heavy gray clouds hung in the trees above the lake, though a brilliant blue sky was beginning to spread overhead. The western peaks reflected the earliest rays, creating sizzling white triangles dancing on the blue background.

"I sure missed Bruce and Nancy last night," Marc said. "Do you think they will really stay broken up?"

"Barb thinks so. She believes once Nancy made her mind up, there will be no turning back," Ricky answered.

The sound of car tires crunching gravel in the drive intruded upon their conversation, and in a bit Billy's Jaguar poked its nose through the trees. Billy pulled the car into the parking area outside the front of the cabin and he, Darren and Bruce climbed out and joined Ricky and Marc on the porch.

～

"How's Andy?" Ricky asked immediately.

"He's going to make it, but it was damned close for a while there," Billy said. "We got him a private room and Beto hasn't left his side."

"Did y'all go back to Tamarron last night?" Marc asked. "Yes," Billy said. "We stayed up in Darren's condo."

"Excuse my manners...would you like some coffee?" Ricky asked.

"Thanks, Ricky, I would—just black," I answered. Ricky disappeared into the cabin and then returned with my coffee.

"Thanks, that looks perfect," I said taking the cup. "Bruce, grab a chair," and turning to Ricky and Marc, "let's sit and talk a minute, men, before I get going."

I sipped my coffee silently and felt the glaze of all eyes on me. I have never felt so spent, but it is important that I summon the energy to say what must be said to these young strangers. I look from Ricky to Marc to Bruce slowly. "I owe you my life, as does Andy and Beto. Know that there isn't anything we won't do for you the rest of our born days. Know also, that I recognize the toll the events of the last few days have taken on you. I chose this life, as did Andy and Beto...and even Billy. You did not. And though I know Billy warned you as clearly as his predictive skills would allow, in reality, you could have no idea what you were stepping into. All I can say is that we are so grateful that you did."

"I urge you to just go on with your lives. You are very wealthy young men. Billy will say more about that in a minute. You are in the unique position to do something very few people can—live almost any life you can imagine for yourselves. There really are no words, so I'll just say again, thanks for your help. Billy?"

Billy, who had been standing behind me while I spoke, stepped forward, "All of the cash is in the trunk of my car. We—Darren, Bruce and I—are headed to the Durango Airport. Captain Richardson is going to pick up Darren and Bruce and take them back to Nassau. Essentially, we're back on plan with everything that Darren set up with the Swiss."

Ricky smiled a wry grin at Bruce, who caught it and nodded sheepishly.

"As agreed, we will establish separate accounts for the three of you and deposit three million dollars in each account. Now, listen," Billy continued, "we're going to put a one-year freeze on your funds in Nassau. We believe this is for your own good. We don't need to have raised eyebrows right now. There is nothing linking any of you to Telluride, but let's take no chances."

"Also, here's a bonus for each of you," Billy said reaching into his briefcase and bringing out three stacks of bills. There's fifty thousand dollars for each of you here—sort of walking around money until next year. Does that sound okay to you guys?"

I got a kick as the three young men's eyes fixed on the money. I suspected none of them had ever seen this much cash in one place, much less hold it in their hands. It seems to have lifted them out of their exhausted states a bit. I was pleased Billy had suggested this surprise.

"Besides that, it will give you a year to think about what you want to do with your new wealth. It's yours to do what you want but consider Darren and me as resources and talk to us before you make any big decisions. We have watched more than a few people inherit or otherwise come into a lot of wealth only to be broke a few years later. We don't want that to happen to any of you."

I stood. "We need to get on the road. Bruce will get your account information to you when we get back next week."

I hugged Ricky. "It was you who made all this possible. After the last little time with you, I believe you would have come to our rescue whether any money was involved or not. Your family raised a fine, young man."

This set off hugs all around. Handshakes just didn't seem appropriate, considering what we had been through together.

I grabbed Marc and after bear-hugging him, looked squarely in his face and said quietly, "You're going to be okay, Marc. Time will heal. Just take it a day at the time."

"I am okay, Darren. Actually, way better than okay. You know how you said that this episode was the first time in your life you had ever been afraid. Well, I woke up this morning thinking of possibilities, not problems. And it's an incredible feeling."

"I think I understand," I said. "You've figured out some very big things as a still young man. It'll be fun watching where you go from here."

In the moment, I sensed Marc's competing emotions—liking Darren Jacobs as a person but not being able to get around his judgment of my morality.

"Yeah, something like that."

Billy, Bruce, and I climbed into the Jag, Billy easing down the lane with Bruce looking out the back window as the space between he and his friends continued to widen.

ᕲ

We headed south through Vallecito Valley toward the Durango Airport. We were a little ahead of schedule, so we stopped in Bayfield at a pay phonebooth, and Billy called Beto to get an update on Andy. Bruce and I didn't have to wait for Billy to report in to know the score—he was smiling ear to ear as he came back.

"Beto says Andy is doing great. Proof positive—he's pissed about the story that he shot himself with his own gun and is swearing revenge for that abomination perpetrated while he couldn't defend himself. "

Billy's report lightened the mood in the car, as we continued toward the airport. I could tell Bruce was excited. He asked one question after another about the jet and Nassau. Billy, driving like a little old man, finally turned off the main highway, through the parking lot at the airport, and stopped in front of the terminal. A white Lear was taxiing to a stop on the tarmac that I assumed was piloted by Richardson. Billy popped the trunk, so that Bruce and I could retrieve the two large suitcases full of our cash.

"I'm not going to hang around, if that's okay, Darren. I want to go back into Durango and check in with Dale Martin, the County Attorney. We went to law school together and I just want to make sure there are no issues on Andy's accidental shooting. What do you think?"

"I think that I like how you are always taking care of business, consigliore." I hugged Billy. "I'll call you from Nassau to check on Andy... and everything else."

I picked up one of the suitcases when Billy put his hand on my arm. "Just out of precaution, Dare, why don't we leave the suitcases in the trunk until you make sure everything is copacetic inside—make sure it's your guy in that jet and not another double-cross."

"Always thinking, Billy. Bruce and I will go make sure the coast is clear and then come back."

We had just come through the door when a man in a solid, dark blue suit, white shirt and skinny dark tie stepped in front of me. "Are you Darren Jacobs?"

Turning, I saw two other white guys in similar suits with flat-top haircuts standing on both sides of Bruce. My heart skipped a beat. I knew a federal agent when I saw one.

"I am. What's this about?"

"Mr. Jacobs, would you and your colleague follow us?" Bruce and I fell into step with the three agents as we walked across the waiting room hall toward a sign, "Airport Security". Over my shoulder, I snuck a glance at Bruce, who was doing a "deer in the headlights".

Fuck, fuck, fuck. How could this be happening? We were home. Our ride is one-hundred yards away. One-fucking-stinking hundred yards to a gorgeous Lear and Nassau.

The lead agent opened the door and our entourage followed him in. When the door clicked closed, chills went up my spine.

Was that sound a harbinger of things to come? I had to shift the dynamics of this episode quickly.

"First things first—let me see all of your ID's. You, first," and I pointed at the lead guy. He hesitated and I stared straight into his eyes, exhibiting bravado that I definitely did not feel. He blinked and then stepped toward me and pulled his ID from his breast pocket.

Ugh...DEA...Drug Enforcement Agency. We are in deep shit.

"Bruce, please take down this information," I said, handing him a small leather notebook with an attached gold-plated pen. The authority in my voice seemed to jolt him into the present. He took the pen and pad and started writing, as I read the agent's name and identification number before casually returning the ID to the agent and turning to one of the other two.

"Now, yours, please," I said addressing the other agents. They took their ID's out but hesitated, looking at the lead guy, who nodded. As intended, I was feeling a shift in the power structure and turned to the head guy.

"Now, maybe you can explain why you are interrupting our travels?" I asked Pencil Neck, as I had now named him, in an attempt to disempower him in my mind. I had won a round. " Just to be clear, am I under arrest?"

He turned to me slowly. "You are not under arrest, though, we hope you will cooperate with us. We have some questions for you, questions generated through extensive discussion with Sheriff Lang of Telluride. You know him, I believe?"

He registered the shock on my face that I had tried with all my might not to show.

Round two to Pencil Neck.

"Actually," he said, now smiling, 'it's only you we want to speak with. Your associate may leave."

This was an offer I wasn't prepared for, and I didn't know quite where to go with it— until I saw Bruce's eyes beseeching me.

"Of course. Bruce, why don't you wait outside while I finish this conversation with these gentlemen? If you see Captain Richardson out there, please tell him that we've been detained a bit and will be right with him."

Bruce didn't hesitate to leave.

I turned to continue my counterattack of Pencil Neck, but, exactly contrary to my intentions, he pushed me into a chair, and when I tried to stand to object, his two goons grabbed me by each arm and forced me back. *No witnesses. Now I see why he was fine having Bruce leave.*

"Sit down, Darren, and quit posturing!" Pencil Neck addressed me. "Lang has been running his mouth ever since he made a deal with us yesterday. We know all about Cortez and Guzman."

He opened my valise. "If you don't have a warrant, you have no right to search my personal belongings."

"Sit your ass down and shut the fuck up!"

I did as I was told.

He rummaged around in the valise, pulled out my passport and shoved it into his pocket.

"You seem to be traveling light for such a long trip. Seems like you should have some luggage or something?'

"No," I replied, "we have clothes and all we need in Nassau."
"Do you have a vehicle outside? We might want to take a look."

"No vehicle. We were dropped off." *Jesus, Billy is a freaky genius. We would be stone cold dead if we had brought the money in.*

"Here's the deal. You are free to go back to Santa Fe and wait until you hear from me.

Right now, there are a lot of people wanting a piece of you. Once we get that all sorted out, we will let you know. Now, Mr. Jacobs, you may join your associate outside."

Pencil Neck opened the door.

When I stood up, my head was spinning, and I had to steady myself on the arm of the chair for a moment. I looked all around the room—seeking my next volley, I suppose—but finding none, I trudged through the door and into the waiting area of the Durango Airport, my vision blurred. I blinked several times to clear the haze and finally saw Bruce and Dave

Richardson talking on the other side of the hall. They hadn't seen me come out, so I began walking toward them, composing myself—I thought—as I walked.

"Darren, Jesus Christ, man. What's wrong?" Dave was holding one arm and Bruce the other, helping me to sit down.

"Are you sick? You are white as a sheet," he went on.

"We aren't going to be going to Nassau, today, Dave. There have been some, er, issues that have come up. I can't say more right now, but, of course, I will compensate your company for the full fare," I said.

"Hell, Darren, don't worry about that. Do you need to get to a hospital?" Dave asked.

His concern warmed my heart and, on the one hand, caused me to blush with shame.

What was he going to think of me when all of this came out, as surely it must?

"No, no, I'll be fine in a few minutes. Two bourbons and I'll be perfect again. I see you met my young colleague, Bruce?"

"Yes, we were just introducing ourselves when you came out," Dave offered.

"Well, listen, I'd like to sit here and chat, but Bruce and I need to get moving. And I'm sure you'll want to scoot back to Denver. Just have your billing people work everything out with my folks. Whatever you guys think is fair, Dave."

We said our goodbyes, and he disappeared through a door marked "Admittance to Qualified Personnel Only". A panic came over me and I wanted out of that place NOW, before the Nazis changed their minds and came back out to get me.

I surveyed Bruce. By all outward appearances, he was doing better than I.

"Bruce, go see if there are any cabs out front of this one-horse-town airport. I doubt it, but if so, hold it and come get me. I will be over at the Hertz counter seeing what they have available." And, under my breath, "Wave Billy off."

Bruce came back and announced, "No cabs, no town cars, no nothing." With relief, I got the message. The only vehicle available was a Toyota Land Cruiser which they were happy to lease to a Gold Card member for a week at some outrageous fee. I didn't care. We found the blue whale of a vehicle in the airport parking lot, and I gave the keys to Bruce. I certainly didn't feel like driving.

As we pulled out of the parking lot, I said "Billy is freaky wise. His intuition saved our bacon. If we had carried those suitcases in there, we would have all been toast." "Where to?"

"Goddammit, Bruce, I don't care!" I yelled. "Just get us the fuck away from this place."

He stammered a bit and then steered us out of the parking lot and turned left out of the airport toward Durango, driving slowly.

We drove a few miles. "Bruce, I'm sorry. That was no way to speak to you. You have done extremely well. I am impressed with how you just handled yourself. Now, let's go to the hospital. I think we will find Billy there," I said it calmly when, in fact, I was close to falling apart.

"The Durango hospital?" he asked.

Jesus fucking Christ. How goddamned stupid are you!

"Yes, Bruce, the Durango hospital. You are headed in the right direction. I will tell you when to turn."

↶

We checked on Andy who was asleep, and the doc said doing really well., before returning to the Land Cruiser where we waited in the parking lot of Durango Memorial for over an hour. I thought Billy might show up. Bruce tried to start conversations twice, but my clipped replies clearly signaled an unwillingness to participate in any needless chatter. I just wanted to think; to sit in the quiet and put all of the pieces together. My life has taken too many body blows this week.

"Bruce, let's head up the condo. If Billy isn't going to come here, Tamarron is the next best guess."

Bruce drove me the fifteen miles north up Animas Canyon to my condo at Tamarron Resort and helped me up to my room, where I kicked off my shoes, curled up on my bed in my clothes, closed my eyes and instantly went to sleep.

〜

"Darren. Darren." When I opened my eyes, Billy was gently shaking my shoulder. "Wake up. We need to talk."

"You're okay? You got away okay?" I groggily asked.

"Yeah. Get cleaned up and come downstairs. I'll fill you in. All is good, though."

I stumbled into my bathroom. When I turned around and saw myself in the mirror, I literally gasped. *Christ, man, you look like shit.* I had aged years overnight, dark bags drooping from my bloodshot eyes and the corners of my mouth turned down in a fixed scowl. The crazy hair and two-day beard growth didn't help. After a quick shave, comb job and intense summoning of courage, I headed downstairs, trying to be prepared for whatever was to befall me.

Billy and Bruce heard my steps and looked up as I came into the living room.

"All right, Billy. I am all ears."

"Well, Bruce filled me in on the details of your ordeal inside the airport, and..."

I interrupted, "God bless you, Billy, your intuition is the only reason I am not sitting in a jail cell tonight."

"Interesting you say that, Darren. I think it was more subliminal than intuitive. After you guys were in the terminal for a few minutes, I got this creepy feeling and drove around the parking lot. There were two black Suburbans with fed plates on them. I wonder if I didn't see them out of the corner of my eye driving in? But, at any rate, I hightailed it out of there."

"Where the hell did you go, man, you were holding for sure?"

"I automatically started to turn to Durango and then, I decided to turn the other direction. Long story short—I drove up to Vallecito and took the money up to Ricky's. We hid it in his crawlspace."

"Genius, Billy. Pure Genius. There is absolutely nothing to tie Ricky to us and he is as trustworthy as they come. I guess we'd better figure out a game plan. That seems the first order of business, though I got to tell you, I haven't a bloody clue at this point," I said to Billy.

"First things, first, Dare. I'll call room service and get some food sent up. Meanwhile, you want to shower and change clothes? Then we'll talk," Billy said.

"I'm in your hands, counselor. Sounds like we at least have a short-term plan," and headed back upstairs to my loft.

IN THE NEXT WEEKS

An article appearing in the Nogales, Arizona, newspaper the following week reported that a meat truck returning to Mexico had been stopped at the border checkpoint and the bodies of seven unidentified men were found inside. Four had been shot, two had their throats cut, and one had been strangled and apparently tortured. The driver had picked the truck up in Phoenix and, after extensive questioning, convinced the authorities that he had no idea about the dead men.

In Telluride, the FBI entered the town in response to concerns of local citizens that the latest rash of crime seemed somehow drug related. Though rumors about Joe Bob Lang had been prevalent for years, the mayor and the town's increasing population of celebrity summer residents reached out, feeling it was time for some outside help. Sheriff Lang just sort of disappeared.

Over the next two weeks, Billy had endless meetings with DEA lawyers, the Attorneys General of both New Mexico and Colorado (both of whom I considered—and still do—friends), and the special prosecutor. Discussed punishments ranged from ten years in federal penitentiary to nothing, the preferred solution of my New Mexico AG buddy. There were real problems prosecuting the case: Lang's credibility, generally suspicious but more so since the "Mescans", as he continued to describe them, were nowhere to be found; the lack of physical evidence (nothing incriminating was found in my house); and the inability to tie me to the operation. Beto and Andy, however, were perhaps more at risk. The real fly in the ointment was Harold Ciro, the federal prosecutor. We hate each other; for us, it is personal. He is not "going to look the other way", as he put it.

Meanwhile, I have been holed up in my office in Santa Fe, going crazy waiting for Billy to call or come over, so that we could strategize the next step...and then, the next. I keep Bruce nearby running errands and doing whatever he can to help. The more I am around him, the more I like and trust him. Though after Paul, it is going to take some time—if ever—for an outsider to have my complete trust.

Truth is—I miss Paul. I suspect part of my current funk comes from some sort of convoluted grieving process over losing him. Of course, I can't share that with even my best friends; Andy and Beto would probably have me committed if I told them that. Besides, they have their hands full dealing with their "people".

This mess has put dozens of folks out of work, many of them close to Andy and Beto. We understand that Cortez's advance crews have approached a few of them, but that's another issue.

I am contemplating taking a run, when I hear Billy's voice—sweet relief from the agony of waiting—exchanging hellos with Bruce.

"Billy, get your expensive ass in here," I shout. "I'm not paying you to talk to the help."

He and Bruce appear smiling. "Well, you seem to have more piss and vinegar today, anyway. That's a good sign," Billy says, turning to Bruce. "Take these files over to the office, please. They're a mess, so get them indexed and sorted."

Bruce left and Billy pulled up a chair next to mine. Ah oh, here comes something he doesn't want to tell me.

"So, Dare—good news—bad news—good news, first. The State of New Mexico, the State of Colorado, and the federal government all have agreed not to bring charges against you, Beto, Andy or anyone else involved..."

"If?...": I say, waiting for the shoe to drop.

"Ciro will not let go of the 'public office' thing. His requirement for the deal is that you agree never to run for or hold public office again. That's his price for the compromise."

The final compromise is a concept I have recommended to other people in a fix like mine, but now find insidious to me. It is an odd creation that the average citizen could not imagine but is actually not all that rare. There are two major tenets. I waive the statute of limitations for prosecution in the event that I, or any of my people, are charged with drug charges, or any other felony, in the future. All of the potential current charges could be brought at that time.

The next one is the most difficult for me. I must agree never to seek public office, again.

This was Ciro's compromise. I will be allowed to complete my existing term but agree never again to run for office. And, if I violate the agreement, the sealed record of all the potential charges would be opened, and I could be prosecuted. Not just me—Andy, Beto, and maybe Bruce and others as well.

My blood is absolutely boiling. But there's no sense taking it out on Billy. I know he's done the best he could do.

"So, what did you tell them?" I asked, trying to appear calm, yet knowing that Billy knows me too well— knows this is tearing my insides up.

"I told them to draw up the documents. Darren, I know you hate this deal, but I think it's the best we can do; and I advise you to take it."

"I know, Billy. You did the best you could—the best anyone could. I will go with you to Ciro's tomorrow."

Tuesday

June 13

SANTA FE, NEW MEXICO
FEDERAL OFFICE BUILDING

*D*ammit, *get a grip. Do not give this chicken shit one gram of satisfaction.*

Harold Ciro is standing at the far end of a mahogany conference table that shines with a dark glow. I look at his hazy reflection in the table because I can't stand to look directly at him.

I hear Billy's voice. "Darren? Darren?"

"Harold, can you give us just a minute alone?" I hear Billy ask.

I clear my eyes and focus on his face that I know as well as my own. Thank God he's here. For longer than I can remember, he's been my advisor, my confidant, and my friend. And now, my lawyer. There's a reason people say "if you did it, get Mercado". But in my wildest dreams—nightmares— it never occurred to me that he would be sitting next to me...representing me...fending off a prick like Ciro.

Harold's nasal whine rings out. "Okay, Billy, five minutes. But when I come back, Darren signs. That's it. No more stalling."

He leaves and closes the door, but I can't quit glaring at the space he occupied. I have never hated anyone so much. And, lately, I have learned to hate some people, believe me.

I feel Billy's arm around me. "Darren, you've got to focus. I know this is a bitter pill to swallow, but—you know this—swallow you must."

Tears come into my eyes. Tears of rage, I suppose. I say "I suppose" because the only time I have ever cried was when I got beat at something. The first time I felt this way seems like yesterday—-I struck out my first time batting in Little League. Definitely the same feeling, just magnified by a million.

"Darren? Talk to me. What's going on?"

"I don't know if I can physically sign that...," unable to find words for the unspeakable. "I just don't know if I can."

"Darren, you don't call me consigliore, but you might as well. That's what I am. And much more—you are like a brother to me. You...are...out...of...options. You have to sign this Consent Decree."

Dammit, this is not what I want to hear. Here we sit knuckling under to a toady, while he gloats at my predicament. *Him and his state school law degree. What a load of shit.*

"Sign the damned decree!" I leap out of my chair and slam the table. "That's the best Billy Mercado, the meanest junk-yard-dog lawyer in America can come up with? And don't tell me I am out of options. Nothing pisses me off more than telling me I have to do something."

Billy shocks me. He grabs my face with his beefy hands and pulls it within inches of his, eyeball to eyeball. "Listen to me, Darren, like you have never listened to anybody before. If you don't sign the decree, a very public trial, no matter the outcome, is going to ruin your life.

Come on, man, put away your child's mind and use your lawyer's mind. You have to know what I am saying is true. Not giving up is one thing, but flat ignoring reality—that is dangerous."

"So, Billy, are you going to come with me to tell my dad I don't want to be in politics anymore? Hell, he's already got 'Darren Jacobs for President' pins printed somewhere."

As always, Billy stays patient with me. "Would you rather tell him that you are going to be prosecuted for serious felonies and have been running a drug distribution network?"

The door opened and Ciro stepped back into the room.

Just like him—it hasn't been five minutes.

"Times up," he says, sounding like an old maid schoolteacher. "Senator Jacobs, are you all right? You don't look well?"

You condescending prick. You don't care one iota whether I'm okay. Special prosecutor, my ass. Beto could put you down—forever—with one punch.

Sweat drips from my forehead, pooling on the table. Cold drops run down my back, as I reach for the pen. *Jesus Christ, I can't get my breath. My tie is strangling me.* I yank it open— but I still can't breathe. The walls in this little room are closing in. *Oh, God, my chest is exploding. I am dying! I am dying!* Black spots dance in front of my eyes. I try to stand, all goes black. I feel myself falling and Billy yelling.

FRIDAY

JUNE 16

Santa Fe Memorial Hospital

Familiar voices pull me out of total blackness into swirling gray. Am I horizontal? I command my eyes to open, but they don't. Summoning all the power I can muster, I feel my head slowly turn toward the voices, and, like a rusty garage door, one eyelid creeps upward. My vision is blurred. Two brighter spots swirl in the darkness.

"Darren! Oh, god, Darren," I hear my mother's voice.

One of the blobs of light moves closer. "Darren? Son, can you hear me? It's your dad, son, can you hear me?"

I blink my eye hello.

"Son, do you know who I am?" rumbles my dad, Doc, in his Ward Bond voice.

I want to say *Geez, dad, don't you think the "son" kind of gave it away?* But I am too tired to say anything—even with a great shot at his rare deviation from logic.

"Darren, honey, how do you feel?" the other light blob asks in my mom's voice.

I open my mouth to speak. It takes every ounce of energy to croak the words "so tired" before drifting back into the darkness.

...back along the river with Beto and Andy floating in inner tubes—not remembering it— really being there, feeling the water— then, just darkness.

I am pretty sure that I'm still alive...but not positive. One minute I am flying through clouds sitting next to Dave Richardson, talking and laughing, but we have no plane; and the next, back along the Rio Grande with Andy and Beto. Then, somebody is poking me with something that hurts, and I open my eyes momentarily to a very ugly, tasteless room, before drifting away again.

"Darren. Darren, can you hear me?"

That sounds like Billy!

I try to speak, but can't seem to form words, and, when I finally do, they are only whispers. I open my eyes fully, and, sure enough, there is Billy.

"Darren, do you know who I am?" he asks.

"Yes," I force out. "Did...I...have a...heart...attack?" "No, man. What do you remember last?"

"At Ciro's—documents. That's...about it," I force out. My head is clearing a little, but I can only grab a snatch of a memory here and another there.

"You passed out. The docs don't know what happened except that it caused you to quit fully breathing. But, Darren, your heart is fine. They really don't know what the problem is.

You've been out for four days, now. Hang on a minute, buddy. Let me go get the doc," Billy offered standing.

"No. No." I look around the room. No one else is there. I hold Billy's arm and signal for him to come close. "Let's just...keep... this...discussion...between you...and me. I'm going to...go back... to sleep...for a while. "

I manage a smile. "I need...some time to think...Billy," and wink at him. "Billy, I didn't sign anything did I?"

"No, man, you didn't sign anything."

There are still lots of possibilities. My condition could take a while to diagnose. You know, it's complicated. Ciro could get hit by a bus— or suddenly transferred to Washington. I still have a huge supply of inventory and cash in very safe places. And Andy and Beto and Billy.

And, best of all, I still have Da Jewel. My mind drifts. Blessed sleeps comes.

ABOUT THE AUTHOR

J. Michael Miller earned his Juris Doctor from the University of New Mexico Law School and is a former member of the New Mexico Bar.

He and his three boys roamed the spell-binding mountains of Southern Colorado, four-wheeling, skiing, hiking, sailing and just generally living large.

Made in the USA
Thornton, CO
06/24/23 02:00:07

3c4d4bed-b695-4b50-9ffd-02cce3199166R02